Also by Rufi Thorpe

The Girls from Corona del Mar

Dear Fang, With Love

Dear Fang, With Love

Rufi Thorpe

ALFRED A. KNOPF

NEW YORK

2016

THIS IS A BORZOI BOOK
PUBLISHED BY ALFRED A. KNOPF

Copyright © 2016 by Rufi Thorpe

www.aaknopf.com

Knopf, Borzoi Books, and the colophon are registered trademarks of
Penguin Random House LLC.

Grateful acknowledgment is made to HarperCollins Publishers for
permission to reprint an excerpt of "Meaning" from *New and Collected Poems:
1931–2001* by Czeslaw Milosz, copyright © 1988, 1991, 1996, 2001 by Czeslaw
Milosz Royalties, Inc. Reprinted by permission of HarperCollins Publishers.

Library of Congress Cataloging-in-Publication Data
Thorpe, Rufi.
Dear fang, with love / Rufi Thorpe.—First edition.
pages ; cm
ISBN 978-1-101-87577-3 (hardcover)
ISBN 978-1-101-87578-0 (eBook)
1. Fathers and daughters—Fiction. 2. Teenage girls—
Mental health—Fiction. 3. Emotional problems of teenagers—
Fiction. 4. Dysfunctional families—Fiction. 5. Domestic fiction.
I. Title.
PS3620.H787D43 2016   813'.6—dc23   2015018750

Jacket illustrations by Tina Berning
Jacket design by Kelly Blair

Manufactured in the United States of America
First Edition

For Sam

Meaning

—When I die, I will see the lining of the world.
The other side, beyond bird, mountain, sunset.
The true meaning, ready to be decoded.
What never added up will add up,
What was incomprehensible will be comprehended.

—And if there is no lining to the world?
If a thrush on a bush is not a sign,
But just a thrush on the branch? If night and day
Make no sense following each other?
And on this earth there is nothing except this earth?

—Even if that is so, there will remain
A word wakened by lips that perish,
A tireless messenger who runs and runs
Through interstellar fields, through the revolving galaxies,
And calls out, protests, screams.

—Czesław Miłosz

Dear Fang, With Love

Chapter 1

———

Dear Fang,

At this moment, we are mental twins. We are each alone, two discrete meat skeletons separated by space, cut off from each other by time, one of us reading a note, the other one writing it, yet we are finally together. Whenever you read this, even if it is years from now, though probably it will be only a few days since I hid this in your underwear drawer, but whenever you do find it: You will be inside my mind because you are reading and I am writing the exact same words. For just a moment, you are not Fang. You are me.

It's neat-o, don't you think?

I will write you lots and lots, I promise. Until, eventually, you turn into me! Even as I am farther away than ever!

With love,

Your silly,

V

I F YOU WANT TO KNOW what kind of girl my daughter, Vera, was, there is a story her mother, Katya, tells over and over. I wasn't there myself, but it is part of the family lore: little Vera, five years old, her dark hair in braids, attending another little girl's birthday. It was an overly elaborate party for a five-year-old girl, with candied violets on the cake, a gazebo, tasteful jewel-toned paper streamers, crowns made of real flowers for each little girl to wear, and a chalkboard listing a schedule of party games in cursive script.

But it was a hot day. The children were beginning to melt. No one wanted to play the games, which seemed to be going on forever. Only the girl's mother, wild-eyed and possessed by the fever of party orchestration, was enthused, and she led them through endless rounds of red rover, musical statues, even an egg-and-spoon race. By the time a game ominously titled "Doggy, Doggy, Where's Your Bone?" was about to start, the birthday girl was crouched under a picnic table crying.

Vera, ever the ambassador, ventured under there to pow-wow. The girl was hot and hungry. She could tell the other children weren't having fun. The party had been going on for three hours and cake and presents were not yet in sight. Why was her mother doing this? Couldn't they at least do one of the fun party games, like the piñata? Wasn't the birthday party supposed to be about *her*? But her mother didn't even care that she was crying there under the table. Her mother was going to make everyone play "Doggy, Doggy, Where's Your Bone?" no matter what.

Vera patted the girl's skinny thigh. "Maybe your mom just doesn't understand how you feel," she said. And so Vera crawled out from under the picnic table, and went and found the girl's mother, tugging at the woman's dress as she was trying to explain the rules to the new game.

"Excuse me," she said politely, "Samantha would like to open presents and eat cake now. She doesn't want to play games anymore."

"Well, right now we are playing games," the girl's mother said, leaning down to Vera's eye level, her hands on her knees. "We have three more to go before it will be time for cake and presents." She pointed at the chalkboard that listed the party activities.

"But maybe," Vera insisted, "you could just skip some. Maybe you could skip to the piñata?"

"Samantha is welcome to join us if she decides she wants to be a big girl. Otherwise, she can stay under the table and cry."

Vera stared at the woman for a moment, and then said, loud enough for everyone to hear, "If you wanted a birthday party so badly, you should have thrown one for yourself."

Vera was always just like that. Almost brutally clear-sighted. Even as a child, she saw through people. Saw the reasons they did things. Saw the machinery behind the façade.

As she became a teenager, her nose for hypocrisy became even keener and her thirst for justice more merciless. One of her high-school English teachers actually got teary-eyed during a parent-teacher conference out of worry that Vera didn't like her. "I feel like she can tell that I'm not actually equipped to challenge her," the poor woman said. "I mean, my degree isn't even in English, it's in education, and I feel like there is a real lack of depth to my analyses sometimes that Vera senses, and honestly, I don't blame her."

If adults were unable to keep from seeking Vera's good opinion, her peers didn't have a chance. They worshipped her in a way that made her disdainful. The fall she was sixteen, she went to the homecoming dance in fleece footie pajamas printed with tropical fish and convinced her boyfriend, Fang, to do the same. They looked like giant, weird, Floridian babies. She also coerced him into memorizing a choreographed break-dance routine with her. I worried the whole thing was deeply misguided, but the dance number was a hit. Everyone thought wearing footie pajamas to homecoming was hilarious and cool.

"You're a trendsetter," I said.

"Ugh," she said. "Gross."

Because she wasn't a trendsetter. No one could hope to be like her. She was one of a kind and, because of this, very much alone. About whether she was pleased with this state of affairs or saddened, I was never entirely sure. Maybe she would have liked to belong. Maybe her cruelty to the girls who would have done anything to be her friends was preemptive because she feared they would never accept her as she was. And maybe that's part of why she and Fang became the way they were.

But all of this is only speculation.

When I first saw Vera in the psych ward, she was wearing paper slippers and eating a banana.

I rushed to the hospital in a hallucinatory state heightened by the paperwork, the waiting room, the complicated buzzing system of locks on the huge doors of the ward. Vera had been transferred during the night from an emergency room to an adolescent unit in a psychiatric hospital in Irvine, so I got there before her mother who was coming all the way from Rancho Cucamonga. Katya, Vera's mother, had called at five in the morning to bark the address of the hospital at me, as well as a jagged, hiccuping slurry of facts and Russian curses and sobbing and bizarre speculation. Maybe it was a vitamin deficiency? Why would her *devochka* do this to her? What could have happened? The police had arrested her at a party, but arrested her for *what*, Katya wanted to know. "Is nakedness now a crime, Lucas?"

The ward looked just like a hospital, but inside no one was in bed or hooked up to tubes. Still, the cues for sickness were everywhere, in the smell of something antiseptic, the tile floors, the bright lights. All the patients were under seventeen. They looked like normal teenagers. Normal teenagers wearing hospital scrubs.

"Are you all right?" I asked, sitting down with Vera in the visiting room at a laminate picnic table that reminded me of school lunchrooms so suddenly and vividly it was like time travel.

Vera shrugged, blinking her puffy eyes. "There's a boy in here who says he can only masturbate to pictures of, like, geological formations or stars. Volcanoes. He keeps a stack of *National Geographic*s in his room."

"He's lying," I told her, grateful at least that I could be sure of that much, could, as her father, contribute sound advice about the scenarios in which young men masturbate. "He's saying that to get attention."

"You think?" Vera asked, seeming relieved. "He thinks he's the next Messiah. He says he likes to come all over the Andromeda constellation. Which has a certain logic to it, I mean what else could cause God to feel desire?"

"Stop talking to this kid—who is this kid? He is not God. How is he telling you all this?"

"Just at breakfast," she said. "The boys and girls eat meals together."

"So what happened?" I asked her. I had a rough outline of events from Katya, but I wanted to hear it from Vera because none of the pieces I had made sense. It seemed that Vera, then only sixteen, had gone to a party she should never have been at in the first place, had stripped naked and begun reading from the book of Revelation. She had then chased several members of the cheerleading squad around the living room, trying to baptize them with sour apple liqueur. "Why baptize?" Katya had cried on the phone. "Is she Christian now? For what *reason*?" Then, in front of everyone, Vera had tried to slit her wrists.

The night ended with Vera strapped to a gurney naked, bloody, raving, and put into an ambulance. Stitches at the emergency room, and then the transfer to the psych ward and the commencement of the bizarre laborious protocol: "a danger to herself or others," 5150, three-day mandatory hold, social workers, and now some asshole who masturbated onto images of the cosmos.

But what had even happened? I wanted her to tell it to me so that it made sense. I wanted her to say it was a weird joke, or a dare, or that she had been shit-faced and didn't remember any of it. Had she really wanted to kill herself? It didn't seem possible, if only because Vera was usually excellent at whatever she did, and the bandage on her arm was high, almost halfway up her forearm. My daughter was not an idiot. She might not know which direction to cut, but surely she knew to cut the wrists.

"Were you"—I began—"were you trying to kill yourself?" I motioned at her bandage. She just stared at me, sighed as though I were annoying her. "They said you tried to kill yourself."

"Of course I wasn't trying to kill myself!"

"Thank God. I didn't think so," I said, "but, please, Vera, just tell me what happened."

She stared into the pale fibers of the side of her banana. "It's like it's woven together," she said.

"Vera?"

She blinked shut her eyes again and rubbed at them with a curled fist. "Papa," she said, in the Russian way, with that long, soft first syllable like a pillow, "you aren't good at this stuff, so why not just let Mama do it?"

"Let Mama do it?"

"Don't make me spell it out for you," she said.

"Spell out what?"

She set down her banana and looked at me. "We see each other on the weekends, and it's fine. You rent whatever movie I want, we order whatever food I want, great, fine. But sometimes you are so desperate for me to like you that it makes me annoyed. You're like a dog begging for attention. It disgusts me. You are honestly the last person in the world I want to talk to right now."

It was like I had awoken to discover I was at the top of a Ferris wheel, the car bobbing over empty space. Vera could do that to me, pull the rug out from under me. It was always a struggle not to let her know how badly it hurt. "Your mother will be here soon," I said. "I know this whole thing must have been scary. Did you sleep at all last night?"

Vera shrugged, raised her eyebrows in a tired way, and continued eating her banana. Every day, she looked more like Katya. Both of them had peculiarly round heads like Persian cats, wide mouths, and thick, shining dark hair. My blond genes had been swept away like nothing but recessive cobwebs. There was something about Katya and Vera that I recognized as biologically different from myself, some cellular Russianness that caused their necks to smell like raisins and made their eyeteeth a subtly different shape than other people's.

Katya and I had only been together for our senior year at Exeter, a boarding high school with brick buildings and marble staircases at which neither of us felt we belonged. Our courtship was brief, only a single year, and we had been estranged most of Vera's childhood. I had never changed one of Vera's diapers, never put her in time-out for hitting the dog. What did I know? I had no clue how to father her.

I had assumed that if I gave it enough time and put in the years of consistently being there, being steadfast, being warm, some kind of authentic intimacy would grow between us. Now she was sixteen, and I was gradually coming to the conclusion that waiting for a teenage girl to want to be friends with her father was like waiting for a cat to want to take a swim. And for my part, I had never developed the set of paternal reflexes and instincts I assumed would assert themselves. I had been only eighteen when she was born. In fact, most people who saw us in public assumed we were dating, which I attempted to combat by loudly calling her "kiddo," which she hated.

"Let Mama *do it*," she had said.

Though what we were supposed to be *doing* to her, whether this was bad behavior or a medical emergency, was still unclear to me. I wished I had stopped to get something to eat. My stomach kept making haunted-house sounds that were embarrassingly audible in the empty tiled room.

When Katya showed up, she came with dark brown bottles of vitamins, a thermos of some green, vile-smelling tea, sure that Vera had just had some kind of aberrant attack. "My daughter is not insane," she said to the doctor, when we finally got to see one. Katya and Vera and I were all seated in the doctor's small office. He was a thin, blond man with watery-looking eyes in his late thirties named Dr. Sneed. He told us he was diagnosing Vera with bipolar I with psychotic features.

I knew what bipolar was in a vague, strictly literary way, but I didn't know the differences between I and II, didn't know the treatment protocols. I didn't know that they were telling me my daughter would never live a completely functional adult life, that she would always be on medication, that the medication would affect her health, that she might not be able to hold a job, that she might not be able to graduate college, that she might not be able to sustain long-term relationships, like a marriage or even close friendships, that she should not have children. I thought they were telling me my daughter was being rebellious and emotional, things I already knew. That was part of what was great about Vera, after all. She was a dervish of a girl, smart and a little mean and absolutely charming. It seemed possible this was just another of her high jinks, a kind of social experiment gone horribly wrong.

But the doctor did not think so. The doctor thought it was very clear. "Normally, I hesitate about diagnoses with adolescents," he said, "but in this case, I think we are better served with a clear treatment protocol that we can move forward with as rapidly as possible."

Vera sighed, annoyed, as though her diagnosis were detention being doled out, and it was difficult to tell what she really thought. But Katya, Katya actually tried to argue the doctor out of the diagnosis as though she were haggling at a swap meet. "She is very young, maybe this is just a phase?" Kat pleaded.

Maybe this, maybe that, Katya went on, describing an aunt of hers who had a vitamin D deficiency that made all the doctors think she had lupus.

Dr. Sneed nodded. "I know how difficult this is to hear," he said.

"It's difficult to hear because it's bullshit," Katya said, suddenly hostile. "Bullshit is what it is."

I was jealous of her ability to believe in Vera, and knew it was a failure in myself that I believed this doctor I had just met over my own daughter. But I couldn't help listening to the doctor—it was some kind of reflexive respect for authority, as involuntary as an eye twitch. However, he could sense this and it caused him to begin addressing all his statements to me, ignoring Katya and infuriating her even further.

"This is a phase," she kept insisting. "I know it is. In my heart. As a mother. It's a phase."

But what kind of phase was it to strip naked and try to baptize cheerleaders with liquor? Who cuts up their arm with a kitchen knife at a party for kicks?

And yet Katya was just trying to protect her daughter. Even Dr. Sneed seemed to understand this and he spent more than an hour with us in that tiny office, gently arguing with Kat until finally Vera asked if she really had to sit through this, got up, and walked down the hall.

After her psychotic break, Vera was only held at the mental hospital for three days. She stabilized remarkably quickly, though I didn't know enough to appreciate that at the time, had zero context for understanding what was happening. But in retrospect, we were lucky. She responded well to the drugs. For a little while, it seemed like maybe we were out of the woods. Vera seemed pissed off, distant, but not insane. We would get through this. She would take the pills. Maybe eventually she could taper down. Everything would go back to normal.

After her release from the psych ward, we said goodbye to Dr. Sneed, and Vera was appointed a psychologist by the state named Dr. Carmichael, who spoke in a high, breathy voice like Winnie-the-Pooh. It was difficult to keep a straight face when he was talking. It didn't seem possible that it was his real voice. It must have been caused by some kind of medical condition, so it shouldn't have been funny, but it was. After our first session, Vera, Katya, and I all stood in the parking lot for a while, awkwardly making small talk, before Katya suggested we get frozen yogurt. It was right next door to Dr. Carmichael's office in the same strip mall, one of those places where you are allowed to serve yourself and the smallest size available is basically a cardboard bucket. The three of us ate sitting at the counter, staring out the window at the parking lot. "Can we please," Katya said finally, "just acknowledge the voice? *What* was going on?"

"What do you mean?" Vera asked. The medication she was on made her slow and literal, or else it was an affectation she was trying out, a way of punishing us by refusing to be her usual loquacious self. She blinked slowly, like a cow.

Katya did an impression of Dr. Carmichael's high, ridiculous voice, and Vera's face lit up, almost in slow motion. She burst out laughing. "I guess it was kind of weird," she said.

Katya went on and on as Dr. Carmichael, *"And how does that make you feel, Vera? Can you think of a better way you could have solved that problem? Let's revisit that a little later. Was that uncomfortable for you?"*

I watched, amazed, as Katya goaded her until Vera was in hysterics, the two of them happily laughing, waving their plastic spoons like batons as they conducted, sentence by sentence, the crushing idiocy of the kindly and ridiculous Dr. Carmichael. How did Katya know how to do it? How could she perform such alchemy, turning tragedy into comedy, like straw into gold? Even as I was jealous, I was grateful for the reprieve, however momentary. Grateful to be included, eating yogurt and watching the two of them laugh.

Ever after that, we all used the Dr. Carmichael voice, especially when we were talking about something boring or something we didn't want to do: asking Vera if she had done her homework, explaining we had to take the car in for an oil change. Probably it was cruel of us, but it was a necessary cruelty, a way of surviving a situation that was actually terrifying.

The absurdity and the banality of the mental health system were almost unreal: the paperwork, the weird scripts of questions used in therapy sessions, not to mention the problems with insurance and billing. And in the midst of it, Vera, beautiful even when zitty and dull-eyed, wearing cutoffs and stained, revolting, sweaty Ugg boots, telling truths that horrified everybody.

About the medical establishment: "You want to police my thoughts, and if I have thoughts you don't like then you say I am mentally ill and you drug me against my will. This is criminal. Show me a brain scan, show me a blood test that proves any of this!"

About Katya: "Mama, you are enjoying this too much, you should try to hide it better. You are not in a movie. This is real life. Nobody cares how you feel. Pull it together."

About me: "Papa, you are so awkward at comforting me it makes me tired just looking at you."

When she wasn't saying these cutting things, she was generally morose and silent. She slept twelve and thirteen hours a night. She was in a support group for people living with mental illness that she absolutely hated going to. There was a schizophrenic there who did nothing but describe various salads he had eaten. It bothered her, the salads, and she complained about them. "How is that supposed to help me?" she would ask.

None of us knew. None of us knew the answers to any of the questions she was asking. We just told her to keep going to the support group anyway and that "things would get better." But she knew we were lying to her.

It wasn't just the bipolar diagnosis. Her psychotic episode had been in October, and by November she was back in school but being bullied. Some shitty kid had taken video of her episode with his phone and posted it on the Internet. I was clueless about it until Vera's boyfriend, Fang, showed it to me.

Fang, having evidently procured my schedule from Vera, simply appeared one Friday at Orange Coast College where I taught English. He found me sitting in the courtyard, avoiding grading papers by means of drinking bad coffee. He sat down at the picnic table with me, though when he did, he eschewed sitting opposite and instead sat down close beside me, making the whole picnic table groan and creak. I thought for a moment that we were going to tip over.

Fang was a confusing and intriguing mixture of things: Mormon, but born on the island of Tonga in Polynesia, huge and hulking, a defensive tackle for Rancho Cucamonga High's Cougars, and yet strangely dreamy and easily bossed around. Vera was constantly making him do small errands and chores for her. In Rancho Cucamonga, there was a surprisingly large Polynesian population, and Tongans were notorious defensive linemen. "Tongan tough, Tongan lazy," the football coaches liked to say, and Vera hated it. "Racist blowhards," she called them, all the while stroking Fang's hair, as if he were an oversize pet, a trained bear or tame lion lounging in her lap on the couch.

But there was no denying the Tongans were a wild bunch. Once Vera went to a barbecue at which a live pig was slaughtered and then roasted. She reported that the boys not only killed the pig with spears but kicked it, punched it, literally fought the pig to death, all in the parking lot of the Church of Jesus Christ of Latter-day Saints. Such things went on in Rancho Cucamonga, though I never would have guessed. From the outside, the town was culture-less, bland, a collection of middle-class families with a propensity for big trucks and eyeliner. Katya worked at the nearby elementary school in special ed—that was the reason they had moved there, so that she could be the director of a new program in the district. Their condo was only about an hour inland, depending on the traffic, from my apartment in Irvine.

For her part, Katya objected not to Fang himself but to his Mormon-ness. "So you have to date a Christian, I get it, it's

Rancho Cucamonga, but did you have to pick a Mormon boy?" she would ask. It wasn't the special underwear, or the idea of getting your own planet, or even the Christianity that really upset her, though she did openly mock all of these things. It was that the Mormons had set about baptizing the dead in an effort to save them retroactively, and in particular, they had been baptizing the victims of the Holocaust. They had even baptized Anne Frank. It was offensive beyond all belief, though the Mormons seemed to have done it in genuine good faith.

Although initially against Fang, Katya finally caved because she liked the boy himself so much, but she still needled him about it, asking him how his grandma Anne was, and saying, "You better distance yourself from those crazies, Fang. You better not go on a mission!" But Fang showed no inclination to go on a mission. He didn't seem overly mindful of the prohibitions in the Words of Wisdom, either, and a Starbucks was almost perpetually in his hand. If he wore special underwear, Vera said nothing about it. And though he went to church semi-regularly, this discrepancy between word and deed appeared not to bother him at all. As to whether he actually believed in God or in the Mormon faith, I had no idea. He was fairly unreadable in that regard.

"Look," Fang said, and pulled out his phone. He opened an app, was loading a video. "There's this kid and he videoed Vera that night. He keeps posting it. Everybody at school has seen it. I didn't know who to come to. You better look at it," he said.

Then he pressed Play with his giant thumb, and together we watched the tiny, grainy, badly lit video in between his cupped palms. It was Vera. She was naked and there was something wrong-looking about her eyes—they were too dark. Her pupils were huge. She was in front of a laughing crowd, catcalling her, as she told them she was God's daughter. No knife could cut her. "I am the immortal light," she said, before reaching up with a long serrated knife and slashing at her extended arm. Laughter, and then, as the blood spurted from her, leaping like little red frogs at the drunk kids watching her, the laughter turned to shouts and yelling, and the kid who was videoing ran out of the house to the dark front yard where you could hear him panting and laughing uneasily, saying, "Jesus Christ, let's leave before the cops get here."

We sat in silence together when the video stopped playing. It was so bright out. I could hear young girls laughing a table away, silly, hysterical, the way only teenagers can be.

"I could beat him up, but I thought I should come to you first," Fang said finally, his eyes worried above the planes of his cheeks.

"That's good you did," I said, though I wondered why he had come to me and not Katya, why he had driven the hour west to seek me out. Perhaps because Katya was still insisting that Vera wasn't mentally ill, that this was all the result of some obscure vitamin deficiency. Or maybe it was an intuitive delicacy that made him prefer not to show such a disturbing video to Vera's mother. Maybe he understood that Katya should be kept from seeing such things at all costs. "Don't beat him up," I said. "I'll go to the school and have him expelled or something."

Fang nodded, as though this was what he had been hoping for.

"All right," he said, standing suddenly, his business clearly concluded. "You're a good man, Mr. Lucas," he said, before lumbering away.

But I wasn't able to get the boy, Johnson, expelled, only suspended for three days, which was fine, except that the video kept being posted and reposted under a variety of names. Vera appeared not to mind the fact that she was openly taunted at school and often came home with spitballs in her hair that she was too out of it to remove. "Why are you so surprised by the potential for cruelty in teenagers?" she said in a sit-down with me and Katya one night. We were all eating grilled chicken breasts and tomato-and-cucumber salad that Katya's boyfriend, Misha, had prepared so slowly and carefully that I had gotten panicky watching him do it. Did he not know how to slice a tomato? Why was he looking at the tomato for so long, turning it this way and that before making a cut?

I did not understand Misha, who was also Russian and exceedingly good-natured and possibly very Zen or else just mentally slow. They had been together three or four years now, but as far as I knew there was no talk of getting married. I suppose it shouldn't have surprised me that Kat wound up with another Russian émigré. Her Russianness could not be eradicated no matter how long she spent here. She was the only person our age I knew who brewed coffee in a percolator. But then, it wasn't really about Russia, it was about Russianness. It was about ways of making tea, raising children, the importance of piano lessons, the incompleteness of a home without nice rugs. I wondered if Misha minded the way she kept the original plastic on the seats of the dining-room chairs. It made a small hissing noise whenever you sat down. But maybe his mother had done the same, maybe he found it comforting, maybe together they both recoiled at the sight of naked upholstery in other people's homes.

"Did you not read *Lord of the Flies*?" Vera said. "This is just how humans are. This is it, guys, so just get over it."

But we couldn't get over it. After almost a month of this,

Fang and his cousins cornered the boy who was with his two doofus friends and beat the living shit out of them. Katya was appalled, but I was glad. I would have loved to punch the kid myself. After that, people mostly stopped making fun of Vera openly, but perhaps they had simply moved on to someone else.

Even if Rancho Cucamonga High was comfortable forgetting, I knew I wouldn't be able to. I would forever remember that shaky, grainy video clip, my naked daughter, her large, mannish hands making her arms look too thin as she held out her wrist, "I am the immortal light." She was God's daughter, she had insisted. I couldn't help but feel it was my absence in her childhood that she was trying to fill, that really this was all my fault, that God had rushed in where I was supposed to be standing.

And as the months passed, that video was the only proof I had that Vera actually was mentally ill. Otherwise, I sometimes felt the doctors were simply trying to medicate the Russianness out of her. Sometimes I wanted to reassure them: "No, no, a perverse interest in nothingness is actually perfectly normal."

That winter, Vera turned seventeen at the most depressing birthday party ever thrown for a seventeen-year-old girl. Katya made her wear a purple tissue-paper crown, and Misha had unexpectedly baked: yellow cake from a mix, chocolate frosting from a can, but he had iced it too soon and the layers were melty and slouching. Vera ate two slices. The medication made her crave sweets like crazy. She had gotten into the habit of eating Fruity Pebbles soaked in half-and-half in the middle of the night. I knew because I found her doing it in my apartment one night on one of her rarer and rarer weekend stays. Katya griped about Vera's new Reddi-wip habit. The girl would just stand at the open fridge, shooting whipped cream into her mouth at intervals. It wasn't that we worried Vera was getting fat. The weight she had gained since starting the medication hadn't quite pushed her into chubby. It wasn't even that we were worried about her health. It was that we could all tell that it wasn't her. That she hadn't always been like this. That it was the drugs doing this to her.

After cake and presents (Katya had bought her the newest iPhone, in which Vera was weirdly disinterested—she didn't even open the box), we watched a movie together on the big corduroy sectional couch. Vera had picked the movie, *Dangerous Liaisons* with John Malkovich and Glenn Close, because it was Fang's favorite film of all time and she had never seen it. I had never seen it either. And after watching it, I was even more puzzled as to who Fang might possibly be. And who was my daughter that she loved him? They held hands at the end, and in the final scene, where Glenn Close wipes at her face so savagely and all the makeup comes away to reveal the pink, almost burned-looking skin underneath, Vera gasped. This movie, about rich, bored, rococo French aristocrats, spoke to her and Fang deeply. Perhaps that was what Southern California had become: a world of artifice, as constricting as a corset. A layer of makeup over their burned skin.

I didn't know. I didn't know my daughter well enough to ask these things. Only to wonder as I drove the long freeways back to my empty apartment, the radio tuned to turned-down static, the window cracked, letting in the buffeting wind and the slithering nothingness of pavement flashing by.

Maybe I should never have taken Vera to Vilnius. It was an absurd idea, after all, whisking her off to a strange Eastern

European vacation in the midst of a mental health crisis, though by that spring she was entirely stable. What worried me most was that she no longer seemed to be trying to find a way out of the maze of her depression. She had simply lain down and gone to sleep inside one of anxiety's winding tentacle arms. I expected resistance to my Vilnius plan from Katya, from Dr. Carmichael, but everyone agreed, a little too quickly, that it might be just the thing.

I had never been there. It hadn't even exactly occurred to me to go, not that I had ever had the opportunity to travel, really. And yet Vilnius in particular, and Lithuania in general, took up a sizable amount of mental real estate in my imagination. It was an almost mythic place to me, a kind of secret garden locked away in the heart of the world, the city they called the Jerusalem of Lithuania, the seat of a massive prewar Jewish cultural flowering.

The idea of the trip came to me in the form of a leaflet placed in my faculty mailbox. "Experience History Firsthand" it suggested in curly white script over an image of a yellow baroque cathedral. It was the kind of thing I would normally have thrown away. These days no one seemed to have even heard of Vilnius, and I liked it that way. It made me irritated to think that this leaflet had been slipped into everyone's faculty mailbox, that just anybody who wanted to could get the idea to go there, buy a plane ticket, and "experience history firsthand." As though that were a thing it was even possible to do.

My grandmother had been born in Vilnius, though her family was Polish. If other kids were raised on Wheaties, I was raised on stories of Grandma Sylvia. Grandma Sylvia had been sent to the Stutthof concentration camp, not because she was Jewish—we were Catholic, though by the time I was born nobody went to mass anymore—but because her father was a journalist who had openly criticized the Reich. Stutthof itself was mostly a camp for imprisonment of the Polish intelligentsia, though by 1943 it had been included in the Final Solution and a gas chamber and crematorium were added. But Grandma Sylvia managed to escape, and in an attempt to flee Germany for her native Lithuania, wound up in Poland and lived for a time with a group of rebels loosely affiliated with the Home Army in the forests outside of Warsaw. Ultimately, she never did return to Vilnius but immigrated to America after the war, where she met and married my grandfather. Together they had a family: my mother, Rose, and her brother, Toby, who died in Vietnam.

Those stories of Grandma Sylvia were the stories my mother told again and again, a prideful insistence in her voice, almost as though the stories, terrifying as they were, could be made tame by being told often enough. They were shadowy things that my mother was forcefully bringing into the light. Grandma Sylvia would never have told me such stories, and in fact any discussion of the past seemed to be weirdly off-limits in her presence, as though none of it had ever happened. My mother only knew the stories because when she was a girl, Grandma Sylvia drank, and she would get sometimes mean, sometimes sad, and whisper horrible, wet secrets as my mother rubbed her back in her dark bedroom. The stories morphed and changed, depending on Sylvia's mood. The versions my mother told to me had been patched together through inference, guessing which of her mother's confessions were true and which were designed to mislead.

There were many stories. There was: The Time Grandma Sylvia Escaped the Gas Chamber. The Time Grandma Sylvia

Stabbed a Nazi in the Neck. The Time Grandma Sylvia Had to Kill Her Own Baby in the Woods So the Nazis Wouldn't Hear It and Find Them. Not all of the stories were so dramatic, of course. There was also: The Time Grandma Sylvia Saved the Family by Clipping So Many Coupons the Grocer Gave Her Everything for Free. Or: The Time Grandma Sylvia Tried to Buy Rabbit Per Pound at the Pet Store.

These stories were impressed upon the soft clay of my developing mind, and they took up rather more room than my memories of the actual Grandma Sylvia. I could remember Grandma Sylvia, but only hazily. I was nine when she died, and so most of my memories of her were nothing but physical details: the ugly orange roses on her teapot; her low laugh, like gravel being shaken in a box; the pale green packets of her cigarettes, Benson & Hedges Menthol Lights; her thin wrists and papery skin that was always cut up from working in the garden; the huge sapphire ring that hung off her hand like a spider's swollen egg sack.

There was one Grandma Sylvia story that dwarfed all of the others. It was also the only story she told openly and forthrightly, though I suspect she did it out of perversity because the story bothered her entire family.

The story was a kind of birthright, or else it was a riddle, or perhaps a curse. My mother told it to me many times over the years. In fact, there was a period when I was ten or so, just after Grandma Sylvia died, when I would request the story over and over again, and my mother always told it in the same thrilling, ritualistic way, making sure to hit on all the beloved details. The whiteness of the field of snow. The red flannel of the shirt. The bitterness of wild onions and how their leaves stuck up through the snow like scraggly hairs. The details were what made it possible to believe the story was real.

Sylvia and her sister were both in the Stutthof camp in the former territory of the Free City of Danzig. They were together, having been separated from their mother and brother before being interned. Grandma Sylvia was, my mother said, the most beautiful girl in all the world, and her sister, well, her sister was not.

On the morning Sylvia and her sister (who was always nameless, my mother claimed not to know her name) were led to the gas chamber, they knew what was coming. They weren't confused or taken by surprise. They had known for months that the camp had been converted into a death camp; they had watched the small gas chamber being built. It was amazing how tedious and bureaucratic the process of death was. They had to wait in line to hand over their clothes to an officer, and as Sylvia handed over her clothes, the officer looked up at her like he had been stung. Such a beautiful girl! Handing over her clothes! About to die!

Sylvia and her sister held hands in the gas chamber, shivering and naked, waiting for death to begin, when suddenly the door swung open. All the naked girls looked up at the officer in astonishment. "You!" he said, and he took Sylvia. He led her naked down the hallway, took her out a back door, raped her in the snow, and then left her there. Before, in the small, crowded gas chamber, holding her sister's hand, Sylvia had been prepared to die, had welcomed death even, but now she was already planning how to live. She sat up, naked in the snow. She thought about what she should do, scrambling up out of the snow, crouching and trying to brush it off the burning skin of her thighs. She would have simply run toward the forest, but she needed clothes and the only source of clothes was the camp. She stood frozen, undecided.

The guard returned, startling her. He threw her some good,

heavy workman's pants, men's boots, a red flannel shirt, a jacket, and a fistful of money. "Go," he said, gesturing at the tree line. "Run!"

She took off running across the field. She thought she'd never get across it. When she finally made it to the woods, she survived by eating wild onions she found under the snow.

"And so your grandmother always celebrated that day," my mother would say, "as her second birthday, her rape birthday."

The term "rape birthday" made me cringe, especially as I got older.

"Why cringe?" my mother said. "He saved her life. Rape happens. Rape is a fact of life. Nothing to be ashamed of."

"I'm not ashamed of it," I would say, but I was lying. I thought that rape was something shameful and terrible that a woman would not want to ever talk about. But I could still remember the cheap supermarket cakes my grandmother would buy for herself on her rape birthday, the blue flowers of lard frosting she would lick off the knife.

"Maybe," my mother suggested, "compared to everything else, the rape was the least bad of the things that happened to her. Maybe when your entire world has been transformed and you have lost everything, your whole family, maybe then rape is just . . ." She trailed off.

"But why did he save her? Just because she was beautiful?" I often asked. It was a point that bothered me. What was the significance of beauty? Was Grandma Sylvia worthy of being saved just because she was beautiful? Was her sister less worthy for being ugly? I didn't like the whole thing.

"I don't know," my mother would say, because she was a naturally speculative creature, too. "Maybe she became human to him. Maybe this is something the guards did occasionally.

Maybe he raped her in order to have a chance to set her free outside. Who knows?"

So I took Vera to Vilnius.

And before we even got there, while we were still on the flight to Helsinki, we got into a terrible argument, the kind that is baffling and confusing and where one of you falls through a trapdoor you had no idea was there.

"When I was little," she had said, deep into the blurry hours of our transatlantic flight, "I pictured tiny men inside me, using levers and pulleys to work my muscles and joints. And I pictured whole cities inside my stomach where they would take the pieces of food and mash them and work them like clay and re-form them into perfect spheres or cubes or pyramids, which they would then set, like little boats, into my bloodstream."

"That's a wonderful image," I said. I had given in and ordered myself a Scotch and I was beginning to feel sleepy.

"But what if that's true," Vera said. "What if we're a collective and not a single thing? What if the idea of being a person is a mistake?"

"You mean, what if there is no 'I'?"

She nodded. She had bought a Toblerone bar at the airport and now was gobbling the dark triangles of chocolate and her breath smelled sweet in the dim cabin.

"But there is an 'I,'" I said. "I mean, that's the reason we think there is an 'I'—because we think there is. *Cogito, ergo sum.*"

"What is that?" Vera asked. "Latin?"

I tried to explain about Descartes and his meditations. Descartes was a figure I found touching. He had been very sickly and spent many hours in bed. They say that was how he invented the Cartesian graph—he was watching a fly on the ceiling from his sickbed and wishing he had a way of charting its coordinates. On the other hand, he vivisected dogs.

"What is vivisection?" Vera asked.

"Like dissection only the thing you are dissecting is still alive," I said.

"What a freak! Who could do that to a poor little doggy?" There was chocolate all over her teeth.

I laughed. "A lot of scientists were . . . like that," I said. "Anyway, *cogito, ergo sum* means 'I think, therefore I am.'"

"I've heard of that," Vera said, nodding, "but it doesn't sound very convincing. Maybe the mind works that way, but what about the body? Did you know that there are one hundred trillion bacteria in the human body? What if they are part of us? I mean—they *are*. They are part of us. So why doesn't that seem to matter to anyone? I mean, maybe I would be a different person if I had your bacteria instead of my own. Maybe I would seem like a different 'I' to myself."

"Maybe," I said. "But I don't understand how the mechanism would work. Are you suggesting they would change your biochemistry?"

"Or whatever," she said. "I mean, we're altering my brain chemistry with medication in order to make me seem like a different 'I' to myself, aren't we?"

That was an uncomfortable question. "Yes, but—"

"And we're doing it against my will. It's a kind of biochemical rape," she said. The word *rape* stopped me, as it always did.

"Is it really against your will?" I asked.

"Yes," she said quietly. "I don't think I'm crazy."

I didn't know what to say. I must have waited too long.

"But you do," she said. "You think I'm crazy."

"No," I began. I was thinking of the video Fang had shown me, her dark eyes, her outstretched wrist: *I am the immortal light.*

"Please don't patronize me," she said. "It was stupid of me to think you would understand. You make a show of wanting to be friends, so it gets confusing. I hope you understand that."

"I do want to be friends," I said, though really I suspected that was my whole problem, the trap of modern parenting: trying to befriend your children. But then, I didn't know how to be a father. What did I have to offer besides friendship?

"I'm going to try to get some sleep," she said, her voice shaky and cold. She took her neck pillow from under her seat, leaned it up against the window of the plane, turned her face into it and closed her eyes.

"Vera," I said.

She said nothing.

"I didn't mean to upset you."

She said nothing.

"Please don't be mad at me. I don't know what I think. Honestly, I don't know."

"Could you please turn off the light?" she asked, not opening her eyes.

"Sure," I said, and I tapped the button above us to turn off the little reading light, and then there was nothing but dim darkness and my daughter who was angry at me and Mario Batali on the tiny television in front of me demonstrating how to fillet a fish.

When we landed in Helsinki, it was like none of it had ever happened. Like the whole conversation had been erased. We walked shakily through the airport and boarded our flight to

Vilnius, but I knew it wasn't all right. There had been a test and I had failed it. And we hadn't even gotten there yet.

I hadn't told Vera the story of Grandma Sylvia's rape birthday, in part because Katya had asked me not to. But even as we got off the plane in Vilnius and wandered the sparkling, efficient little airport, where the air smelled sharp and clean, and where all of the people were dressed so beautifully and formally (I had somehow managed to spill wine/grease/dark stuff all over the front of my polo shirt), I still thought maybe Vilnius had the magic that Vera needed, the magic that was so painfully absent in Dr. Carmichael's office, the magic that I myself lacked and was unable to give her. In a way, Vilnius seemed like my last chance.

But a chance at what? To save Vera? To wake her up from an enchanted slumber? It was absurd. Possibly my motivations were more selfish. Vera identified as Russian because her mother was Russian, and she had grown up speaking Russian at home. She identified as Jewish because her mother was Jewish, and she had been raised going to temple, had gotten bat mitzvahed and everything. She did not identify as Polish or Lithuanian, nor did she have any interest in my family's faded, sentimental Catholic memories. Then again, why should she? I myself hardly identified as Polish or Lithuanian. Even my mother didn't speak a word of Polish, though her mother had been fluent. We didn't have a culture to offer her so much as the ghost of a culture. And maybe the Grandma Sylvia story had something to do with that. I worried that at bottom, I just wanted Vera to be interested in me, in my family, to ask me questions and hear my stories and make me feel like *not* the worst father in the world.

Still, as we waited for our bags in the Vilnius airport and

looked around hopefully for the person from the program who was supposed to meet us, part of me thought that if Vera could find in herself that hardness, that ability to lick the frosting off the knife, maybe she would be better able to play the hand that life had dealt her.

Vera redid her messy, rat's-nest bun, and said, "Hot Jewish Johnny Depp at two o'clock."

"What?" I asked. I had just spotted her Hello Kitty suitcase tumbling down the chute and onto the baggage carousel.

"I said the hottest guy I've ever seen is walking over here right now. Don't tell him you're my father."

"Are you Vera and Lucas?" asked Johnny Depp, his voice stunningly American and reassuring in the midst of so much susurrus murmuring. He was wearing a fedora and flashed glaringly white teeth. There was an air of fate about his swagger, as though we had stepped into an absurdist film. I could already feel reality shifting.

"Yes," I said, touching Vera's shoulder. "I'm Lucas. And this is my daughter, Vera."

Chapter 2

——

Date: 7/7/2014 11:43 PM
From: Vera.Abramov@gmail.com
To: FangBoy76@hotmail.com
Subject: Fairytale on Jew Street

Dear Fang,

Already my neurons are like tragic little fireflies trying to find a mate before they die, that is how fucking tired I am, and the apartment I am in is weird and smells like tea bags and plastic that has been microwaved, and I am a pathetic, puffy, bloated creature who has not pooped in, I swear, like three days, and who got rained on, and then went to a weird concert, and then got a little tipsy off free chardonnay in plastic cups, and then had a heart-to-heart with a really old lady who wanted to buy pot, and OH MY GOD FANG it is weird here, it is so so so weird, and yet it is kind of wonderful. I thought this whole trip to Lithuania was going to be a drag because, well, reasons, but I have this feeling in my guts like when a plane takes off or when you have just shoplifted something, only I can't figure out what I have stolen or what part of me is about to be launched into the air.

1. The buildings here all look like wedding cakes and the streets look like alleys. The street our apartment is on is called

Žydų gatvė, which means "Jew Street," or, I guess, "Jewish Street." Because the people of Vilnius are mad straightforward like that. I don't know how to describe what is both creepy and beautiful about this town, Fang. It's surrounded by forests and swamps, and in the middle of, like, WILDERNESS there is suddenly this little medieval town with all these quaint buildings. Only it doesn't feel old and ramshackle but instead very modern and European and civilized, except that amid bicycles and taxicabs there will suddenly be a babushka selling mushrooms out of a red handkerchief. I would not be surprised to meet a Nobel Prize–winning scientist in a café, nor would I be surprised to encounter a gnome. It is just that kind of place.

2. I've decided that the problem with my dad is that he is trying to be likable all the time. Inside his head there is some sinister laugh track going on that either guffaws or boos, and no one can hear it but him and he lets it rule everything he does. God forbid someone not like him. That's the tragedy he is constantly trying to avoid. I'm going to try an experiment of just being excessively nice to him and praising him for everything he does and see what happens.

3. The concert we went to was possibly the most insane event I have ever attended, and yet it was totally normal. Here is what happened: We had to walk there, getting totally lost, through the rain, without umbrellas. By the time we got to the concert hall, we were soaked and then it was really air-conditioned in there, so sitting through the music was kind of like a specialized torture technique. The music itself was just a pianist and a singer, and the singer was an incredibly short fat little man who was shaped just like a teapot, only he was wearing a tuxedo. He must have had it specially tailored. He was really the most oddly shaped man I have ever seen, and he wore shoes polished to a

mirror shine. But Fang, his voice. It was like bronze and chocolate melted together and flung through the air in spangles. It was like something stretched impossibly taut, a piece of silk against the sky, and then something that sags, soft and dead, the belly of a shot fox, the clicking jaw of a dying mink.

He was singing in Yiddish, but it didn't matter that I couldn't understand because I was still almost crying through every single song. So was my dad. It was the first time I have ever seen him cry. He does not cry gracefully. He looked like he had an eye infection. Anyway, the teapot man kept singing song after song and, keep in mind, we had just flown for like twenty hours, I hadn't slept in thirty-six hours or so, we were freezing cold and shivering and wet and this tiny little teapot man is FLAYING us alive. Anyway, during the last song this old man next to me completely loses it and begins sobbing and then he says sorry to me and asks if I can understand the words, and I whisper no, so then he kind of translated for me, just the chorus really, but it was a lullaby about a mother and child whose house has just burned down and the mother is telling her child that they must walk into the fields, but the fields are dark, are an abyss. God, like a horrible interstellar wind, is pulling them into that darkness, intent on erasing them and the whole world. All that is civilization is ash. She is telling her child to be brave. They have no choice but to walk on into nothingness. She says not to worry. She says little birds are singing, attending them as they walk toward death.

I am going to try to google the lyrics tomorrow and see if I can find it. Because isn't that exactly right? That we have no choice but to walk out into the abyss? Death will find you warm and cozy in your bed, or will find you in the bloody dirt-mound trenches of a war, in the first world, in the third world, in the past and in the future, death remains the same, is capable of being only itself:

the darkness before there was light, the nothing before there was something.

4. Did you know that my Russian sounds wrong here? It does. I don't know if it is the accent around here or if the people I am talking to are actually Belorussian. But it isn't just that, it's me. At the reception after the concert, a man actually laughed at me because I said "drive-el," like conjugated the English word "drive" but in Russian. My cousins do it all the time. I didn't even think about it. And my case endings are all wrong, I know it, I sound like a child, like a toddler who doesn't know grammar.

I wish you were here with me. If you were here I would be too tired to give you a handie, but I feel certain you would forgive me, and instead snuggle me in my weird room where the ceiling is slanted and low. It is thundering and lightning outside. I'm sorry the Wi-Fi here is so slow that we can't Skype, and I tried to talk to my dad about the possibility of phone cards but he acted like I was asking him to perform nuclear fission. So it is going to be old-fashioned e-mails for us. I promise there are no cute boys here and I will have eyes for no one else and I will report to you daily on my thoughts and doings so that it is like we are together the entire time, and, in fact, by the end of this trip you will be sick of me!

With love,
From Vilnius,
Your crazy,
V

A T THE RECEPTION after the concert, which had been an unexpected spiritual ordeal that left both of us shaky and confused, Vera had a mini freak-out about, of all things, her clothes. Everything had seemed to be going fine; we were eating the cubes of sweaty cheese and chocolate-covered strawberries familiar from every reception that has ever been held in the history of time—for all I know it is illegal to throw a reception without cubes of cheese and chocolate-covered strawberries—when I somehow lost track of Vera. This worried me because she had been filching glasses of free chardonnay all night. She kept stealing them as fast as I could confiscate them.

I saw Johnny Depp, the guy who had picked us up at the airport, and on whom Vera had an obvious and instantaneous crush, the kind that is big and painful like cystic acne. He was standing with a young woman who was evidently his date. She was radiantly beautiful and wearing an orange knit dress that made her look like an Italian movie star. She too had beautiful teeth. I imagined her and Johnny Depp bleaching their teeth together. It must be weird to be part of such an attractive couple. Why would they even watch pornography and ruin their eyes with the specter of people less beautiful than themselves?

"This is Rūta," Johnny Depp introduced her to me. His real name was Adam, but Vera continued to refer to him as Johnny Depp and I found myself unable to think of him otherwise.

"Nice to meet you," I said. "Have you seen my daughter anywhere?"

"Uh, I did see her earlier, I think," Johnny Depp said.

"So nice to meet you," Rūta said, in a lightly accented English that I immediately recognized as not-Russian.

"Are you Lithuanian?" I asked. Despite being in Lithuania for almost a day now, I had mostly only met other Americans here for the history tour. Even the cabdriver and the shopkeepers I had met seemed to be Russian or Polish.

Rūta nodded. "I am sorry if my English is poor."

"You sound very good," I assured her. "I need to learn some Lithuanian. My daughter speaks Russian, which is good, but . . ."

"Yes," Rūta said, understanding immediately, "most people will understand her, but it will not . . . endear her to them."

"That's what I was wondering about," I said. I knew that Lithuania had been under Soviet rule and native Lithuanians must have very mixed feelings about Russians, even though they had learned the language. Lithuania had only gained independence from the Soviet Union in 1990, so it wasn't exactly ancient history, either.

"Some people still will not go to the symphony," Rūta said and made a sour face.

"The symphony?" Clearly I had missed something.

"The KGB offices were right next door," Johnny Depp explained. "They would schedule torture for while the symphony was playing so that the music would cover up the screams."

"My God," I said, and Rūta nodded emphatically, all the

while smiling brightly in a winning way. She had an ease and an intimacy with the idea of torture that would be impossible to find in an American woman.

"If you see Vera, tell her I'm looking for her. It was very nice to meet you," I said, before plunging back into the crowd.

A woman tapped me on the shoulder. "Are you Nikolai?"

"No," I said, unsure if I had heard her correctly, though clearly she had not said, "Are you Lucas?" She was holding two glasses of champagne and wearing a top with many sparkly beads on it.

"Somebody said you were Nikolai. The writer."

"Sorry to disappoint," I said, still scanning the room for Vera.

"Do you want champagne anyway?"

A man behind us laughed very loudly. I still couldn't see Vera anywhere. It took me a moment to register that the woman had pressed a plastic champagne flute into my hand, and I looked back to her.

"Are you looking for someone?" the woman asked.

"I'm sorry," I said, realizing that she was rather beautiful. She had a cloud of frizzy strawberry blond hair, and she was older, perhaps in her fifties, but her eyes were a liquid brown and large. I immediately wanted to sleep with her. It was just something about her, about her skin or the way her head sat on her neck. I knew I wouldn't because I was traveling with Vera, but it still occurred to me. "I'm looking for my daughter," I explained. "I don't want her to get into any trouble."

"How old is she?"

"Seventeen."

"My son is seventeen," the woman said. "I wouldn't have thought you were old enough to have a teenager!"

I nodded, sipped the champagne. It was an observation I had heard many times. "I was a baby when I had a baby," I said, my standard limp joke. There was actually something about the woman that reminded me of my mother, so probably sleeping with her would trigger some kind of Oedipal curse and should be avoided at all costs.

"Well, I'll keep an eye out for her," the woman said.

"Thank you." I intended to go on and say something nice to make up for my rudeness, but when I turned back to her again she was gone.

I found Vera outside smoking a cigarette under the portico, positively radiating unhappiness. She had been so happy before, giddy to be at the party, delighted to be stealing wine, that I didn't know what to make of it.

"I was scared I'd lost you," I said. "You shouldn't be smoking."

"Whatever," she said.

"What's wrong? I thought you were having a good time."

It had begun to rain again, but we were sheltered by the colonnade. I worried, as I always did, that something was wrong, that she was having another episode. I was constantly scanning her for reactions or emotions that seemed off, which probably made me seem horribly distant and humorless, but I couldn't help it.

"I need different clothes," Vera said. She blew smoke out of her nostrils like a dragon.

"What?"

"None of my clothes are right here," she said, suddenly on the verge of tears. "I look like Rancho trash! No one dresses like this here!" She gestured to her outfit, a garment she had earlier assured me was called "skorteralls," which was ridiculous in the first place but which looked even sadder having gotten wet and then dried on her.

I was so relieved that her problem was not existential in nature that I almost laughed. She was not being insane. She was just being a teenager. Which was a different and altogether more manageable form of insanity. "You want new clothes?"

Vera nodded. She dropped her cigarette and pinched the bridge of her nose.

"We can get you some new clothes," I said, walking over to her. I held out my arms tentatively, afraid a hug was not what she wanted, but she practically fell against me, shivering from the hours in the air-conditioned hall. She hugged me tight and hid her face in my shirt.

"I want to look like *her*," she said into my shoulder.

"Who?"

"I want to look like *Rūta*."

She said this while hiccuping so forcefully she squeaked.

"We'll get you new clothes," I promised her. "Tomorrow. First thing. We'll get you new clothes."

The next morning, I awoke with the novelist Judith Winter drinking coffee in my kitchen. Evidently she was housed in our building, just one flight down, and she and Vera had become friends the previous night.

"Vera is out buying provisions," she informed me. She looked oddly formal, even though she was wearing a robe and pajamas. Maybe because she had on red lipstick.

"Is that coffee?" I asked. And like a merciful angel from heaven, she motioned for me to pour myself some from the pot on the stove.

"I packed it in my suitcase," she explained. "I didn't trust the Lithuanians to have coffee up to my exacting standards. And I am very old and unwilling to compromise."

"As well you should be," I said. The coffee was pitchy black and smelled glorious.

I sat with her at the table, trying to think up some safe conversational gambit. She was writing busily in a journal and it seemed rude to interrupt her, but also strange to sit silently. She looked up. "Have you ever been on a history tour before?"

"No," I said. "Have you?"

"My husband and I used to love to take history tours, especially of Jewish places of interest or historical sites. We've been on many, but I think this program is particularly unique."

"How so?" I asked. Ridiculously, I had not done any research on history programs in general, it never having occurred to me that I could use that little pamphlet as a jumping-off point to find other options. Vilnius was Vilnius, and that pamphlet had been more of a portent to me than a piece of paper. But it was turning out that there were many aspects of being on the history tour that I had not entirely anticipated. Like the fact that Vera would be the only teenager and would feel out of place in rooms filled exclusively with gray-haired, bespectacled, fanny-pack-wearing retirees. It had also somehow not occurred to me that everyone on this trip would be Jewish since Vilnius was a place of Jewish cultural interest. I didn't mind any of this, I had just failed to realistically picture the whole scenario.

"Well, it's idiosyncratic. The program. The main historian who runs the tours is a preeminent scholar of Vilnius. This city is his life's work. So I've heard the walking tours are just masterful. But I also think the program has a bit of a literary bent. Somehow it turned out that Nikolai Azarin, the poet—have you heard of him?"

"I haven't read him, no. I've heard the name," I said, though truthfully I had only heard his name for the first time at the reception last night from the sexy redhead who looked like my mother.

"Well, he's friends with the people who run the history tour, and he visits Vilnius every summer, so he always does a reading with the program. And he sort of spread the word through literary circles about this amazing tour, so a lot of the people here are actually writers. Novelists, but also memoirists, journalists. And then, of course, you have the Owl People."

"The Owl People?"

"Oh, you know, didn't you meet them last night? That couple from Wisconsin who have those matching thick glasses that distort their eyes? And they look out of place anywhere you put them?"

I knew exactly the couple she was talking about. They had also been wearing matching brightly colored plastic gardening shoes. "Oh, them," I said. "I did meet them."

"Well, there are always those kind of history weirdos on tours like this. Nice people, but the kind who collect spoons or bird-watch or whatever. Not that there is anything wrong with collecting spoons." Judith shrugged. "I'm just saying, most history tours are about eighty percent Owl People and twenty percent intellectuals, and I've heard that this tour is the inverse. Which was part of what spurred my interest."

"I have a terrible feeling I might be one of the Owl People," I said.

"Nonsense," she said. "What do you do for a living?"

"I'm an English professor."

"No. Plus you get extra cool points for bringing your daughter," she said, taking a sip of her coffee, which she had poured into a small bowl instead of a proper mug. "But I didn't see many possible romantic candidates at that reception last night despite the better ratio of Owl to intellectual, so I'm afraid I'm rather blue."

It took me a moment to catch up with her. "Oh, so you're on this tour looking for love?" I asked.

"It's been a year since my husband died. I'm not sure I'm looking for love exactly, but I'm tired of grieving. I'm exhausted from being sad. I think it's safe to say I'm looking for sex." She smiled at me, and I laughed. I liked Judith Winter very much.

Vera burst into the apartment then with a huge bag of groceries, babbling about a beautiful clothing store she had seen and could we possibly go before the walking tour? I was confused by how animated and awake she was. I would have preferred to sit around drinking coffee and eating some of the appealing little pastries she had brought back with her, but this was out of the question. Vera had that look. She had seen something she wanted in that window and every second that she was not able to get back and find the thing she wanted was killing her. She was hopping around like a little kid who has to pee as Judith and I chatted.

When we said our goodbyes, Judith asked permission to stay in our apartment so that she could "be close to the food source," by which she meant our refrigerator, while I took Vera shopping, and of course we said yes.

The store Vera wanted to go to was only a few sunny blocks away, but once we were inside she was transformed into a velociraptor stalking prey. She hardly noticed I was there until it came time to pay. I was just sitting on a chair as she tried things on and decided to check my e-mail on my phone. I had turned off my cell service to avoid charges, but there was Wi-Fi in the store because of the café next door. I had seven e-mails from Kat. Guilt lurched my stomach. I hadn't called. I hadn't called to tell Kat we got in safe. I hadn't even sent an e-mail.

"Did you let your mother know we got in safe?" I asked Vera through the dressing-room door, though obviously I knew she hadn't.

"No," she said. "Oh my God, *you* didn't?"

"No, I didn't."

"You're gonna be in big trouble," she said, laughing.

"Should I try to Skype her or what?"

"Call."

"If I turn on my phone it will be like eighty bucks."

"Call," Vera said.

So I stepped outside to call. Katya was understandably furious. I let her yell at me as I leaned against a metal utility pole, which, I noticed, was plastered with a poster advertising a reading by Nikolai Azarin. There was a black-and-white picture of him, hollow-eyed and serious, on the poster. He must be some kind of big deal, I thought.

"You are trying to kill me," Kat said. "You are trying to give me a heart attack."

"No, no," I said. "The time change just really threw me for a loop and we had to get into our apartment and then attend this concert and then we just fell asleep. But I promise—everything is fine. Vera is safe. It's all good."

"No, no, no," Kat said. "It isn't *all good*. Be a grown-up. You can do that, Lucas, I know you can. Don't make me regret saying yes to this trip. Just pretend. Just pretend you're a grown-up."

"I am a grown-up, Katya," I said.

"Are you?" she asked.

It wasn't an entirely insane question. Katya had been dropped into adulthood as though from a helicopter by Vera's birth. Meanwhile, I had meandered my way through the prolonged adolescence of graduate school. There had been long periods of my life where my entire plan for a Sunday was to watch football from the time I woke up to the time I went to bed, at some point leaving the house to buy a rotisserie chicken and a six-pack of beer. Since I had given up on ever finishing my dissertation and had started teaching at a community college, I had at least mastered showering more regularly and showing up places on time, but honestly not much else had changed. I closed my eyes there on the street, leaning against the face of Nikolai the Writer. In the private dark of my mind there was only her voice. Just me and her.

"Probably not," I said.

Unexpectedly, she laughed. "You drive me crazy," she said.

"Do you ever miss me?" I asked, my eyes still closed. The connection was good, just as good as if we were both in the States. I could hear her breathe.

"Of course," she said. I pictured the tendons in her neck, the soft, almost shiny skin over her collarbone.

"I miss you so much sometimes," I said.

"No," she said, "you miss being eighteen."

"Maybe."

"Truth. Go. This call will cost a fortune."

And we hung up. I stood on the street, a little stunned. Katya and I did not normally have such intimate moments. I had not heard that tone in her voice for almost eighteen years. To keep from thinking about it, I went ahead and called my mother to let her know we were safe. When I came back in, Vera was waiting patiently by the cash register. She had chosen a purple sundress and a pair of gray slacks, some little leather loafers and a couple of shirts.

"Loafers?" I asked.

"Shut up," she said. "They're the right thing."

And she was right. They were the right thing. She put the slacks and the loafers on with her white T-shirt and she looked suddenly Lithuanian. And older. And prettier. I knew nothing of clothes or what it takes to fit in with teenage girls, but even I could tell this was an upgrade. Vera was ecstatic.

"Papa, thank you," she said, as we hurried, late to our history tour.

"You are very, very welcome," I said, embarrassed by how grateful I was for her gratitude.

I don't know what I had been expecting of the history tour, exactly: lectures from various speakers, trips to museums, old women in spectacles and droopy sweaters. Instead, our program consisted almost entirely of one single human specimen. There were lectures and readings of course, and there were museums, and there was Johnny Depp, who turned out to be an American Fulbright Scholar at the University of Vilnius and who was our day-to-day liaison, and there was his girlfriend Rūta, who also appeared to be employed by the program in some fashion, and who was the person to see if you didn't like your room or wanted reservations for dinner, but the heart of the history program was Darius.

We were to take walking tours with him every day. He spoke at length without notes, reeling off dates and titles, facts and

figures in an inhuman way, almost as though he were possessed by a daimon like Socrates, a spirit that resided within
his skull, giving him a priori access to all human knowledge.
Judith was correct: The city of Vilnius was Darius's life's work
and watching him talk was like watching a prodigy at the
piano. The city itself would be our classroom, and most of the
things we would study were not housed in museums but were
simply places, ordinary ones, with pedestrians hurrying past.

But the things Darius said were rarely straightforward and
his observations veered away from the purely historical and
toward the hermeneutical. He was very concerned with the
etymology of the word *Vilnius,* for instance. Vilnius itself was
named after the River Vilnia, of course, though the exact loca-
tion of the town had been chosen for spiritual reasons. It was
built on a sacred pagan site where people came to communi-
cate with the dead. The word *Vilnia* was etymologically related
in Lithuanian to the words for "the departed," "ripple," and
"devil."

Darius's English was lavishly fluent but was accented and
slightly nasal, and he had an odd habit of punctuating his
thoughts with the exclamation "Well!"

"So already, we see that, again, Vilnius is at a crossroads.
Well! It is the portal between Eastern and Western Europe,
but it is also the portal between the land of the living and the
dead, the place where reality is thinnest and contact with the
outside is possible."

The outside? I looked over at Vera as we walked, following
this strange blond historical daimon through the cobbled
streets, but her attention was rapt. She was actually frowning,
she was listening to Darius so intently.

"Even though," Darius went on, "Vilnius seems to the West

to be Eastern Europe, and seems to the East to be the start of Western Europe, it is actually at the exact geographical center of Europe, which makes any exploration of Vilnius an exploration of Europe, and yet Vilnius figures in Europe's story of herself not at all. Well! This is an interesting problem, I thought. To be so central that one is completely marginal!"

We had to pause for a moment at a red light, and the group clustered tight around Darius as he went on. "Even stranger, Vilnius appears on early maps under a variety of names. To the Germans, Vilnius was called Die Wilde, because it was surrounded by wilderness and swamps. But the irony of a city called the Wilderness is not slight. Well! The Poles called her Wilno, the Lithuanians called her Vilnius, the French and Russians called her Vilna. It is also, of course, Vilna in Yiddish. Sometimes Vilnius appears multiple times on the same map, as though she is a pair of entangled particles that can exist in two places at once. In some ways, it is difficult to think of Vilnius as a single city at all. Czesław Miłosz famously wrote a poem about Vilnius called 'City Without a Name.' So how shall we think of this city then?"

I nudged Vera on the shoulder. This idea of Vilnius as being some kind of concatenation of multiple half-imaginary cities, a city that refused to be known by a single name, reminded me of the fight we had gotten into on the plane.

"Hey," I said, tugging Vera's sleeve. The light had turned green and our group was slowly shuffling across the intersection. "Vilnius doesn't have a single self either."

Vera squinted at me, like she had no idea what I was talking about.

"On the plane you were talking about there being no self. That the 'I' is an illusion." It wasn't that I wanted to dredge up the fight again, but I also didn't want that whole conversation to be erased. If it never happened, then it could never be repaired. I didn't want her to think I thought she was crazy, even if I *did* think she was mentally ill. Maybe it was an impossible line to walk, but I didn't see any other path available to me.

"I didn't think you were listening," she said.

"I was," I said, nodding. "I always am."

"Hmm," she said, and just kept walking, trying to listen to Darius, trying to catch his words over the traffic, but I could have sworn she walked several inches closer to me than she had been, and at least twice she turned to give me a look when something Darius said was interesting.

And I felt like I had won the goddamn lottery.

Chapter 3

―――

Date: 7/9/2014 9:47 PM
From: Vera.Abramov@gmail.com
To: FangBoy76@hotmail.com
Subject: Suck my imperfect pearl

Dear Fang,

So there is a thing called baroque architecture, and the word baroque means "imperfect pearl," which I think should be made into a sexual euphemism for clitoris. Screw "the little man in the boat." My clitoris is not some dude doing forced labor. (I don't know why I think all rowing is forced labor. I think I am thinking of Roman slave ships or something.) Anyway, my clitoris is an "imperfect pearl" and shall be called such henceforth. Really, the possibilities are endless. Guys that like eating pussy could be called "really into the baroque." You could say, "I'm off to go stroke the baroque!" Do you see the potential?!

Anyway, I really like this idea of the baroque because basically people started to think that not everything should look like an austere Greek temple and maybe buildings could get a little crazy and weird, so they started doing all this ornamentation and asymmetrical stuff, and they painted the buildings hot pink and bright yellow and purple and wild colors, and everyone was just amazed because this was beautiful too. Things didn't have to be perfect to be beautiful. They could be weird and fucked up and insane and still be beautiful, and can you really believe that dudes were only just figuring that out? And they were figuring it out by BUILDING CHURCHES. I mean, the world is really a very weird place, Fang. Anyway, Vilnius has a ton of baroque cathedrals because I guess they didn't get the memo when the rest of Europe got tired of baroque and they just kept on making more and more baroque buildings that got weirder and weirder and now there are no buildings like these anywhere else in the world.

As you can tell, the history tour has started. Fang, our tour guide is amazing. Let me just give you the particulars without commentary:

He is definitely like six foot four.

He is definitely blond, like blond the way children are blond. I have never seen a grown man this blond.

He is definitely extremely attractive (don't get mad) but too clean and upright to be sexy exactly. Probably he has transcended having genitals and has been given some other, more interesting organ instead.

He is also maybe the smartest person I have ever met and I think that it actually causes him some kind of physical pain to explain basic things to us or when someone asks a stupid question.

I think he might have metal instead of bones. That is conjecture, but still, I'm trying to paint a portrait here.

He has an accent and a really nasal voice and it reminds me of Werner Herzog, so you know, there is that wonderful creepy factor. "Civilization is like a thin layer of ice upon a deep ocean of chaos and darkness." Seriously, that is the kind of thing that Darius could just straight-up say, and because he is the leader or whatever, everybody nods and keeps following him. It is AWE-SOME.

Update: The being nice to my dad experiment is going super well. He's totally relaxing and it's making him way more likable. Sometimes I really wonder: Was he always this way? Did he ever love Mama? Was love something he was once capable of, or was he always just sort of numb and bumbling and like: *Whoops, I got you pregnant, so sorry!* I just can't picture it. I can't picture what she ever saw in him. And I know that at least *she* did really love *him* because there was one time when she totally lost it with me in a Macy's dressing room when I was seven and I was whining about wanting to get a dress that was too expensive and she just snapped and she was like, "You are the reason he left. You think everything is about you, that you deserve everything, but did you ever think about what I gave up in order to be your mom? Did you ever think about everything I lost?"

She never said anything like that ever again, but I never forgot it, obviously. I can even still remember that dress. It was so stupid that I wanted it—it was green taffeta and black velvet, the kind of thing you would only ever wear at a holiday party. I don't even know why I wanted it except that it reminded me of the Samantha American Girl doll who was like the only brunette role model I ever had.

The other thing I totally forgot to tell you about is the old woman who is also staying in our building, Judith Winter. This woman is my idol, Fang. I want to grow up to be her more than I want almost anything. For one thing, she wears red lipstick and no other makeup, which is a sure sign of someone who knows what's going on. Also, she just turned seventy and her husband died only a year ago and this trip is her brave foray into the world and her attempt to live a life without him even though they were married for most of her life and he was her one true love. Also, she is a novelist and she has written eight novels and they have won awards. And of course, she is a Real Jew who has lived in Israel and whose husband was studying to become a rabbi but was also some kind of Buddhist priest or something? I don't know, but shit, it all sounds amazing. She also had a freak-out after the concert and asked me if I had pot because she is a pothead but she couldn't bring any weed on the plane. I felt really bad that I couldn't help her out.

All of the Jews on this trip are much Jew-ier than me, Fang. I honestly feel a little out of place. I mean, Dedushka Pavel and Babushka Inna aren't religious at all, like, at all, and when I was really little we never went to synagogue. In the Soviet Union, being observant would have meant no jobs, KGB investigations, it was illegal even to study Hebrew. They knew nothing about Judaism when they came to America. My mother said she asked them once, when she was a little girl, why they had to be Jews, and they said, "Well, someone has to be, I guess. The way some people are ugly or beautiful, or tall or short. It's just a misfortune." And that bothered my mom, I think. She thought they had no pride in themselves, and it was all also caught up with Dedushka Pavel's coin dealership and him wanting to make money and be American and have a nice car, and my mom hated all that. So then right around when I turned twelve she developed this manic thing of suddenly we had to be Jews! She was going to give me the Jewish upbringing she never had! I mean, seriously, before that I'm not even sure we owned a menorah, though I do have childhood memories of playing dreidel and conning one of my cousins out of all his chocolate coins. And certainly we celebrated Rosh Hashanah.

Anyway, we started going to temple every week and I had to have a bat mitzvah and go to Hebrew school, which I wasn't that into, to be honest, and it mainly felt like I was playing catch-up because I was so behind everybody else. I was shit at Hebrew, I was really terrible at it, and then I found out we had to do this service project? I was supposed to tutor this girl for a year for free, only I really hated doing it and she hated doing it, I mean—we kept meeting, but I wasn't trying very hard, and the long and the short of it was that she failed math and it was all my fault and her parents were very, very angry at me. But it was too late to do something else so we just let it slide, but I always felt like I wasn't really a bat mitzvah. I always felt like a fraud. Which is part of why I stopped going to temple, but also because that was right around when we moved to Rancho and we never did choose a new temple to start going to and whatever phase my mom was going through seemed to have died down.

Sometimes I feel so moved, like at the concert, at that Yiddish lullaby about being chased into the abyss of the world, or learning about the Holocaust, and I think: This is my heritage, these are my people. And it feels authentic. And I feel like it's important.

And then other times I feel like an imposter and I think: Bullshit. You don't know anything. You are a suburban little white girl who hasn't done one single hard thing in her life. You are more of a Californian than a Jew! I don't know. Is it enough that Hitler would have killed me? Is that enough to make me Jewish? I'm getting weird, I'm sorry. I'll stop.

Stopping, stopping, stopping!!!

Anyway, it's awesome that your brother's band got that gig—I'm jealous I don't get to go! I am totally fine with you going, by the way, but you are not allowed to dance with anyone and you are not allowed to even talk to any girls who are hotter than me. It's not that I don't trust you, it's just that I'm a reasonable human being, and do NOT let any of your cousins drive, they are always saying they are fine to drive when they are totally hammered.

Okay, I've gotta go, I'm exhausted, but FYI, it is almost ten at night here, and guess what? THE SUN IS STILL OUT. Do you see how deranged this town is?

With Love,

From Vilnius,

Your Imperfect Pearl,

V

PS: I left you a note in your underwear drawer. I have been waiting for you to find it, but you have said nothing about it and I am an impatient creature. Please tell me you are changing your underwear regularly while I am gone.

S OME KIND OF HAPPY SURREALITY began to take hold of both Vera and me the longer we were in Vilnius. It took a few days to get into the swing of the program so that we weren't checking the schedule constantly, worrying we'd missed something, but by day four we were old pros at following Darius around. The routine of it reminded me pleasantly of school, and yet following Darius around was nothing like school. The stories he told us were bizarre and beautiful, and Lithuanian history, which was already complicated and difficult to understand, became a sloppy stew of stories and characters and details in my mind. Vilnius was a city of many peoples: Jews, Lithuanians, Poles, Russians, Belorussians. It was a city of many languages, of many graveyards, of many histories. Part of what made Darius's stories so confusing was that Vilnius kept being taken over by different powers, becoming part of first one country, then the next, sometimes changing hands two or three times in a single year.

I had never imagined Grandma Sylvia arising (and I did in some way picture her as not *born*, but *arising*, thrust upward out of the sea foam) from a place so complicated or so multicultural. My feeble imaginative powers had been spent on the details of her escape from the camp, the brutal years as a rebel in the forests, her voyage to America. About her life before these things I had pictured—what? Sheep? A butter churn? It was a joke. I had not even really considered what it meant that Grandma Sylvia was Polish, nor had I understood that when she was a girl Vilnius was home to so few native Lithuanians. "There used to be a saying," Darius told us, "that in Vilnius the façades were Russian, the interiors were Polish, the streets were Jewish, and the ghosts were Lithuanian."

I was slowly coming to understand the implications of a history I had always technically known: that Poland and Lithuania had once been one grand combined state, which was part of why both Poles and Lithuanians called Vilnius home. In fact, many Poles considered Lithuania just a special, rather mysterious and pagan part of Poland, while many Lithuanians saw themselves as culturally assimilated and repressed. Darius, quoting somebody, had said, "Poland is like a pretzel—everything that's good about it is in the outer crusts, and inside there's nothing."

I had always imagined Grandma Sylvia as a victim. It was startling now to frame her as an oppressor.

Walking around the real Vilnius made me suddenly consider questions I had not ever bothered to ask: Did Grandma Sylvia get along with her parents? What had her parents even been like? To whom did she feel closer, her mother or her father? How had the German occupation changed her daily life? Had she continued to go to school? How long was it after the occupation before her family was picked up, just a matter of days, or did it take a while for the Reich to get organized and assess their enemies? The whole thing seemed realer to me now in a way I could not have anticipated.

But I avoided the subject of Grandma Sylvia with Vera. I had not told her the true story of Grandma Sylvia's rape birthday, and I suppose I was afraid that I would accidentally reveal something if we talked about her too much. The truth was that I wanted to tell the story to Vera. To me, it was the piece that made all the rest of the portrait make sense. It was the heart of the mystery. But Katya had asked me expressly not to mention it.

"She has issues about rape," Kat had said.

"What do you mean?" I asked. This put me immediately on edge, worrying that it indicated some kind of psychological stress I had been completely unaware of. Since when did Vera have issues with rape?

"She gets obsessed with it. It started with that damn movie, you know the one, with the long rape scene and the girl is dressed as a boy? It was a big dramatic thing this winter with her English teacher because Vera tried to write some paper on rape. Oh, it was garbage, Lucas. Something like if there is no such thing as free will then rape is not a crime. She spent forever on this paper, it was thirty pages, well researched too, but very much insane. The teacher flunked her and after that Vera refused to turn anything in. Just don't mention it to her. It's the one thing I ask."

"Why didn't anyone tell me about this?" I asked. I knew that Vera was failing all her classes, but no one had said anything about an obsessive term paper about rape.

"I called you about it," Kat said, "but you said, 'Call me in the morning when you are sober.'" She did a mean imitation of my voice, a doofus Southern California accent.

I remembered the night she was talking about. Katya had called me, quite drunk, saying that the genes for mental illness came from my side of the family. Somehow, since Vera's initial episode, Katya and I had managed to switch places: She had gone from not believing a word the doctors said, claiming that Vera was just going through a phase, to worrying daily over Vera's medications and attending support groups for the parents of mentally ill children. If anything, I got the sense that it was the Christian elements in Vera's manic episode that had gotten to Kat. It creeped her out. The stuff about reading from the book of Revelation. Trying to baptize the cheerleaders with liquor. That her daughter was even reading the New Testament was disturbing to her. Vera's doctors, meanwhile, had referred very casually to Vera's tendency toward delusions of grandeur. I don't think they used the phrase "messiah complex," but that was what they were talking about. Vera was now lumped in with the boy who masturbated onto images of the cosmos, and this bothered and upset both Kat and me in our different ways.

"Why not Moses?" Kat asked. "If she must have a messiah complex, why not at least have a Jewish one? It's like Christianity seeped into her through the groundwater. Or maybe through Fang."

"I don't know," I said, trying to be agreeable while not actually committing to any of these hypotheses. I didn't exactly want to point out the fact that I was Catholic and Vera's father, since Katya didn't seem to be making the connection. But it made me feel even more responsible for Vera's condition than I already did. It seemed obvious that the Christianity, if it had "seeped in" from somewhere, had seeped in through me.

"You know what I think it is? I think Judaism is more about questions, whereas Christianity is more about answers, and so when she gets confused—it's a place to go."

"Mmm," I said. But I didn't really think that was it. I actually didn't think there was a profound reason why Vera's mania had resulted in such a Christian outburst. I suspected it was more coincidental and arbitrary than that. I had noticed this, about the people in her group therapy: Their delusions were often painfully stupid. They never believed the FBI was following them. It was always Dick Tracy, or some other equally absurd figure. It was Mickey Mouse who told them to stop brushing their teeth. Something about the way your mind made connections when you were in that state had a random, chaotic element to it, as far as I could tell.

But as Kat became more and more convinced of Vera's illness and committed to her care, I became less and less sure of anything the doctors said. It wasn't that I doubted Vera had some kind of brain chemical imbalance—there was no getting around the video of her that night, her claim to be God's daughter. When they had breathalyzed her, she came back completely clean. She hadn't even had a beer. So there was no other choice but to believe that she had a problem. But even if I believed that Vera had a problem, in fact, especially if she had a problem, there was no possible chance that Dr. Carmichael was going to have the solution. It was also painfully, visually obvious that the medication she was on was poisoning her: She'd gained thirty pounds in a matter of months, her skin was bad, her hair was falling out in a big patch in the back. She slept all the time. It was a nightmare.

"You didn't say anything about a paper," I said, "you were accusing me of having the genes for mental illness!"

"But that's what I was going to tell you about."

"How could I have known that?"

"She had come home, so angry about getting this F, and I said, well, let me read the paper. She threw it in the trash. I picked it out and read it later that night. Lucas, it was insane garbage. No normal person could write this. That's when I knew."

I nodded, trying to be sympathetic. I had heard as much in her voice that night, the despair that I had felt in the beginning, the panic that it was true, that Vera was really mentally ill.

"Do you still have the paper?" I asked. I wanted, badly, to read it myself.

"No. I threw it away. Garbage. Don't talk to her about rape. It is an obsession. It's not good for her. Promise me?"

"Sure," I said, still wondering over what exactly Vera's thesis had been. If there was no free will, was it possible even to give consent? And if there was no such thing as consent, was it possible to be raped? Or were human beings more like billiard balls, randomly, even violently clacking against each other, or like planets or asteroids, smashing into each other then re-forming in the vacuum of space, pulled into orbits around the nearest star? Possibly such a paper, while insane and even wildly offensive, could be logically consistent and, in its own perverted way, brilliant. No wonder Vera had not wanted to turn in any more work to that teacher.

What I didn't understand was why she was so concerned with rape in the first place. I had grown up being told the bedtime story of Grandma Sylvia's escape. I had eaten the rape birthday cake year after year. But Vera didn't know about any of that. Why had it been on her mind? I worried that something had happened to her.

I wanted to talk to her about it, but I had no idea how to bring it up. I couldn't even force myself to be specific about it in my own mind: When, how, by whom did I really think she had been raped? I couldn't imagine the scenario in which it might have happened, not concretely enough to start asking questions, anyway. I also did not want to undermine Katya's authority as a parent, and so I did not tell Vera about Grandma Sylvia being raped in the snow and surviving on wild onions, or rather, I told her a highly edited version of the tale wherein the Nazi guard simply felt bad for her and set her free outside without explanation. "She never knew why," I said. And at least that much was the truth.

"It's you again," a woman said to me on our next walking tour, and I started. It was the woman with the red hair, the woman who looked like my mother. "Mr. Not Nikolai." She laughed.

"Yes," I said. "I'm sorry I was flustered that night. I was trying to find my daughter and then I was so rude to you."

"Not at all," the woman said, falling into step beside me. I looked around for Vera, but she was already talking to a guy in his early twenties whose name I was pretty sure was Daniel. His khaki pants were ordinary enough, but he also wore a billowing white shirt that was somewhere in between a dress shirt and part of a pirate costume. It was unbuttoned to about halfway down his tan and hairless chest. He had taken her arm as they walked.

"So if you're not Nikolai, then who are you?" the woman asked me.

"Right. Sorry, my name is Lucas."

"I'm Susan," she said.

"Nice to meet you."

"Are you going to have the genealogist look you up?"

I had no idea what she was talking about.

"Did you not read your packet?" she asked. "They have a

genealogist you can meet with to track down your family tree here. Some people even have living relatives still in the city."

We were stopped in front of another building and Darius was explaining something, but it was too difficult to hear over the traffic, so I settled into chatting with Susan at the back of the group. "Wow," I said. "My grandmother was from Vilnius proper. I bet they might have some record of her."

"They might," Susan said and smiled. We were walking through a kind of park set in an oversize median between the two lanes of a major thoroughfare. There was a massive bronze cubist sculpture and a fountain and a young woman talking on a cell phone, her baby carriage several feet away. You would never see a woman wander that far away from a baby carriage in America. All American women were convinced that their children were about to be stolen at any moment. It was the small differences I noticed most about Lithuania. The way shopkeepers preferred to keep quiet and never tried to talk you into buying things. The way even major businesses were marked with tiny, unobtrusive signs. The lack of bill-boards. The peculiar substantiality of the puffy white clouds that looked made of sparkling marzipan. I couldn't help but try to imagine Grandma Sylvia here: a young girl, wandering through the city awhirl with different languages and different cultures.

"Well, I'm gonna do it," Susan said, clearly trying to nudge me toward also seeing the genealogist. I wondered if she was flirting with me or if she was just being friendly. My normal rule of thumb was that all friendliness was a sign of sexual attraction, but it seemed possible the rules were different on a history tour, a social setting where being chatty and friendly with people was simply expected.

"Are your people from Vilnius?" I asked.

"On my father's side," Susan said, and then launched into an inventory of her genealogical stock. "All of which is a long way of saying that I'm hoping to turn all of this into a book, like a nonfiction family-memoir type thing. If I can find out anything about my father's brother. Are you a writer?" she asked. "It seems like everyone here is a writer."

"No, I'm just an English teacher," I said.

She laughed. "Well, so am I! I feel like all I ever do is grade papers anymore. My mind is slowly being poisoned by undergraduate prose."

"But you have a project," I said. "You came here and made this trip happen. It's very admirable."

She shrugged. "Why did you decide to come to Vilnius?" she asked.

"For my daughter."

"Is she interested in Vilnius?"

"No, actually." I laughed.

"Weird plan."

"I think I was hoping to surprise her with it. With the place."

"Of course, and you in no way wanted to come for yourself. To see where your grandmother was from."

"Of course not," I said. "In fact, I think I stopped having personal emotions seven or eight years ago."

"Oh, me too, me too," she said. "Next I'm going to give up eating, and then shortly after that breathing."

I laughed. I was beginning to sort of hope that Susan *was* flirting with me.

"You know that famous Tolstoy line?" Susan asked, as we walked. "Happy families are all alike; every unhappy family is unhappy in its own way."

"From *Anna Karenina*." I nodded. She was walking with her

hands clasped behind her back in a way that seemed wonderfully old-fashioned to me.

"Well, I've been thinking about it, and I think that might be wrong. I mean—do you think that's true? It seems to me, if anything, that happiness is the more idiosyncratic thing, and unhappiness is this sort of chronic disease, where really it's the same for everyone: They feel unloved or unseen, they resent the people around them, blah blah blah. I mean, doesn't it seem crazy to you? To say all happy families are alike?"

"I think you may be on to something," I said.

"Are you happy with your wife?"

"Oh, I'm not married to Vera's mother. We were never married," I explained. "We were just teenagers. I didn't even get to be part of my daughter's life until she was four. Big drama." This small lie, about reentering Vera's life when she was four, had become routine for me. It was true: I had first met her when she was four. But the intervening seven years before I actually reentered her life were simply too damning to say to someone casually.

"But you never got married after that? To anybody?" Susan asked, clearly shocked.

"Nope," I said, and tried to smile as though I were unaware that this might be raising some kind of red flag for her.

"How old are you?" she asked, still staring at me like I didn't make sense.

"Thirty-five."

She made a noise in her throat, a kind of skeptical groan, before nodding her head. It was as though she had been told the number of jelly beans in a jar and was having trouble reconciling it with her own estimation. "Well," she said, "I loved my husband very much. And I still do. We're friends now. Which has its own challenges. Anyway, he's an alcoholic, he's in recovery. But I spent a long time going to Al-Anon meetings, which are for, like, friends and family of alcoholics, and all the stories I heard there—they were all the same. It was all different, but it was all the same. And I started to think that really the thing none of us could ever say, because it was so unique, so personal that it was almost unspeakable, was what happiness had been like. When it was good. That was the thing that I started to get interested in when other people were talking: I would try to imagine what it had been like when they were happy. Had there been mornings of NPR and coffee and burned toast, just quietly sitting together and feeling safe? Or had it been torrid? That was the thing about my parents, they were always fucking each other's brains out!"

We had wound up near Vera and Daniel and I tried to eavesdrop enough to make sure everything was all right.

"Is that her?" Susan asked. "Your daughter?"

"Yes. Vera."

"She certainly doesn't look seventeen! I thought she was in her twenties."

"I know. It terrifies me." The day was hot and Susan was sweating slightly. I had a flash image of myself licking the dew from her breastbone.

"Well, I think having a teenager is all about being terrified," Susan said.

Of course, there was no way she was talking about the kind of terror I experienced loving Vera. "You learn self-control in a mental hospital," Vera had said to me once. "If you have a freak-out, they get you with the booty juice." Booty juice was what the kids in her ward called being held down and injected with a sedative in the buttocks. That wasn't the kind of story one told a stranger though, and so I nodded and agreed that teenagers were very difficult.

"Would you like to go out to dinner?" Susan asked.

I did want to go out to dinner with her. I imagined laughing with her, drinking wine as the sun finally set, hearing her husky voice in my ear telling me things, things about her life, about her ex-husband, things about being a writer, things about why she had wound up on this odd tour in Vilnius. But I couldn't imagine abandoning Vera, nor could I imagine letting Vera tag along, although surely Susan was aware that I was Vera's guardian and any dinner with me would involve Vera as well. I wasn't able to read her intentions quickly enough to answer, and I was interrupted by Darius. "This will be all for today, my ducklings. Oh, but I must tell you one more thing. There is a legend that upon once visiting Vilnius, you are destined, or perhaps cursed, to return. So I am afraid all of you are already committed to this journey much more seriously than you might have imagined."

Darius gave a queer little laugh. Vera came out of nowhere and grabbed my hand.

"Let's get out of here," she whispered, and my daughter and I slipped away without saying goodbye and set out alone in the city.

At twelve, I had confessed to my mother that I worried I would never have a girlfriend. "Is that possible," I asked, "that it could just never happen?"

"Oh," my mother said, drawing air into her deep lungs and then giving one of her low, beautiful chuckles, "you will have so, so many girlfriends, Lucas. I promise you."

My mother, Rose, was an actress and it hadn't been a sure thing that she would make the dangerous crossing from ingenue to leading lady to character actress. She was so blond and pretty and short that for a time she had despaired completely. These traits had made finding work easy when she was twenty but miserable when she was nearing forty. I remember her wailing about it when I was little. I would hold her hand as she sat at the kitchen table sobbing, telling me about this or that evil casting director, tossing her long curly hair. I was my mother's confidant, always. I suppose you could say I was a mama's boy, except that having no father, no brothers or sisters, it didn't seem I had much of a choice.

After my father, who was also an actor, turned out to have no interest in fatherhood, I became my mother's little companion, some cross between child, toy, and friend, and she took me everywhere with her: to plays and bookstores, on long car trips to Santa Barbara and back for no reason other than to drive in the rain and listen to the radio. She told me everything, allowing me full access not only to the adult world but to her world, which was not entirely the same thing as the real world, stuffed as it was with Shakespeare and odd bits of remembered novels and family mythology. When I was five, I found her diaphragm on the lip of the bathtub and she explained explicitly what it was for and how it worked. When I was ten, she liked to joke that Gushers candy lunch snacks had been invented to get girls used to the idea of swallowing surprising liquids. She dated throughout my childhood, but she was never with one man for long and I rarely met any of them. She never remarried. "Why would I remarry when I have you?" she would say. "I'm never going to love anyone the way I love you, Lucas, so what's the point?"

She had perfect pitch and an unbelievable mental recall for

song lyrics, and so she would often burst into song in public places to embarrass me. She would sing "Danny Boy" through the door when I was on the toilet. Once, she kept up an Irish brogue for four days, though I begged her to stop and even started crying at one point. And yet, she was everything to me. Once Grandma Sylvia was dead, she was literally my only family in the world.

That day, as she smoothed aloe on my back—I was badly, chronically sunburned as a child—she told me all about the many girlfriends I would have. The first one, she said, would just be sort of awkward and painful. We would go to a school dance together and we would slow dance and I would smell her shampoo in her hair and neither of us would know what to talk about. But then, my mother went on, things would get better. The next girl, she promised, would have a great big wonderful laugh, and would snort when she was surprised, and would love *Star Wars* and skateboarding. Our love would be familiar and real and wonderfully normal. A sane love.

But I was not sure I wanted a sane love. "Tell me about the next one," I said.

"Oh, the next one?" my mother asked. "The next one will break your heart."

"How will she do it?" I asked, excited.

"Even I can't predict that," my mother said, clicking the cap of the aloe vera bottle closed and patting my shoulder to let me know she was done. "But everyone gets their heart broken at least once. The secret is to try to enjoy it."

I was positive I would enjoy it. I wanted to get my heart broken more than anything.

———

Still, it had been a surprise to fall in love with Kat.

We attended Phillips Exeter Academy together, a New England boarding school so old and prestigious that every other New England boarding school was a kind of copy of it. She was in my biology class. When I first met her, I was more a dreaming embryo than a person. Something about the harsh winters had scared my California soul into deep hibernation, or else it was simply that having escaped the suffocating and yet intoxicating intimacy with my mother, I was haunted and lonely. That is the thing about living at school: No one touches you. The teachers are not allowed to. You have no parents. Occasionally, your friends punch you. And that is about it. Eventually your whole body starts to ache.

I also felt profoundly out of place. I didn't belong at Exeter, though I couldn't exactly express why. Part of it was money. I was there on an academic scholarship, not because I had connections or power. I was there to be a nerd, though I was also there to escape my mother, or else I was there to stop being myself and somehow become a character in a novel, only I had not become a character in a novel, even as everyone around me appeared to have successfully done so. I alone, of all my peers, had remained homely and real, and I assumed that this was transparently obvious to everyone.

The things that had happened to Grandma Sylvia hadn't happened to me, and yet they altered me. In high school, that SS officer and my grandmother hovered just outside the realm of the visible, giving the lie to the grand glory that was Exeter, the easy confidence of those brick buildings, those Latin inscriptions, the beautiful children of powerful men scuttling up and down marble staircases in their blazers, laughing in dining halls over jokes that were no more insightful or interesting than the jokes told in any school cafeteria anywhere in

America, but which were confused and amplified by the self-importance of youth and money. I did not feel self-important. I was not capable of it, even though in retrospect I can see that there was a kind of morbid egocentricity to the way I held myself apart.

I indulged the ghostlike feeling that would sometimes come over me even when I was with a group of people, in the locker room after wrestling practice, in the common room of my dorm. In the midst of raucous laughter or the most absurd pseudo-philosophical argument, I could become suddenly silent, pulled away to some other non-real space that I associated, whether rightly or wrongly, with the gas chambers.

What Sylvia had lived was a life. What I was living was some sort of cheap knockoff of a life. Never would anything as exciting, as epic, as painful, as important happen to me. What was worse was that I worried that if I ever were put in the same sort of situations as my grandmother, I would fail miserably. It is embarrassing for a young man to grow up feeling his grandmother was more of a man than he, but the idea of fighting Nazis hand to hand in the forests of Poland terrified me. Not only was my life a cheap knockoff of the past, I was a cheap knockoff of a person.

And so I studied Russian, wrestled, told jokes, and ate gross amounts of Top Ramen at night with my friend Taisei, a boy from Tokyo whose parents had unfathomable amounts of money. I quietly and hungrily read the poems I was assigned in English class, and sometimes got choked up in my room, smoking a forbidden cigarette out the window, thinking about my grandmother. If the other guys were thinking about such things, they did not let me know it. And so my isolation felt as simple and complete as the snow.

But from the moment I met Kat, everything was hypercharged, overly vivid, awkward, frantic. There was no chance for me to hold myself apart, I was plunged into reality like being shoved into a swimming pool. Kat often made fun of me, and yet she kept wanting to see me. After a week of awkwardly crossing paths (I was following her around), she began inviting me to do homework with her in the library, a wonderful brick building with huge open spaces designed by Louis Kahn. That library always made me feel like we were hiding inside some kind of puzzle toy built for giants.

She knew of an old abandoned bathroom on the basement floor of the Academy Building, which she could pry open with her ID card and which we used as our secret hangout. The knowledge of this secret room, which was filled with huge, basketball-size dust bunnies and housed a collection of broken radiators in one corner, was a secret passed down through her dorm, Amen. Amen girls were reputed to be weird and prudish, but perhaps this was because they kept their wonderful bathroom a secret. Only one girl in each grade was told about the bathroom, and that year it had been Katya, who had elected to tell no one but me. She would give me hand jobs with peach-scented lotion while I read Allen Ginsberg's "Howl" out loud in the echoing silence.

She was a maddening girl, prone to eating baby food out of jars with a tiny spoon and defending the possibility of extraterrestrials. The walls of her room were papered in images of Marilyn Monroe. She convinced me to sneak out one night and meet her in the woods where we tried to get high on a bottle of Robitussin. I remember she had stolen a red carnation from one of the tables in the dining hall, and she was wearing the wilted thing tucked behind one ear, the red hyper-vivid against her dark hair in the moonlight. We did not get high, just felt terrible and sick, but she let me kiss her for more than an hour, standing in the woods, swaying with the trees, and I remember I had my hands on her rib cage and I could feel the little pull and push of her bones as she breathed in and out. "Lucas," she would say, "you are mine. Tell me you are mine."

"I am yours," I would say, flabbergasted by the drama of those words. Life was finally happening to me. Everything else had been a dry run, a dress rehearsal for this.

"That lady was totally into you," Vera said at dinner. "Can I order a beer?"

We had decided to try out the Belgian place that was the ground floor of our apartment building.

"You shouldn't drink alcohol on your meds," I said.

"Mom lets me."

"I don't care," I said. "And that lady wasn't into me."

"Was too," Vera said. "And I approve. Anyone is better than Amanda."

I was flustered. What had been bad about Amanda? I had been unaware that Vera even had an opinion. "Well, Amanda and I aren't seeing each other anymore," I said.

"Good. When did that happen?"

"A few months ago."

"Way to keep me in the loop. Was it mutual?" she asked.

I shrugged. I hadn't told her because she'd had enough going on in her life at the time. And it had been mutual in the sense that I had slowly begun to feel like I was suffocating to death but was unwilling to do anything about it until finally Amanda broke up with me for not having proposed marriage to her in a timely fashion. Actually, my arguments as it was happening were all fairly rational: If we weren't ready to have kids, there was no point in getting married. The wedding industry was a mega scam, it was just a way to get people to spend money they didn't have. Maybe she wanted a wedding more than she wanted me, blah, blah. But the sheer relief I felt once it was over made me understand that she had been right all along. I hadn't wanted to marry her. It was a crushing kind of realization, really. I was thirty-five and unmarried. It seemed indicative of something pretty damning, even though I wasn't sure exactly what the damning thing was.

"Well, you could do way better," Vera said. "She was younger than you and everything, but she was kinda fat."

I sighed. "This is one of the areas," I said, "where the fact that you are only seventeen is really pertinent, because you don't know what the fuck you're talking about."

Vera laughed, clearly delighted to have someone to spar with. "Oh, I don't? Explain it to me."

"I don't even want to. The amount you don't understand is just—" I made a motion like my head was exploding.

"Oh, I get it!" she said. "You like them chubby!"

Against my will, I blushed flame red. I don't think I had blushed so hard since I was eleven or twelve years old.

"You do!" she cried.

Just then, the waitress came and I ordered us both moules-frites, myself a beer and Vera a lemonade. I did like them chubby. Honestly, I liked them all. I liked them any way they came. Blondes, brunettes, white girls, black girls, skinny girls, fat girls, I liked them all. I thought my friends who had a very narrow definition of a woman's physical attractiveness were insane. And as much as I had failed to want to marry Amanda with the proper urgency, and as profoundly relieved as I had been by our breakup, she had still inspired in me a tremendous tenderness that made me not want to talk about her to Vera anymore. There would be no explaining the lovely creatureliness of Amanda to Vera. Vera was not capable of that kind of soft, mammalian sentiment.

"So how was that guy, Daniel?" I asked. "Is he really a pirate, or does he just wear the shirt?"

"Shut up," she said.

The outside patio where we were sitting was pleasant, and we were brought a bowl of delicious rolls. The beer, when it came, was very good.

"Did you love Mom, ever?" Vera suddenly asked me. Her face was painfully earnest and I was confused: What else could Vera think? That I had never loved Katya?

"Of course, I loved her," I said.

"The way you felt about Amanda?" she asked.

"No," I said. "The way I felt about your mother was much more serious than the way I felt about Amanda."

"It was. So then—what happened? Why did you leave?"

I was baffled. I had never expected this question from Vera because I had thought the reasons for Kat's and my split were out in the open. There was nothing secret about them. On the other hand, I had no idea what Katya had told her. I had always assumed that she had told her some toned-down version of the truth.

"Well," I said, "at the time, we were living on a commune, and we were very young. We had run away from home. And Katya wasn't getting any kind of prenatal care. Not even from a midwife: nothing. And she wanted to have the baby, I mean *you*, naturally at the farm. And I just got panicky that we were doing the wrong thing, I guess."

I paused, took a sip of my beer, waiting to see if that would be enough.

"So why didn't you guys just leave the farm and stay together?" Vera asked.

"Well, your mom was really mad at me. She was very mad at me. And I had, I guess, betrayed her by calling my mother and telling her where we were. So then she wouldn't speak to me. After she was back at home with her parents, she wouldn't speak to me when I called or answer any of my letters."

Vera stared at me, considering this. A large black crow cawed from somewhere overhead, and at the table next to us a boisterous Dutch man and his much younger mistress began laughing.

"We discovered that we were really different people," I said. "And I couldn't be who she wanted me to be."

Vera nodded. "So you're saying it's all her fault?"

"God, no," I said. "It was no one's fault—it was inevitable. It was the kind of thing that couldn't be avoided. It was a calamity, like an asteroid hitting the earth or something. It was nobody's fault."

But I was lying. It was definitely my fault. It had always been and would always be my fault.

Chapter 4

———

Date: 7/11/2014 5:47 AM
From: Vera.Abramov@gmail.com
To: FangBoy76@hotmail.com
Subject: Destined to return to Putin

Dear Fang,
    Why can't I sleep??? Ugh. I just lie here in my creepy room that smells like tea bags and scroll through news stories on my phone. Fucking Putin is insane. Like, I think he is literally mentally ill. I finally did sleep for a little while, only it was like the difference between Pringles and actual chips, like someone took sleep and then put it through a horrible industrial machine, made it into a paste, and re-formed it and baked it into a shape that was supposed to *look* like sleep but was not anything even close. Then I woke up at 4:00 a.m. because THE SUN CAME UP. That's how far north we are. The fucking sun came up. It is five in the morning right now, and it is as bright as midday outside. I even got up and got dressed and wandered around outside for a while, but nothing was open. Papa is still snoring like an ogre next door. Why do old people snore? Is it because the cartilage in their nose hardens and becomes a big grumpy whistle? Or is it just because they get fat? I think it is because they get fat.

I've been thinking about what I wrote you before, about being a bad Jew and about not really being Russian. Growing up I never wanted to be American, but I think what I really wanted was to be like my mom. I mean, Fang, she was so beautiful. She is beautiful now, but when I was a little girl, I was just in awe of her. She kept her hair long then, and it was so heavy and thick and shining, I would pick it up off her shoulders and I swear it weighed like three pounds. When I was seven and eight she was only, what, twenty-five? Twenty-six? Anyway, she was so into being Russian, and I think it was natural for me to mimic that. But—I mean, why didn't she ever start identifying as American? She never did. She's lived here almost her whole life, and she still acts like maybe it's just temporary. Or, no. It's not that, because she would never go back to Russia. I think it would terrify her, to go back, even to visit. It is more that being Russian is a way she has of being better or more interesting or more internally conflicted than other people. And I wanted to be like that too. The less American I was, the easier it would be, I thought, for her to love me. And I needed her to love me because there was no one else to do it. No father or brothers and sisters, I mean.

I wound up having an interesting conversation with my dad about why he left and it's funny, the story he told was almost exactly the same as what my mom had told me, and yet it seemed completely different. Basically, my mom had always said, "He was afraid to have a baby," like, *Ugh, men, they are so afraid of commitment, but we women must wade into the gory blood and guts of life without hesitation because that is our destiny.*

But my dad was really being kind of REASONABLE, Fang. I mean, she was wanting to have me on this farm with no doctor or anything, and she hadn't had any prenatal care and they weren't talking to their parents, and he just got freaked out and called his mom. He was only eighteen. He was one year older than I am now. I can imagine many different scenarios in which I would get freaked out and call my mom. But my mother always acted like it was this unpardonable sin. And to her, it really was. But they could have patched it up, you know? I don't understand why he didn't just try harder. Didn't he know her at all? He must have understood that some phone calls and some letters apologizing weren't going to do it. He needed to show up at her house with a guitar and flowers and stay on his knees singing her love songs from her driveway for three straight days. That's how my mom does shit. Surely he knew that?

Anyway, I'm thinking of telling him what really happened the night of my episode. I think he would believe me. We've gotten closer on this trip. I have no idea how I am gonna bring it up or when I am going to say it, but just: Wish me luck. You know, we really should have told my mom in the early days, back when she still thought it was all a big mistake. But I never imagined she'd start to believe that I was really sick. I never imagined she would turn. I was so confident that she would go on believing me, it didn't seem like there was any point to admitting it.

OH MY GOD, a cat just jumped into my room. I am not kidding. I had opened my window because it is sunny today and the breeze was nice, and the roof is at a really steep angle, like, literally if I sit up in bed, I will hit my forehead on the roof, so the window is in the angled part of the roof and a cat jumped through and then walked over to me on the bed and now its sitting here and looking at me. What do I do?

Do you think it is a nice cat? It hasn't made one single sound, not even a little mew or a purr, which seems sinister to me, like maybe it is a spirit cat and not a real cat. Okay, now it is purring, so everything is fine. I'm petting it. But it better not get stuck in here because I have no idea where it would go to the bathroom.

You know, Darius said an interesting thing the other day, he said that there is an old saying that anyone who visits Vilnius is destined to return to it one day, which, you know, isn't that just a way of saying that anyone who comes to Vilnius will eventually be forced to leave? Because you have to leave in order to come back, right? But then I was also thinking, maybe I'm not Russian, but maybe I have to keep returning to the idea of Russia. Like, I'm not from there, but I'm destined to keep returning to it. It's part of the dance of my identity. Which, you know, what if identity is more of a dance or a pattern than a thing? Like, what if it isn't so much a noun as a verb? And in the same way, I am destined to keep returning to my own Jewishness or lack thereof. It's a part of the pattern of the way I am existing.

Do you feel that way about being Tongan? Do you dream of going back for more than a visit, but to live? Whenever you talk about it, it seems like just a vacation, or like a pilgrimage, or something, but do you think you could ever actually live there and belong there again? Or would you be destined to leave, re-enacting that initial departure when you were little, returning just so you can leave again, and then returning once more to make sure you really can leave one more time, and on and on?

Maybe that is why I love you so much: We are both doing dances with cultures that aren't ours and your empty spaces form the perfect foil to my empty spaces so that when you are dancing with death, you are also dancing with me, and vice versa. Because in the end, isn't it all about death? HAHAHAHAHAHA-HAHAHAHA. Sorry, I'm cracking myself up.

There you have it, right from the horse's mouth: It's all about death. Then again, I've always been a *nei-ei-eigh* sayer.

With Love,

From Vilnius,

Your night-mare (get it?),

V

PS: Darius told us about Napoleon's campaign on Moscow (big fat disaster, like major, major cock-up in the deep doo-doo) that ended in 40,000 French soldiers descending on Vilnius only to push people out of their homes, steal all their food, and die anyway because they were so starved they weren't able to digest the food. They even broke into the university and ate the jars of organs preserved in alcohol. CAN YOU IMAGINE HOW HUNGRY YOU WOULD HAVE TO BE TO DO THAT? More French soldiers died in Vilnius than there were inhabitants of the city, and it was winter, so there was no way to bury them because the ground was crazy frozen. So naturally people began stacking the dead soldiers around buildings as a layer of extra insulation. Holes in the walls of the hospital were stuffed with hands, feet, heads, trunks, whatever would fit. For real, Fang. For real. The spring brought a terrible thaw and . . . wait for it . . . plague! Which, I mean, duh, but still.

MOST PEOPLE ASSUMED THAT KATYA had gotten pregnant by mistake, and often I let them believe this because the truth was very difficult to explain. The truth was that I had been blindingly in love and eighteen and Katya had whispered in my ear one night, "Let's make a baby, baby," and we made a blurry, moonlit decision which, through careful lack of critical thinking, grew into a plan. We would turn our backs on the corrupt world of money-grubbing, status-hungry adults and start our own family. We would live a real life, safe and far away from all the phonies. The summer after our senior year at Exeter, we took a road trip, cut off contact with our parents, and finally settled on a communal farm in North Carolina, nestled at the base of the Blue Ridge Mountains. It took me only a few weeks to discover that I hated it.

I remember mostly being sunburned and eating beet greens and lentils and other food that was too healthy to taste very good. Farming, which I had thought sounded noble and interesting, turned out to be very boring. Everyone on the farm was dopey and friendly, and there was a lot of group sex and partner swapping going on. I wanted to be like them, many of whom were older than me, guys in their twenties with beards, wearing overalls and no shirt and Birkenstock sandals, playing music in the evenings, talking earnestly about the concept of personal liberty. But the idea of being a father, the insane permanence of what Kat and I were doing, gave me a perpetual fever of panic, a swaying wobbly feeling that our lives were out of control.

Katya was only three months along and not really showing. She hadn't been to a doctor. She said she didn't need to, that her body knew what it was doing. Sometimes I believed her. Her pregnancy kept away most of the sexual advances from other men. There was a rule against monogamy on the farm. "There is no ownership here," they said. Still, most guys felt like a pregnant woman was somehow off-limits, and for this I was grateful. I was so in love with her that I think it would have literally killed me to stand by as she slept with someone else.

But her pregnancy wasn't enough to keep other women away from me. One girl, Chloe, was the most persistent, following me around as I did my chores, making gestural sex jokes with a zucchini. She was a runaway, and as far as I could tell, every guy on the farm had slept with her. One night, I saw three of the men playing with her at once, passing her around. Chloe seemed to be more than fine with all of this. She had been smoking pot, but they all had. There was nothing forced or nonconsensual or even coercive in what I saw, except for the sheer visual wrongness of it: She was short and small, built almost like a child, and she simply looked like a victim when she was making out with three adult men.

Katya called me uptight. "She's a free person," she said, "those boys shouldn't make her do anything, and you shouldn't make her not do it either." One day I came into our room to find Kat and Chloe on the bed together. Kat grinned at me wickedly.

That was what I hadn't understood, I think. That she wanted all of this. That she had chosen the farm, not just because it was a way of rejecting the world, rejecting Exeter and sport coats and aspirations to become a member of Congress, but because this was what she wanted. This wildness, this heat and sunburn and freedom. There was a kind of triumph in her eyes as she beckoned me to the bed where she and Chloe were in their underwear. She wanted to trick me into it, sure that if I just did what she said, I would find it as wonderful as she did. Of course, I got in bed with them. I didn't even have words for what I found objectionable about the whole thing, and the feeling in my stomach, like hot static, seemed indicative of a crucial lack of virility.

The sex was, in retrospect, fairly comical. Chloe explained early on that she was non-orgasmic and taking this off the table left me completely unable to know what to do with her. It was a lot of making out, a lot of awkward taking turns. It probably wouldn't have been remarkable if Chloe hadn't started softly crying afterward in our bed. Kat cradled her, comforting her, and extracted from Chloe only that she was very homesick. "That's all," Chloe kept saying. "I just miss my mom."

The next day, someone mentioned in casual conversation that Chloe was fourteen. It was like an explosion that seemed to impair my hearing. I went around deaf all day. I told Katya, and she was unfazed. "Just because she's fourteen doesn't make her less able to make her own decisions," she said. "You remember freshman year. Do you think you were not a 'real' person then?" I did remember being fourteen. And I had felt like an adult. But had I been? Did an adult draw the Dead Kennedys icon all over their shoes? But it was true that Chloe was close enough to Kat and me in maturity that I hadn't even guessed she was so young. Though now that I knew, I couldn't see Chloe as an adult, I could only see her as a child. I couldn't see the farm as an Eden, either, but only as a place where a cluster of losers had gathered to fuck each other.

That night I called my mother. What a ridiculous and weenie-ish thing to do, to call your mother, blubbering and scared, late at night, hiding in the communal kitchen that smelled of nutritional yeast flakes and old curry powder, and confessing that you have knocked up an intoxicatingly beautiful and possibly mentally unstable Russian girl who was in your biology class and who now you found yourself lying to continuously:

"Yes, if the baby is a boy we should name him Absalom."

"Yes, I too believe that the moon landing was faked." (In my experience, nearly all Russians harbor at least a tiny hope that the American moon landing was faked.)

"Yes, Western medicine is probably entirely a fraud perpetrated by the drug companies and most people could heal themselves by eating dandelion greens."

My mother had been hot with rage on the phone, wanting to talk about my betrayal, about how hurt she had been by my disappearance, but I couldn't even take it in, I just kept saying: "Kat needs prenatal care. She needs to be with her parents. I need to get a job. We can't stay here, Mom. It isn't safe here. Please help. I know I fucked up, but please help."

My mother had flown out that very night and arrived in the morning in a rented Ford Taurus to return the cursing, spitting, wrathful Katya to her parents. Everyone in my life assured me I had done the right thing. But of course I also worried that I was nothing but a coward, so scared of myself, scared that I had fucked a child, that I gave up knowing my own.

Throughout my life, a sort of flickering ghost hovered, a mirage of who I might have been had I stayed there with Kat on that farm. Who I would have become instead of myself.

The first time I met Vera, she was already four years old. Katya agreed to have breakfast with me at an IHop so that I could finally meet my daughter. I brought with me to this meeting a pale purple teddy bear. It was winter in California and it was lightly raining, and the bear's fur had gotten wet on the walk from my car, and the toy looked exactly like what it was: a bribe, too late and not enough. Vera was shy in a way that I know now was perfectly normal for a four-year-old, but which at the time I found devastating. Our meal was short—it is impossible to have a protracted meal at an IHop, anyway. I had never been around kids. I had no idea how to engage Vera. Katya pointedly did not help and would only murmur things to the girl in Russian. The breakfast experience was so awful that I didn't ask Katya to see Vera again for seven years. The whole thing lasted maybe half an hour.

One thing that went wrong with that morning was that I was hungover. I was almost always hungover in those days, it is true, but I had not intended to be hungover that morning. I was in my senior year at Reed College in Oregon and this visit was happening on one of my trips home to California, specifically my Christmas break, and the night before had been New Year's Eve. My mother and I and some asshole she was dating named Jerry had gotten wrecked drunk at a Hawaiian-themed bar that served oversize hamburgers. I had not understood heading into the night that it was going to be so insane. Who knew middle-aged people even liked to drink that much? Who could have imagined my mother would wear a plastic lei and begin dancing barefoot on the bench of our booth before being asked to stop by the management? Jerry was footing the bill so the drinks just kept coming, and it was the first New Year's I had spent legally able to drink so I may have gotten carried away.

But I had not anticipated any of that, and so it had not seemed unreasonable to agree to this New Year's Day breakfast date with Katya and Vera. In a way, it had even seemed appropriate to me: A new year was beginning, a new era of my life in which I would be a father. This misconception seemed laughable and bitterly ironic as I drove, squinting in the glare between rain clouds, to the IHop where I was to meet my daughter for the first time, sad purple bear in tow.

Katya was living with her parents in LA by then, surrounded by a nest of extended family and Russian Jewish émigrés who made that city home. Her mother watched little Vera while Katya took classes at UCLA, slowly reclaiming her life after our time on the farm and her ensuing pregnancy had derailed everything, causing her to defer and then ultimately give up her admission to Brown. Needless to say, her parents hated me. Katya hated me, too. For calling my mother to come get us. For bringing her back to her parents. For not believing in our love, and worse, for not telling her that I was having second thoughts myself but allowing my mother to do the talking for me. I never talked to her about the night with Chloe, never tried to put into words the wrongness of it, in part because I already knew she couldn't see whatever it was I saw. There was some insult to Kat in the fact that I saw Chloe as a victim, because really, what was the difference between Kat and Chloe? A few years?

But I think Kat also hated me for going ahead with my own plans. I was the guy, and so I got off relatively scot-free. In my defense, at the time I made the decision to go to Reed as planned, she wasn't speaking to me at all, refused to see me. It didn't seem there was much point in sticking around and giving up college in the hopes that she would change her mind. I had already been accepted by Reed the previous year, and so actually going was the path of least resistance. I never did see Kat fully pregnant, belly swollen and round. I didn't see Vera as a baby, only pictures. Our parents hashed out a child-support agreement and that was that. None of this was done in court—my name wasn't even on the birth certificate. Katya had insisted on leaving it blank.

Sometimes I would get drunk and heartsick at Reed and write Kat long, incoherent e-mails about how much I loved her and how sorry I was. I would try to bring up fun times we had at Exeter, remind her of our inside jokes, call her by the pet names I used to then, my Rusalka, Russian for mermaid, or the more peculiar "Cabbage Face" that had come from a joke about how weird the French were. Most of the time, she did not respond, but sometimes she sent me e-mails with no words, just pictures of our daughter. Vera was so beautiful it was crushing. There was nothing Katya could have done that would have made me feel worse. I could not even write back, so ashamed did I feel, and I would resolve to leave them alone, since that was what Kat seemed to want, what her parents told my mother she wanted, what she herself told me once, in the very beginning, in a long handwritten letter that she sent just after Vera was born.

But time would pass and I would long for them. They were a secret I had. I didn't tell everybody I met in college that I had a child. I didn't even tell some of the girls who were my girlfriends. I didn't actually consider those girls my girlfriends because I imagined that I was wedded to Katya in some awful, eternal way. The territory of my body and soul belonged to Katya still. Katya and Vera began to live in my consciousness in the same invisible space Grandma Sylvia inhabited, in the gas chambers of my imagination. At night I would scroll through Vera's baby pictures to torture myself. Vera on a sheepskin blanket, a chubby dumpling of a baby, naked except for a diaper. Vera on Kat's mother's lap, looking serious and jowly. Vera looking mistrustfully at a cooking spoon. Vera laughing on a swing, a yellow barrette in her dark hair. Her beauty was the beauty of all children everywhere, the beauty of youth itself, of life, of flowers, of perfect cells newly divided.

I was so caught up in this, in my own martyred suffering, in images of the two of them as eternal archetypes, that I did not spend a lot of time wondering what life was like for Katya. Did she enjoy being a mother? Was it hard? Did the baby keep her up all night crying, or did they sleep together peacefully, the bassinet beside her bed? Did she like her coursework at UCLA? Did she regret not going to Brown? Did it chafe, having to live with her parents after failing to achieve their dreams for her? I did not think about any of these things at the time, though now they seem like the only questions.

Probably, things were grim for Kat in those years of Vera's early childhood. Kat's father, Pavel, was a fat and pouty man with unpredictable moods and fairly conservative values. He had gotten his family out of the USSR in the 1980s when Jews could request visas to move to Israel, and from Jerusalem they had rerouted to LA where he had opened a coin and autograph-memorabilia shop that did quite well. He had an innate gift for telling when something was authentic just by touching it, a sixth sense that people in collectibles claimed was real. He was a believer in America, in capitalism, and he wanted his children to have everything. Katya was the eldest and he had sent her to Exeter, paid through the nose for four years, and then she had come home pregnant. Luckily, or perhaps unluckily, Kat's little sister, Tamara, was better able to live up to their parents' expectations, attending the University of Chicago for a degree in business. I imagine this created something of a divide between the sisters. Certainly it meant that Tamara was not around much during those first years when Kat was a young mother. I realize now that Kat must have been very lonely.

Her mother, Inna, was around, but she and Kat were not very close, at least not back when Kat was in high school and I was privy to her life. When Kat was a girl, Inna had harbored bizarre hopes that Katya would become a child star and dragged her all around LA on auditions. Finally, at eleven or so, Kat had rebelled and refused to go anymore. She never got cast anyway, and she hated it, she told her mother. They hadn't been close after that. For a time, her mother had taken Tamara around, but Tamara was not as pretty as her sister and so eventually this too was dropped.

But that day in the IHop, I was not thinking about any of this. I was not prepared for a real Vera and a real Katya. I had been living with them for so long as characters in my mind, that seeing them in person was a bit grotesque. I had a searing headache and it felt like my temples had been bound in ice-cold twine that was slowly being tightened by an invisible hand. Possibly I was going to need to leave the table and vomit in the bathroom at some point. Katya was wearing unflattering eye shadow, too much of it, and her hair looked crunchy with hair spray and she wouldn't meet my eyes or smile at me. Vera didn't answer any of my pandering, awkward questions, but stuck to her pancake with its whipped-cream smile. She was hesitant even to take the bear, and then when she did, she frowned. "It's wet," she said.

"I guess it is," I said.

How many times have I gone over this exchange? How many solutions to this problem have I come up with over the years? I could have said, "Yes, it's raining outside—do you like the rain? I love the rain. Have you ever jumped in rain puddles?" I could have said, "I know, that silly bear! I kept telling him to hurry but he wanted to try to catch raindrops on his tongue and now he is all wet!" I could have said anything, any stupid thing.

But instead, I said, "I guess it is." What is a child supposed to say to that?

"Say thank you," Katya insisted, and Vera stared at me with round calf eyes.

"Thank you," she said, as though I were the grim reaper or some other terrifying figure that only politeness could keep at bay.

The omelet I had ordered was disgusting, and so as Katya neatly cut her eggs and toast into squares and placed them in her mouth, almost as though she wasn't eating but sorting papers or something, and as Vera moved the whipped-cream globs around on her giant chocolate pancake, I stumbled on, trying to present my plan, my ridiculous plan, to Katya.

I had applied for a PhD program in literature at the University of California at Irvine. If I were accepted, and I would hear in just a few months, then I could be close to them and possibly be a more active participant in Vera's life. I had also applied to NYU and a few other programs, in case I didn't get into UCI, but I didn't mention that part to Katya. Vera could stay with me on weekends. I could babysit. I could play whatever role Katya wanted and we could take it slowly, as slowly as she felt comfortable with.

"Where would she sleep?" Katya asked.

"Well, I would get an apartment down here," I said. It hadn't really occurred to me that Vera would need her own bed and bedroom. I felt sick even thinking about how I would pay for a two-bedroom, if that was what Katya was suggesting.

"Lucas," Katya said, then faltered.

"It isn't unreasonable," I said, "for me to be part of her life. Come on, I'm her father."

Katya set her fork down, struggling for words. "Lucas," she said, "you know nothing about children. You don't know when a fever is serious and when it's not. You don't know what is safe and what is not. I don't even trust you to feed her regularly! You think you can just take a little girl and put her in your grad-student apartment and she will be happy?"

"I could learn all that—I could read books, and I could—"

"Books?" Katya laughed.

"Yes, parenting books," I said.

"Lucas," she said, leaning forward. "You stink of booze. Do you realize that? Do you think we can't smell you at this tiny table? You show up for the first time you ever meet your daughter, and you're still obviously drunk. And then you think that I am going to let her come live with you on weekends?"

"It was New Year's Eve," I started, trying to explain.

"Yes, it was New Year's Eve last night in my world too, but I have a daughter, so I didn't go out and get wasted like an animal and not even bother to shower! Lucas, you don't understand what being a parent means. You just don't get it," she said.

"You could teach me," I said. "I could learn."

Katya didn't say anything, just crumpled her napkin in her hand, shaking her head.

"Can we go now?" Vera asked.

Katya said something to her in Russian, leaned over and kissed her on the head, then got up to leave. "I assume you are fine with paying for breakfast?" she said.

"Of course," I said.

"Say goodbye," Katya instructed our daughter.

"Bye bye," Vera said, and handed the purple bear back to me. They left and I sat, waiting to get the check, holding that stupid purple bear, its fur still wet.

When I was accepted by NYU's comparative literature program, I went.

During graduate school, I didn't see Vera at all. What little money I didn't send to Katya, I spent on beer, which was about pleasure and revelry to be sure, but which was also a form of penance. There was something about being hungover that I sought out, that I needed. I would watch ESPN all day, skipping class, drinking warm blue Gatorade, feeling deep in my guts that nothing was okay and that I was a horrible person.

I spent the next seven years in New York. It was during this period that my mother began her bicoastal career path, doing Shakespeare in the Park during the summers in New York, and then making her real money by filming commercials and bit parts on TV during the winters in LA. We shared a tiny studio apartment during the summer, and I lived in it alone during the school year. I learned to be many things during those years: a scholar and a writer of research papers, a rider of subways, an eater of squid, an estimator of danger, a buyer of marijuana and sometimes other things, a seducer of women, and a reader of books. Oh, above all else, I learned in those years how to be a reader. My life was worth nothing except the books I read, and I spent years, literal years, reading in that studio apartment.

What I did not learn was how to finish my dissertation.

What I did not learn was how to become a father.

When I returned to California, after finally confessing to my adviser that my dissertation was not "almost done" and in fact would probably never be done, Vera was almost twelve. Katya had changed. When I asked to see Vera, she said, "Please do. She is constantly asking questions about you." Vera was allowed to come stay with me without even a cursory inspection of my apartment. Evidently, the idea of a thirty-year-old man taking care of a twelve-year-old was less problematic than a twenty-two-year-old man taking care of a four-year-old. I didn't have to buy toys or car seats or learn about fevers. All I had to do was be myself.

And from the start, Vera absolutely terrified me. She was like Katya on steroids, dark and funny and biting and capricious.

"So," she said, the first time she came to my apartment, "you're poor."

"So," she said, over dinner, "why didn't you ever want to meet me?"

"So," she said, before we went to bed, "my mom says you're an alcoholic."

It was exhausting and thrilling, and I was also very relieved to drop her off at her mother's the next day. After that we saw each other on and off, sometimes every weekend, sometimes not seeing each other for a whole month. I always tried to let Vera's enthusiasm be our guide. If she had plans with her girlfriends for the weekend, I stepped aside. I didn't want her to feel like time with me was an obligation. I wanted her to like me.

But she never really did start liking me. Maybe she couldn't forgive me for not being part of her childhood. Maybe it would take not just years but decades to make up for the time I had lost. Or maybe, I sometimes thought, compared to her violent, moody world, I was a little boring. Vera and Kat were painted in bright acrylics, and I was in washed-out watercolor. They could barely see me. I was like a ghost wandering through their world.

I decided to go ahead and see the genealogist after all. Even though I had failed to take the proper steps to make an appointment, Johnny Depp was able to get me in. It was Friday, the end of the first week of our tour, though it felt like we had been there much longer. I left Vera with Judith in the apartment, eating farmer's cheese and discussing the possibility of love at first sight, and went to the Vilnius University library to meet the genealogist, whose name was Justine.

Justine was not what I was expecting. For one thing, she was young, perhaps in her late twenties, and she had a narrow, officious face with a lean beauty and dark hair cut close to her scalp. She was also the only black person I had seen in the entire city of Vilnius. I guess I was expecting a more grandmotherly type. I associated genealogy with the elderly for some reason.

We sat together at a table in the large echoing hall. I gave her Grandma Sylvia's full name and date of birth, as well as the names of her parents. I explained that Sylvia was Polish and that her father was a journalist who was perceived as a threat to the Reich, which is why the family was interned at Stutthof instead of being taken to the pits at Ponary, where most of the Vilnius Jews had been executed. I didn't know much more about it than that, I told her.

"That's fine," she said, continuing to scribble in her notebook. She had an accent that sounded vaguely French, but I wasn't expert enough to tell if she was from France or a Francophone country in Africa. I wanted to ask her how she had wound up here, but worried this would be invasive. She was not a chatty sort of person and was really just trying to do her job.

I felt bad that I didn't have the name of Grandma Sylvia's sister, the one who died in the gas chamber, but I was able to tell her that Grandma Sylvia's brother's name was Henryk.

"And he also went to Stutthof?"

"No," I explained, "my grandmother and her sister got separated from their mother and brother on the train. They never found them at the camp. We don't know what happened to them."

"And your grandmother died in Stutthof?" Justine asked.

"No, she escaped," I said.

Justine set down her pen. "How exactly did she do that?"

I paused. It hadn't occurred to me that I would wind up telling this particular story today, and I wasn't geared up for it, but the moment I set my mind to telling it, the old words came back to me. I always told the story the exact same way, using the very words and phrases that my mother used when she would tell it to me. It was something memorized, deep in my bones, like the Lord's Prayer or the Pledge of Allegiance.

When I was done, Justine tapped her pen tip on the page in a fine constellation of dots. "Rape birthday," she said.

"She would buy a cake and everything," I said.

"What did she do when she got to the forest?" Justine asked. And so I explained about fleeing Germany and the years spent as a part of the Home Army in the forests outside of Warsaw. I even told the story of the baby who had to be killed so the Nazis wouldn't find them.

"Who was the father?"

"She had a forest husband."

"Do you know his name?"

I admitted I did not.

"And the child died. Did it have a name?"

"Not that I know of," I said.

"Hmm . . ." Justine set down her pen and briefly massaged her temples. "It's a very odd story," she said. "The gas chambers at Stutthof were small and they tended only to gas those who were too weak or sick to continue working. Which makes your grandmother's story harder to believe."

I shrugged. I didn't understand exactly what she meant.

"I'm just saying, women who have already been in a camp for months, women who have had the last of their vital essence drained from them, women no longer able to work—are typically not terribly sexually attractive. Or beautiful, as you say."

I didn't know what to say to this. Grandma Sylvia's beauty had always been presented to me as the reason for her salvation. I had never questioned it. But now, as I sat there with Justine, a more horrifying prospect presented itself to me: that maybe the guard's desire had been awakened not by admiration, but by pity. Perhaps some internal calibration in him had been rewired by his work in the camps, so that desire and pity were one and the same. I thought, involuntarily, of the boy who masturbated onto images of stars. Of Vera's question: "What else could cause God to feel desire?"

"Well, I don't know," I said finally. "That was always the story I was told."

"I'll see what I can dig up," Justine said, concluding our brief meeting with a smile so formal it gave me the shivers.

As I walked home through the winding streets, I kept thinking of her phrase "what I can dig up." Maybe because we had just come back from a trip to the cemetery with Darius, the phrase seemed to have a sinister, grave-robbing ring to it. The morning had been foggy and the graveyard eerie. Darius pointed out that some of the Christian headstones in the shape of crosses were carved to look like tree branches. Stone transmuted into wood transmuted into a cross. Almost as though the cross wouldn't mean anything if it weren't made of wood. And this too had to do with life and death and resurrection: trees, the way they lost their leaves and then were reborn each spring. It was a pagan thing, Darius said, the love of trees.

That was another part of the puzzle of Vilnius: its pagan roots. "The pagans of Lithuania were really appalling to our first visitors," Darius had said, laughing. "A priest from Italy claimed that there were people in the forest outside of Vilna who worshipped fat black lizards as gods and kept them in their homes as pets. And of course, most of the houses were built without chimneys and so blindness was almost an epidemic, from all the smoke. They used to say that nowhere in the world were there as many blind people as in Vilnius. Well!"

I wondered if Grandma Sylvia had had any lingering pagan

sentiment, even though she was a Pole. I thought of the way she devoted herself to the garden, the way she preferred the company of plants to the company of most people. She'd had a real drinking problem when my mother was young, but all of that was over by the time I was a child. By then she was just a cranky old woman obsessed with her rosebushes. I had never wondered before why she had named my mother Rose, but now it seemed possible that the name was terribly literal: Perhaps she had just really liked roses. Maybe Grandma Sylvia was secretly a pagan. It was a comforting idea. Maybe her fierce pagan heart was what made it so easy for her to let the fabric of Catholicism slip from her hands, like a curtain that was simply drawn away. We had never needed it. We had only ever been pretending to believe. Or maybe what she had learned fighting in the forests had made the nicety of God an impossibility for her. And after God, what was there besides the simple beauty of plants?

On the bus on the way back from the cemetery, I had wound up next to Darius, standing in the aisle, clinging to the straps as the bus navigated the narrow curves of the old streets. I said something, something stupid, about how the tour was sometimes depressing, so much death.

"But imagine," Darius had said, in that clipped, strange accent, "without death, there would still be so many Nazis. Death is wonderful in that way."

I nodded, unsure whether he was being serious or making a joke.

"Like a magic eraser! Well! And how lucky for the Nazis if there is reincarnation! Now they are all clean little babies who do not have to remember what they've done. Little babies with a chance to start over. Isn't that nice to think about?"

I agreed that it was. I tried to imagine Grandma Sylvia reborn as a clean little baby, a baby with no memory. I imagined the grim reaper taking his scythe and scraping the grooves off the record of her life until it was all completely blank, until there was nothing. Once my mother had suggested to me that perhaps it was Grandma Sylvia's sister who was the lucky one.

I had been such a young man at the time that the idea appalled me. What could she possibly mean, I demanded. My mother shrugged. "There is a certain kind of poison to being beautiful," she said. "There is a weight to it. I don't know. Being alive is very *difficult*, Lucas. It takes energy. It's messy. That's all. There is a kind of agony to it. That's all I'm trying to say."

I hadn't understood her then, but her words came back to me as I wandered after my meeting with Justine, head down, toward our apartment on Žydų gatvė. Once, I had broken one of Grandma Sylvia's glasses, I suddenly remembered, when I was five or six, just an ordinary water glass. She had yelled at me and I had started crying and she had looked at me, disgusted, repulsed by my weakness. But I had only been a child. I could not figure out now why she had been so upset with me. Where had my mother been? Had Grandma Sylvia been babysitting me? She must have been, but I found I had no recollection of whether that was a regular thing. It reminded me of something my mother had always said, but that I had never thought deeply about, which was that Grandma Sylvia didn't like children very much.

I shivered. Coming to Vilnius was making me feel closer to Grandma Sylvia, but getting closer to Grandma Sylvia wasn't exactly a warm and fuzzy experience.

Chapter 5

———

Date: 7/13/2014 9:33 PM
From: Vera.Abramov@gmail.com
To: FangBoy76@hotmail.com
Subject: Ho Ho Ho

Dear Fang,

If you are going to cheat on me with other girls, you should try harder to make sure no one fucking takes a picture and then posts it on Facebook and fucking tags you in it. Also, Stephanie Garrison? Are you fucking serious? She has no lips and her mouth looks wobbly like she just got back from the dentist.

I am guessing you already know that we are no longer together.
Fuck you,
V

Date: 7/13/2014 9:50 PM
From: Vera.Abramov@gmail.com
To: FangBoy76@hotmail.com
Subject: Re: Ho Ho Ho

So you just randomly had your arm around her in a friendly way—that's your argument? You think I am an idiot. You have always underestimated my intelligence. Have fun. Enjoy her. I hope she does anal. Mazel tov.

   V

PS: You should never begin a letter to a woman with "Calm down." It's insulting. I will decide when I am calm and you know I am sensitive about that anyway so it comes as a double fucking whammy.

Date: 7/13/2014 9:53 PM
From: Vera.Abramov@gmail.com
To: FangBoy76@hotmail.com
Subject: Re: re: Ho Ho Ho

NO. NO. FUCK YOU FUCK YOU FUCK YOU FUCK YOU. You're heartless. Do you even know what that means, to be so heartless? You are disgusting. With your lies. You are filthy. It is unclean, what you are doing.

Date: 7/14/2014 12:43 AM
From: Vera.Abramov@gmail.com
To: FangBoy76@hotmail.com
Subject: Re: re: re: Ho Ho Ho

Dear Fang,

   I was talking to Judith Winter yesterday and she said an interesting thing, she said, "Well, the major lesson from the Holocaust was that the rest of the world will talk a good game, but they won't do anything to save you. Your neighbors, people you've known for years, will just watch as you are systematically exterminated." Imagine how surreal it must have been. As the ghettos were created, as your belongings were confiscated, as it was announced that you must wear a patch, or a badge, that you could only shop in the market at certain times of day. Imagine watching your Christian neighbors and thinking: Really? You aren't going to say a thing? This madness, this madness seems *fine* to you? By the time it came to the death camps, the Jews must have been completely unsurprised. They had already learned everything there was to know about human nature.

That's the thing, Fang. You can't know anything about a person by looking into their eyes. You say, "Trust me." You say, "When have I ever lied to you?" You say, "If I had video footage of every second you've been away, you would see that I'm innocent. But there is no way for me to defend myself if you are determined to believe I cheated." You say all these things, but who can trust anyone? Who would even believe the things humans are capable of?

Deep in the seam of being there is an evil, evil splinter. The garden of life is filled with rotten apples breaking apart into seeds. You can take a bite of anything, even a bite of young love, and there will be a seed, a little something extra, a tiny pebble of evil, of something that can kill you. I know you love me, Fang. Whether you fucked Stephanie Garrison, whether you just kissed her, or whether as you say it was just a photo where you happened to have your arm around her—whatever the truth is, I know it doesn't change the fact that you love me. Or at least that you think you love me.

It isn't about that. It is about the fact that even love is not enough.

From Vilnius,

V

O N MONDAY, DARIUS STARTED IN the lecture hall. I had caught Vera and Judith smoking pot together that morning, and I wasn't pleased. I barked at them incoherently, I was so mad. It wasn't that I was scandalized by a teenager smoking pot, that was probably part of their mission directive from God, after all, but it seemed weird and inappropriate for Judith to be the one toking her up. Something a little incestuous about smoking pot with Grandma. Maybe it was all in my head. Mainly, I had no idea how marijuana would interact with Vera's medications. Surely it couldn't be good, though her doctors had never discussed it specifically. Vera had put on too much perfume in an effort to hide the pot-smoke smell on her clothes and now my sinuses were beginning to swell in an allergic reaction as we sat there, listening to Darius.

"Today," Darius told us, "we are going to visit two sacred places: the Great Synagogue of Vilna, which was the center for Jewish life in Vilnius, and the Cathedral of Vilnius, the heart of Catholic life in Vilnius. Two sacred places in one city, though the visitors of one are not the visitors of the other, so that for each group, there appears to be only one holy site. But of course, one of these places does not exist. And so we must visit it with our minds." The room went dark and Darius flipped on the projector. For a moment it was just a blue screen and then a black-and-white lithograph of the interior of a large and beautiful building came up.

"This is the Great Synagogue," Darius said. "Which stood at one end of Žydų gatvė, or Jewish Street."

"That's our street," Vera hissed.

"I know," I whispered back, and Vera reached over and clutched my hand as though we were about to go on a roller coaster.

"It was first built in 1573," Darius told us, clicking through various images of the building, all of them interiors, some drawings, some blurry black-and-white photographs. "But the interior was remodeled in the eighteenth century. It was built upon the site of a Jewish house of prayer that had been there since the 1440s. The Great Synagogue was built below ground, because no synagogue was allowed to be taller than a church, so from the exterior, the building was unremarkable, but inside it was five stories high, so magnificent that Napoleon himself is said to have stood on the threshold, wonderstruck, frozen with awe. It could hold five thousand worshippers. The interior was done in the Italian Renaissance style." He clicked through images of the massive columns and ornate decorations, though all the pictures were so dark and blurry that I began to feel like I was going blind.

"Well!" Darius said. "Are you ready to visit the Great Synagogue of Vilna?"

Everyone was excited and there was murmuring as we stood to go. Darius led us out onto the street where it was lightly raining, a relief from the heat. Umbrellas were popped open and Vera and I wound up borrowing one from the Owl People who had brought two and were generous enough to share. Our group was small that day. Judith hadn't come because she was exhausted, she said, and didn't want to be dragged through the rain, though probably it was just because she was high. Who wouldn't want to stay inside, cozy, smoking pot and eating apples and farmer's cheese? But I didn't see Susan or Daniel in the group, either.

Darius himself marched through the streets without an umbrella, unstoppable, like an automaton who did not feel the rain. Vera and I followed, not talking to each other. It wasn't that I was still mad about her smoking pot, I was over it, but she had something else going on, some kind of internal drama that I wasn't invited to participate in. She carried herself like a dishonored queen. Even the way she held her head at an angle as she considered the buildings around us seemed watched and pretentious, and I thought about my mother saying there was something toxic about being very beautiful. It must be terrible to be a woman. I honestly thought that, looking at my daughter in the rain. I thought her life would have been better or easier if she had been born just a little bit uglier. When had she gotten so beautiful anyway? The weight she'd gained this past year seemed to have melted off again. There was no more bald spot at the back of her head, or else she had figured out a way to hide it by wearing her hair in a bun.

Darius stopped us in front of a playground. There was a building on the back half of the lot that appeared to be some kind of kindergarten: There were children's paintings hung up in the windows.

"Here we are," Darius said. "This is the Great Synagogue."

We all looked at him, confused.

"It was partially destroyed by the Germans during World War II, but the entire complex was torn down by the Soviet authorities. They replaced it with this park and kindergarten so that no memorial could be erected."

We all stood there, looking at the rain-soaked park with its swing set and mud puddles. Perhaps it would not have seemed so sad if there had been children playing, but there were none. It was impossible to imagine the Great Synagogue, though we had just spent forty minutes watching a slide show of images of it. It was impossible to imagine anything other than the playground in front of us, its puddles glimmering as the rain continued to fall. Vera whimpered, and when I looked over, I saw she was crying.

"Whoa," I said softly and put an arm around her. I had experienced this temple-turned-kindergarten revelation as surreal and sad, but it was clearly hitting Vera much harder.

"Three pieces survived the destruction," Darius went on. "And we will visit them at the Vilna Gaon Jewish State Museum tomorrow." He described the pieces, but I was distracted. Vera could not seem to stop crying. It was no longer just tears silently slipping down cheeks, but audible, hiccupy sobbing.

"Are you okay?" I asked, which caused her to duck her face into her hands. She started hyperventilating.

"When they destroyed the Great Synagogue," Darius was saying, "there was a rabbi who tried to save it, refusing to leave, so they took him out front and put a garden hose down his throat and turned it on until his stomach exploded inside him and he died."

Vera was now crouched on the ground, her face completely hidden in her hands. I squatted beside her.

"What's going on?" I asked. "Are you all right?"

She didn't say anything.

I was trying to understand if we should attempt to continue with the group or just depart and give up on the rest of the tour.

Vera was struggling to breathe. "There's so much violence," she said, gasping. "It was a house of God. How could you look at it and tear it down?" She slapped her hands down in a puddle then cupped the rainwater in her hands and splashed her face so that her cheeks were wet and streaked with mud.

Vera poured more of the muddy rainwater over her head, wetting her hair. It came to me very quietly, the knowledge: that it was happening, that Vera was having another episode. It was like a whisper inside my mind, but I knew. I had never even truly thought it could happen while she was on so many meds. But now I knew it, and I was filled with the cold calm of emergency. Continuing on with the tour was no longer an option.

"Are you okay?" the Owl Woman mouthed to me.

I nodded. "We're fine, just go on ahead," I said, and motioned for her to rejoin the group that was slowly making its way down the street.

"Vera," I said. "We're going to go back to the house, all right?"

She nodded, biting her lip, holding her wet hands out in front of her, but she sat down on the curb. I crouched in front of her.

"God must be so disappointed in us," Vera said, wiping her eyes. I didn't know what to say to this. I didn't entirely believe in God, not in that way. I didn't believe in a being who had personal feelings like disappointment. On the other hand, I could empathize completely with the devastating emotional realization that this is what human beings were: the kinds of animals that built Great Synagogues, and the kinds of ani-

mals that shoved garden hoses down the throats of holy men
and then watched as they died. I rubbed her shoulder in a way
I hoped was soothing.

Maybe I was wrong about this being part of an episode.
Maybe her reaction to the destruction of the Great Synagogue
was because she was a Jew and I was not, or maybe because
she was stoned, or else because she was seventeen and understanding the full cruelty of human history for the first time.
But God, she had never looked more like Katya than at that
moment.

"Your mother would get upset like this when she was your
age," I told her. "Only for her it was about American slavery."

Vera looked up. "She did?"

"Yeah," I said. "I remember she had a breakdown in the
middle of American history class. They were watching *Roots*
and she had to leave the room and go throw up in the bathroom. She said it was like it was happening to her, watching it.
She said it was okay to experience the suffering of the slaves,
because at least that was pure, but what made her throw up
was feeling inside herself the cruelty of the masters."

"That poor rabbi," Vera said, starting to cry again.

I nodded, though I did not want to think about the rabbi,
had built up ramparts in my mind against that kind of information long ago.

"I'm really hungry," Vera said.

I took her wet, gritty hands in mine. "Then let's get something to eat."

We wound up in the Belgian restaurant that was the ground
floor of our building, again. This time we both ordered the
borscht. "I'm sorry I got so freaked out," Vera said, tearing into

one of the rolls in the basket and dipping it in the rich pink broth of her soup. She had gone into the bathroom of the restaurant when we first got there to clean the mud from her face, and her hair was still wet and slicked back from her forehead. It made her look vulnerable. "But then why should I be sorry—who can hear something like that and just stand there? You know, it's sort of disgusting, all of us here on vacation."

I nodded. It was swelteringly hot out, but it continued to rain. Our table was right by the window and I watched the drops coming down and hitting the steaming cobblestone street. "But it's also about memory," I said, thinking of Darius, of his peculiar unbending rigidity. "Remembering. There's nothing gross about that—trying to hold on to the memories of your people. That's important."

"I have to tell you something," Vera said.

My fatherly ears pricked. No one announced they were going to tell you something before telling you unless it was something big. Or something bad.

"One time," Vera said, setting down her roll, leaning back in her chair, "Fang and I were lying in this field, and it was fall, before the episode, but it was really sunny, a really pretty, pretty day, and the grass was green, and we were lying there, just watching the clouds, and I was thinking that we would never be that young again. That every moment that passed, we were moving closer to death, and I felt like I could feel myself rotting. I kept thinking I could smell us rotting, just underneath the regular smells of sweat and skin and perfume or whatever. I remember thinking that it was my job to keep Fang from ever noticing that we were dying. I started doing this thing, of kissing him between his eyes, and in my mind, I thought I was keeping his third eye shut so that he wouldn't see, so that he wouldn't know that we were dying. And maybe you think that's crazy, but at the same time it was true, you know, every day you live, you get closer to dying. That's a fact."

She eyed me uneasily, as though she were waiting to see if I would agree. "Death and taxes," I said. "They're inevitable."

She nodded, seemingly reassured. "And then," she went on, "when I had the episode. Part of it was that I thought, well, that there is so much more to life than what's cool or uncool in a high school in Rancho Cucamonga. I was watching these cheerleaders getting drunk and I started to see the muscles under their skin, and their skulls, and all their veins, and I realized they were rotting too. They were dying and they had no idea. They were like corpses in party dresses, worried only about who had the cutest shoes. It was revolting. Revolting the same way it is revolting to watch everyone just listen, nodding, as Darius talks about murder, about that poor rabbi, about all of it—the mass graves, the torn-down buildings, people's whole lives erased. How can the world go on? How can you just go out to lunch like we're doing right now?"

"I don't know," I said, wanting so badly to steer her, to force her to think about it differently, less melodramatically, even though on some level I thought she was right. "What else is there to do, though?"

"Papa," she said. "Do I sound insane to you? Are the thoughts I'm thinking really insane? That's what I want to know."

I sighed. I didn't want to contribute to some kind of delusion that she wasn't mentally ill. That was one of the recurrent themes in all the narratives of mental illness I had read in books, on message boards, in forums: The desire to believe that they weren't actually crazy was one of the chief dangers for the mentally ill. The suspicion would build in them until eventually they stopped taking their medication and then they would have another episode and their lives would unravel further. But at the same time I worried I would lose Vera—that this tenuous intimacy would slip through my fingers. And I didn't think what she was saying was truly crazy. Kat and I had said far, far crazier things to each other when we were her age. "No," I said. "You don't sound crazy to me."

She nodded, leaned toward me over the table. "Okay," she said, taking a deep breath. "Now I need to tell you the big thing. And you are going to be really, really mad at me, okay?"

I nodded, unsure what she was going to say and praying, just praying that she was not going to tell me she was pregnant. I don't know why, it was the only thing that occurred to me: that she was pregnant with Fang's baby and she was going to try to convince me she would be sane enough to mother it.

"The night of the episode," she said, "that night at the party? Fang and I had taken acid. I was on acid that night."

This new fact was like something injected into my bloodstream and for a time I was unable to say or even think anything as it traveled through me causing a series of chemical reactions, complex recalculations that I couldn't compute fast enough. My mental state was really more like a strobe light than an opinion.

"I didn't want to tell the cops I was on drugs!" Vera rushed on. "It was one of those decisions you make at the time that then you can't take back, and also, well—it was complicated. Papa, are you listening?"

"I'm listening," I said. I had never done acid myself—it had been one of those drugs that scared me a little. But it was starting to click together—Vera's story, her own sureness that she wasn't mentally ill, her scorn for the doctors and for all of us, her worry that the self was not a solid thing but instead a swarm of chemicals, a collection of the little men inside of her. Dear God. If she wasn't mentally ill, had we been drugging her, poisoning her, all this time for no reason? It was terrible to think about, but also building in me was a wild, irrepressible hope that it was true—that she was not mentally ill, that it had just been a big mistake.

"So what you are saying is that you don't think you have bipolar?" I asked.

"Well," Vera said, "I don't really know. I mean, Fang was on acid and he didn't take off all his clothes and start telling the cheerleaders they were sinners. So I really did think I had an episode, and I just didn't want to tell the drugs part, but then over the past few months me and Fang have been thinking, well, what if I'm sane? What if it was just the acid?"

I took a sip of my beer. "I'm not going to lie," I said. "I'm so relieved that I don't even know what to say. I should be furious with you, but right now I am just—fuck it—I'm overjoyed."

"You are?"

"Jesus," I said, "I'm sorry—I'm reeling. There's a lot to consider. We need to tell your mother. We need to get you off the medication. We've gotta call your shrink."

Vera made a face. "Fuck," she said.

"What? I know it's scary, but we've got to." My mind was already a scrolling marquee of to-do lists. I was thinking that I would turn my phone on and to hell with the charges and we would start calling people that very afternoon. Everything could be handled. Everything could be sorted.

"No," she said. "There's something else. That I have to tell you."

"What?"

"I went off my meds three weeks ago."

There was a heavy pause. She was holding her linen napkin in her lap, twisting it in her hands until it was a thick little rope. Of course she had. I thought of the way her skin had cleared up. Of the way she had seemed to come out of herself and get excited about the trip to Vilnius. I had thought it was Grandma Sylvia luring her, tempting her back into the land of the living, but of course it wasn't.

"Vera," I said. "That's really serious. You need to taper off medications like that, and you really shouldn't have done that without getting your shrink involved."

"We did taper off!" she said. "We did—Fang looked it up online, and we figured out how to do it, and we just did it over a couple of weeks."

"Christ," I said, feeling grim but also giddy. She had gotten off her medication and she was *fine*. She was going to be fine.

"It was making my hair fall out," she said apologetically. "I thought maybe if I could just see—because then I would know for sure whether I was or whether I wasn't before I told people."

I almost laughed—it was so much a teenager's line of reasoning. It was so stupid: thinking about being in trouble for taking acid when her mental health was on the line. Worrying about her hair falling out. And Fang—Fang I wanted to just strangle. Giving her acid. Playacting at doctor.

I looked at her. "What you did," I said, "was reckless and stupid and worrisome."

"I know," she said.

"Let me finish," I said, leaning over my untouched bowl of borscht. "It is most worrisome because it indicates a complete lack of faith in the adult world. You found yourself in a scary fucking situation and the only person you took into your confidence was Fang."

She nodded.

"And that just breaks my heart," I said. Really, it did more than break my heart. But that hackneyed phrase was all I had to describe the disorienting way it shifted my mental landscape, the way it splintered all the assumptions I had made, had let my reality rest upon. It recast the entire past year from her point of view. I had been so unable to overcome my own awkwardness, concerned with whether or not she liked me, injured by my own inability to be her father, but I was not the one who was injured. I was not the one who paid the price. I had let her pay the price in full.

"Papa," she said, "I don't have a way of describing exactly what it is like being on that many drugs, but I was trapped in a fog bank. I was literally tranquilized out of even being able to talk or make decisions. So please don't take it personally. I was so passive, I don't think I could have even formulated a plan to get off of them myself. But Fang was crazy worried about me. He could see that I was just gone. The lights were out, you know?"

I nodded. I had known too. I had been worried about her. I had seen that the lights were out, that she was gone, and I had done nothing. I had left my problems to be solved by a teenage football player.

"Most days, by three in the afternoon," she went on, "I literally could not keep my eyes open. And that was always sixth period, which was Algebra II, and I would put my head down and go to sleep. And the teacher would yell at me, but I can't even describe—I just didn't care. I could barely understand what he was saying to me. Like, I literally couldn't understand the words. One day we got into this fight, and he asked me if I was on drugs. And I was like, 'Yeah, I'm on a lot of drugs.' And he says, 'What drugs?,' and so I start listing all my medications, and he got so angry that he threw his dry erase marker on the ground, and said, 'I meant real drugs!' And I was so confused, really, Papa, I didn't know what he meant, and so I said, 'I'm pretty sure they're real.' Which made the class bust up laughing and made him even madder, but honestly I wasn't trying to be funny. Anyway, after that, he just let me sleep and failed me, and all the other students felt so bad for me, they would put their sweatshirts on me to keep me warm while I slept, so I would wake up and there would be a pile of sweatshirts on top of me."

The waitress came over to see if everything was okay. Neither of us had eaten our soup but we had her take our bowls away. I wanted to murder people. I wanted to murder her math teacher and her shrink and her social worker. I wanted to murder the cops who had arrested her for not noticing or not even considering that she might just be fucking high.

"So did they not test you for drugs?" I asked. "When you were arrested?"

"I have very little memory of that part of the night. I know I took a pee test. I've always kind of wondered about it, but Fang's cousin said that they don't test for acid with a pee test. I have no idea."

"I want to kill your math teacher," I said.

Vera laughed. "It's not his fault," she said. "Although how he didn't get the memo that I was diagnosed I really don't know. Public school."

"It must have been so weird for you," I said, finally starting to catch up with her, to what her version of reality must have been like. "Having all of us so convinced you were insane."

"I was convinced I was insane!" she said, laughing again. There was a lightness to her now, an almost physical relief to having her secret out that showed in her face and in her eyes. "I kept having thoughts, like, not hallucinations, but sudden thoughts that I thought were part of it."

"Like what?"

"I thought the glistening in Mom's eyes were demons telling her that I was crazy when I wasn't. That she wouldn't believe me because there were these things, these beings, inside her eyes occluding her vision."

"Occluding," I echoed, surprised and pleased that she knew the word.

"I used it right," Vera said defensively.

"No, you did. You absolutely did."

"And I thought I was getting the strength to keep going from touching Fang's skin. It was a blue light, coming off his skin. I thought he was loaning me his life force, but I felt really guilty about it because I knew it would mean he died sooner. I actually think about that a lot."

"Fang dying?" The demons in Kat's eyes and the blue light coming off Fang's skin concerned me, but I wondered if they could have been acid flashbacks or something.

Vera nodded. "Do you think that's crazy?" she asked.

I sighed. "People think a lot of things," I said. "People think all sorts of weird things and that's not what makes them crazy. Crazy is . . ." I trailed off. But I didn't know what crazy was, where the line was. I could remember thinking bizarre and wondrous things when I was a teenager, long winter afternoons at Exeter, thinking that birds were music made into animals, thinking that Katya's body was a bell and God was the tongue inside making her ring with beauty, thinking Grandma Sylvia was watching me, disappointed, as I ate Oreo after Oreo alone in my dorm room. But that was different than seeing blue light on Fang's skin.

Yet who was anyone to police someone else's thoughts and decide which were sane and which insane? Who were doctors to inspect my daughter's brain, determine that her ideas were delusions, her mind unfit? That was the thing about bipolar—there was no blood test, no brain scan, nothing that went into the diagnosis except one person deciding another person was insane.

"I'm just so angry," I said finally. "I'm so angry that we left you alone with all of this. I'm so angry that even when we thought you were ill, when you needed our help most, all we did was try to alter you, medicate you, control you. I mean—I never even asked you any questions! I never even asked what it was like inside your head!"

Vera laughed. She wiped a tear away with the back of her hand. "It was weird inside my head!" she said.

"I'll bet it was!"

Chapter 6

_____

Date: 7/14/2014 9:16 PM
From: Vera.Abramov@gmail.com
To: FangBoy76@hotmail.com
Subject: What's done is done

Dear Fang,

I don't forgive you. I don't know what happened, I don't know what to believe, I don't know how to behave, but the truth is that I need you so much that I simply don't care. Fuck Stephanie Garrison for all I care, fuck her silly, just please, please don't leave me alone in this world. I need you. I need you so desperately.

I told my father. I told him about the acid, but also about getting off my medication. HE BELIEVES ME. Fang, he believes me! I don't know why I didn't understand before, but now it seems so clear. My father was the only person who would ever have believed me because he is the only one of them that is really and genuinely simple. I don't mean he is stupid, I mean he is impractical. He is lacking in cynicism. He thinks he is world-weary, but he is not, he is more like a child than a man. My father believed me, Fang, because I was telling the truth. That is how simple it is with him. And it is simple with him because he is simple. Why did I not understand this? I always thought: Oh, he is so simple, what an idiot! But there are also advantages to simplicity, and one of them is purity. He is like clean water. He is like a piece of quartz. TELL ME I AM CLEVER! STROKE MY HAIR AND CALL ME BABY! I DID IT!!!

My mother does not believe me. We waited until it was seven in the morning California time and called her and she told him that acid can trigger bipolar and blah blah blah. He got really mad at her! I've never seen my dad mad before, and it is true that it does make him look kind of impotent because he holds it in too much, and he turns all pink, but at the same time it was really kind of impressive. He threw his cell phone against the wall after she hung up, and it broke into two pieces, but then we had to quick-fix it so he could call my doctor and see what my doctor had to say, but it was easy to fix. It was just that the plastic casing had popped apart. Thank God the screen didn't shatter because I left my phone in Cali.

Dr. Carmichael said I had to get back on my medication. Which, I mean, what else is he gonna say, he doesn't want to get sued, right? And I'm all the way over here, he can't evaluate me. And you know what my dad says? He says NO!!! Fang, he said no! And he called Dr. Carmichael a joke! He actually said that, he said, "You're not a doctor, you're a joke." All sorts of insane things began spewing out of him: "My daughter's life is on the line here," "I *am* serious, sir, I'm deadly serious," and, my favorite, "What exactly would she have to do to make you reconsider your diagnosis? Walk on water? Swallow a sword? I mean, really, once you've diagnosed someone is there anything they could ever do that would make you reconsider, or are you infallible?"

I mean, Fang, he lost control. He totally did. Not that Dr. Carmichael didn't deserve it, he is a joke, but still, my dad is supposed to be a grown-up, he should never have said any of that stuff, but you know why he did?! Because he is simple!!! Wonderfully, lovably, adorably, perfectly pure and simple!!!

After the phone call to Dr. Carmichael, which ended a little anticlimactically with scheduling an appointment for as soon as we get home, it was like he was transported by what had just happened into the locker-room scene of a football movie, and he sat down at the table with me and he said, "Listen, Vera. I need you to listen to me. This is not going to be easy to undo. It is not going to be easy to get people to believe you. But we will fight. And we will win. We will win, Vera."

I legitimately got the shivers!!! Oh, it was amazing, Fang. I wish you could have been here.

With Love,

From Vilnius,

Your triumphant,

V

PS: I totally got caught smoking pot with Judith Winter this morning. But just GUESS who she got the pot from?! That little tenor shaped like a teapot from that crazy concert the first night! She says he is a total sweetheart. Judith is absolutely the best. Also there is a ton of Vilnius stuff I need to tell you about, but I am too happy and too excited to talk about it now. I am going to go just sprawl on my bed thinking about how perfect the world can sometimes be.

THE MOST DISTURBING THING ABOUT Vera's confession was that it didn't "change everything," so much as it revealed everything as having been other than it had seemed to be. Nothing had changed, in fact, it was just that I now knew more about what had happened and so it all looked different to me. I had heard a story once of an Amazon tribesman who had lived his whole life in the jungle where line of sight was limited to thirty paces or so. The first time he was taken on a road and driven through fields where you could see long distances, he saw a building far away and asked what the miniature house was for. Having never had to calculate perspective, his brain simply didn't know how to do it. That was how I felt in the days after Vera's confession: like a man baffled by miniature houses that got mysteriously bigger as you approached them.

It wasn't just seeing Vera as suddenly sane that was a mind trip, it was also the literal trip we were on: It was Vilnius. It was seeing Grandma Sylvia differently, and by extension seeing my mother differently. It was seeing European history differently by getting to know this peculiar and really rather small city, which didn't seem to be a city so much as a concatenation of different cities happening on top of one another, both simultaneously and consecutively. War, genocide, and even the weather had conspired to make Vilnius a place people were constantly fleeing. Darius mentioned quite casually Vilnius had lost ninety percent of its prewar population. With such an unstable population, Vilnius was literally a different city than it had been. For this reason, it was a city without memory. A city of strangers, Darius called it.

The day after Vera's confession, our history walk was through the district of Užupis, technically the Republic of Užupis, a small area that, either in earnest or in prolonged jest, had proclaimed itself independent of all of Lithuania, Europe, and the world, though its statehood was recognized by no government. It was difficult to know how seriously Užupis took itself, Darius explained, since they declared their independence on April 1. I hadn't known April Fools' Day was a thing in Lithuania, but when I asked, Darius looked at me with his ice-blue eyes, unamused. "You think America made up April Fools' Day?"

I had already framed Vilnius in my mind as a liminal place, a portal between East and West, but also, as Darius had mentioned, a portal between the living and the dead, and I didn't like the idea of crossing the river into Užupis. It made me think of the River Styx. But the River Vilnia was narrow and picturesque, not haunting or misty, and the bridge railings were bristling with love locks. It was a custom around there, Darius told us, for young couples to have their initials engraved on a lock, which they attached to the bridge, and then together they would throw the key into the river. There were hundreds, maybe even thousands of locks on the bridge, covering every bar of the railing. "They do this now in many cities," Darius explained, "but it has been a custom in Eastern Europe for at least a hundred years." Vera was clearly delighted by them, and ran her hands over the clumps of padlocks as we passed by.

On the other side, there was a sign letting us know we had entered Užupis. Darius translated: "Smile, drive slowly, create masterpieces, and be careful of the river." The Republic of Užupis was small, only a little over half a square kilometer with seven thousand residents. Užupis even had its own army, Darius said, though it was comprised of only eleven men. "This is the artists' country," he said. "The president himself is a poet, musician, and filmmaker. Everyone here is either involved with the arts in some way or wishes they were."

I wondered what Dr. Carmichael would think about such a place. Would he become furious and begin impotently writing prescriptions for every passerby, or would he melt with repressed desire and throw himself at the foot of some tangle-haired poetess and beg to be remade? I thought it was rather more likely to be the latter, honestly. Dr. Carmichael, as hateful as he was, didn't ever seem to enjoy being himself.

It was a big group that day. I noticed that both Daniel and Susan were with us. Even Judith had come and was walking along steadied by Vera's arm. I forced myself not to turn around and catch Susan's eye, but I couldn't help being aware of where she was in the group, closer or floating farther away, as Darius led us around.

He took us to a square with a statue of the angel Gabriel blowing his horn to rouse the artists, or else to announce the end of the world. Previously this square had housed a statue of an egg, but the egg had now been moved to another part of town. "There were a lot of empty plinths," Darius said and stared at us, pausing, almost as though he were uncertain if he would go on. Was it worth it to explain the history of his country to these people, most of them idiots? I was aware of my own beer gut, of the Owl People in their bright clogs, of the general distracted, ragtag appearance of our group and I felt embarrassed, but also thought that what Darius was doing in taking us on these history tours was possibly heroic. "When Lithuania became independent of the Soviet Union and all the statues of Lenin were torn down, there were many empty plinths. Užupis actually began as an idea two years before the republic was founded when a group of artists decided to erect a statue of Frank Zappa. It is not in Užupis, however, it is over by the children's hospital. If anyone wishes to go looking for it."

I was unsure if I was hearing Darius correctly. No one else in the group guffawed—they were all listening patiently. No one seemed amazed that in Lithuania, in order to deal with the end of communism, local artists had made a statue of Frank Zappa. It didn't seem to strike anyone but me as odd or wonderful or funny. Vera whispered, "Who is Frank Zappa?"

"And now Frank Zappa has become sort of a patron saint, if you will," Darius said, "of Užupis, but also of Vilnius and even Lithuania as a whole." He paused again, squinting in the bright sun. "This area," he gestured around us, "was really just a slum. These warehouses were filled with homeless, with prostitutes. The artists who founded Užupis were mostly squatters living in these buildings. There had been no life for them under communism. They just, well, mainly they drank all the time. They used to call alcohol 'ink.' They would say, 'I have to go to the store and get more ink,' because they really believed that drunkenness and the artistic process were one and the same. A lot of those guys are dead now. They all died very early from liver failure. It was very sad, but, I guess—well! I guess they did it to themselves, you could say."

As we continued along, I could feel Vera buzzing with excitement. She loved it here. She kept exclaiming in wonder over murals, pointing out hidden statues to Judith. This was exactly the sort of place she always dreamed existed, the sort of place that could never come into being in safe, ordinary Rancho Cucamonga.

On one of the pockmarked walls on a narrow cobblestone street the constitution of Užupis had been translated into twenty languages and then engraved on great slabs of shining mirrored metal so that as you read them, you had to face yourself in the mirror. The items ranged from the profound to the whimsical.

Everyone has the right to live by the River Vilnia, while the River Vilnia has the right to flow by everyone.

Everyone has the right to be idle.

Everyone has the right to love and take care of a cat.

Everyone has the right to look after a dog till one or the other dies.

A dog has the right to be a dog.

A cat is not obliged to love its master, but it must help him in difficult times.

Everyone has the right to sometimes be unaware of his duties.

Everyone has the right to be happy.

Everyone has the right to be unhappy.

Everyone has the right to be silent.

Everyone has the right to have faith.

No one has the right to violence.

Everyone has the right to encroach upon eternity.

It ended with these simple instructions:

Do not fight.

Do not win.

Do not surrender.

"Hi," Susan said, coming up beside me. Vera was a few paces away, reading the constitution printed in Russian with Daniel, and maybe that was why Susan had decided to approach me.

"Hi," I said. We stared at the constitution, which also meant staring at ourselves in the mirror. I was uncommonly sexually attracted to her. It was uncanny. It was frankly uncomfortable because at the same time she did strongly remind me of my mother. The silence stretched between us so long that it became surreal and suddenly anything could have been on the table. I could have reached over and kissed her. She could have reached over and honked my nose. Or punched me in the face. Or grabbed my crotch.

"How are you?" she asked. It was such a female question. The other famous female question being: What are you thinking? "How are you?" was the easier of the two to answer.

"Disoriented," I said. "How are you?"

"Dizzy," she said. We stared at each other some more. It was hot out. I wanted a beer. I wanted to be alone with her at a picnic table in the shade by the river drinking a beer. "I couldn't sleep all last night," she said.

I nodded. "The long days have been throwing me off. I keep waking up at four in the morning."

"But isn't that why we travel? To get disoriented. To be changed."

"What do you think about this?" I said, gesturing at the constitution in front of us, but then more loosely to the buildings around us, to the project of Užupis.

"I think it's kind of wonderful," she said.

"See, I think I'm just being a stick in the mud."

"How are you being a stick in the mud?" she asked, nudging my shoulder with hers.

"I'm suspicious of it. I'm suspicious of the whole thing:

alcohol as ink and this faux free society where everything is a joke at the same time as it is for real and everyone is a drunk or a whore but with a heart of gold. I mean, was the poetry they wrote any good? Were their paintings really good? I don't know." I didn't like the world of Dr. Carmichael, the world sucked dry of anything that might be magic—but I wasn't willing to live in this world, either.

"Oh, I think that's a fair question," she said. "I don't think that's you being a stick in the mud."

"Hmm . . ." I said. But I knew that what bothered me about Užupis was that it reminded me of the farm.

"You disappeared the other night," Susan said. "I hope I wasn't too forward in asking you to dinner."

"No, not at all," I said. But I didn't say anything else and she didn't either. We just continued to linger, standing next to each other, waiting for the group to be led wherever we were going next. I looked over at Vera. She was laughing up into Daniel's face with his arm around her. I wondered what it meant, what it meant about her and Fang. And what had ever happened to her crush on Johnny Depp? It was almost as though Daniel had simply stepped into the vacuum created by Vera's initial desire.

Surely Daniel didn't realize she was only seventeen. I would have to have a talk with him. I didn't want to embarrass Vera by being too direct about it, but I could at least make him aware that she was so young. Although it occurred to me that I could choose not to. That I could just let myself slip into this prickling, delicious dream. That I could give in to the part of myself that wanted to lick Susan's sternum even though she looked like my mother. That I could order a beer in Užupis and watch the River Vilnia flow past. That I could let my daughter, who was now sane, no longer my charge but a person in her own right, a young woman, just a few months shy of eighteen, that I could let her flirt with a handsome young man in a pirate shirt in the town where my grandmother had been born.

What could go wrong? What was it that I was so terribly afraid of?

After darkly pointing out a memorial marking a Jewish cemetery destroyed by the Soviets, Darius returned us to the central square of Užupis and set us free to go find dinner. Susan and I stayed close to each other, wordlessly willing ourselves to wind up in a cluster of people who would all go to dinner together. Vera and Judith and Daniel drifted over. Everyone was chatting. A small man named Kenneth who had a reddish beard and thick plastic bifocals inserted himself into our group. He was in his mid to late forties, old enough that I never interpreted him as a peer, and truthfully, I had been avoiding Kenneth for reasons obscure to me. If I hadn't been under some peculiar spell, standing there with Susan, I would have simply taken Judith and Vera and gone off on our own for dinner as we did most nights. I hated splitting the bill in a big group. But Kenneth was very friendly. He was from Kentucky. He clapped his hands together. "Let's go!" he said. "I know a great little place!"

And so we all allowed ourselves to be led blindly by this man whom none of us knew. We were tired and no one made a lot of conversation as we followed him. Daniel had sweated through his maroon silk pirate shirt in big dark circles at the armpits.

The restaurant that Kenneth brought us to was in a basement, brick walled with low arched ceilings, and one entire wall was cold case after cold case of fine beers. During the hubbub of pushing tables together to accommodate our large party, I floated over to the glass case to ogle. All the labels were in Lithuanian, and they all appeared to be microbrews.

Once seated, Kenneth and I were transformed into comrades by our mutual excitement over the beers. We proceeded to over-order a multitude of beers for the table to sample. The food menu was quite limited, however, and it turned out that Kenneth had brought us to a bar and not a restaurant. We ordered fried bread and charcuterie and a cheese plate.

Judith was very upset that there was so little to eat. She was a vegetarian, so the charcuterie was useless to her.

"I must learn to be thin, like you," she said to Vera.

"Nonsense, you must eat," Vera said, and reached across the table to snag Judith some of the fried bread.

It was very hot down there and the only light was candlelight and very quickly we were all drunk. I did not even try to stop Vera from having some of the beer, though I did try to keep track of how much she drank. She was almost eighteen, which was the legal age to drink in Lithuania anyway, and honestly, it had always seemed to me like kids were better off drinking around their parents who could look after them and make sure things didn't get out of hand. I said these things loudly inside my own head as I watched her at the table, her face luminous in the candlelight, smiling over something Daniel had said.

Vera and Daniel were speaking softly at one end of the table, which left Judith, Susan, Kenneth, and me in a foursome. Kenneth was not a writer, and he was also, he mentioned, not Jewish. He was very red in the face, perhaps from the beer, perhaps from the heat. "But I find Jews very interesting. I like to study them," he said.

An awkward silence fell. There was something off in the way Kenneth had phrased this, but I was sure he meant well. He was just clumsy, like the Owl People. A bit tone-deaf. After all, this was a largely Jewish history tour—we were all here because we found the Jewish experience interesting.

"They're mysterious!" Kenneth went on, laughing. "Always keeping to themselves, refusing to mix with the rest of us."

Judith cringed politely as though Kenneth had just blown his nose into his napkin at the table, but she nodded and said, "It is true—the extent to which Jews, especially in Eastern Europe, were uninterested in assimilating does imply that they did not find the pretty glass beads and top hats of Western civilization to be of much value."

"Oh, but Civilization, man," Kenneth said, "you can't ignore her! She's coming for you! Can't turn your face away from steam engines and guns or you wind up like Anne Frank!"

I was just drunk enough that I was having a hard time keeping track of exactly how outrageous Kenneth was being. In some moments, especially in the dim light, Kenneth's sweaty red face seemed animal and gross, and I was sure he was an anti-Semite come to this history tour out of some dark impulse, the way a serial killer likes to revisit the crime scene. I knew a boy in high school named Scotty Nicholson who collected Nazi memorabilia, plates and cups engraved with swastikas, hidden under his boarding-school bed. Maybe Kenneth was like Scotty Nicholson. Or maybe, Kenneth was just some fumbling average Joe, unable to couch his very human observations in a politically correct way. It was unclear and I wished I were more sober.

"Civilization as some kind of advancing monster," Judith mused, clearly trying to be generous.

"I sometimes think part of it," Kenneth said, leaning in

conspiratorially, "part of the Jew Hate, is that they kept their women so covered up."

There was a heavy silence at the table, though at the phrase "Jew Hate" both Vera and Daniel had tuned back in.

Susan cleared her throat. "I'm sorry, what? What did you just say?"

"Covering their hair and everything, doesn't it kind of imply that other people aren't good enough to even look at their women? I think it's part of why people don't like Muslims, either. Subconsciously, I mean."

Susan made a "hmm" sound and nodded, but around the table there was the growing feeling that Kenneth was a creepy weirdo. But was he enough of a creepy weirdo that he must be stopped? In a group of mostly women like this, any confrontation would fall to me. I accepted this as part of being an adult and an able-bodied man, but I was also a naturally conflict-avoidant person. I didn't have a lot of practice at drawing lines in the sand.

"As a Jew," Susan said, and I was grateful that Susan had thought to do that—to make Kenneth aware that he was talking to Jews and not just about them, "it is hard for me to relate to what you're saying."

"Sorry, sorry, sorry!" Kenneth cried. "Jesus Christ, are you all Jews?"

Susan and Judith and Vera and Daniel all nodded, and I realized I was the only non-Jew.

"I'm not an anti-Semite or anything," Kenneth said, holding up his hands as though to say, Don't shoot. "I'm just a history teacher!"

There was a deflation of tension at the table—he was a history teacher! To each of us, this instantly meant that he was on our side: the side of human knowledge, the side of rationality. There was a collective sigh of relief.

"These history tours are tax deductible," Kenneth explained, "and they're great fun. I've done them all! And, I gotta say, I do just find all the Jew stuff fascinating."

Kenneth went on to talk about his job teaching history at a community college, about his recent divorce and his ex-wife who was apparently very coldhearted. He was in a confessional mood, and he became maudlin when discussing his dogs. Apparently, he bred cocker spaniels and one of his bitches had been impregnated by some neighborhood monster, some Doberman or something, who got into his yard.

"I was going to let her keep the puppies," he said, "but then they exploded inside her."

"What?" Susan said.

"Killed her. Pups got too big, just exploded her insides."

None of us knew what to say to this, except Judith who said, "Well, that is horrifying!"

But then Kenneth didn't respond. He was staring at Vera and Daniel who had paid no attention to his story and were in their own world again. Kenneth's eyes were very glassy and there was a nasty expression on his face.

He set down his beer. "She was the only reason I wanted to have dinner with you all, but it looks like he beat me to it!" He gestured at Daniel.

The idea that Kenneth had thought he was a possible suitor for Vera was so shocking that I had a hard time even making sense of the words. As soon as I did, I wanted to punch Kenneth in his fat red face. I stood up without thinking about it, but then just stood there, swaying at the table.

"What did you say?" I asked.

Vera and Daniel looked up from their end of the table.

"Don't get so uptight, man," Kenneth said.

"I'm not being uptight," I said. I wanted to hit Kenneth, or shove the table, or do something, but to throw a punch or break glass in a bar was a serious thing. And besides, Kenneth was still sitting down and he was older, there was white in his red beard, he was drunk and wearing glasses that were smudgy with finger grease—I could see all this in the candlelight.

"Maybe you should just go and call it a night," Susan said, touching Kenneth's arm.

"Guess that's my cue, eh? Thanks for dinner," Kenneth said, and chugged the rest of his beer, stood, and threw his napkin on the table, then walked out of the bar, so drunk he was weaving.

Watching him go, it occurred to me that maybe there was something wrong with people who decided they wanted to visit the past on vacation. Maybe what was obviously broken and weird in Kenneth was more subtly present in all of us. Judith was barely able to function or open her own apartment door and she wore a red beret and red lipstick at all times. Daniel was wearing a pirate shirt. I, myself, was so inwardly tangled that I wasn't able, even to myself, to admit what I wanted, or even that I wanted. I was a fool. We were all fools. And possibly creepy fools.

"Well!" Judith said. "That was an adventure!"

Susan cracked up and then could not stop laughing. There had been so much tension that the laughter was contagious and manic and it overtook all of us, not because anything was genuinely funny but because we were all so relieved. There had been something about Kenneth and his constant forays into creepiness, about the way the candlelight played on our faces, making our skin seem pink and shiny, the hollows of our eyes so deep, our expressions exaggerated and plastic. We had been in a subtle kind of nightmare for almost two hours, and now it was over and the relief was immense.

Judith was pinching the bridge of her nose and laughing, hunched over, saying, "It hurts! It hurts!"

"His dog exploded!?" Susan crowed. "Did he really say that? I mean, Jesus Christ!"

Even Daniel was laughing, though he kept his mouth closed and so he sounded eerily like Winnie-the-Pooh or Dr. Carmichael. "The Jew Hate?" he asked, and we all moaned, laughing so hard we were crying.

Chapter 7

——

"Stage 2"

Word doc
Created by User on 7/15

I have lost contact with ground control. That's what it feels like, this blockage between me and Fang. I'm untethered. Maybe that's part of what made me come clean with my dad. I had been wanting to tell him, but the situation with Fang forced my hand. Telling my dad was a way of tethering myself just a little bit to him so that at least one person will know what is going on with me. So that I won't feel so entirely alone.

I know rationally that there is a possibility that Fang is telling the truth and he just had his arm around that girl to have their picture taken. People do that. They put their arms around each other when someone says, "Say cheese!" They just do, although why it is better to be clasping each other in a picture is really mysterious when you think about it, I mean, why not just sit side by side! But people do all sorts of weird things in pictures. I had a friend once who compulsively made the peace sign. She just couldn't not. Tracy Arbuckle. I wonder whatever happened to her.

Anyway, sometimes my mind runs along that track, and I think that mostly everything is exactly the same as it was before, that Fang sees me and I see him, that we are in the same world together, and that that is rare and sacred and worthy of being protected. It feels almost like an act of violence to mistrust him. Every single hour I take the marble of my mind and I place it on this track, the track that goes: Nothing happened ==> Everything is fine ==> You and Fang still love each other. And every single hour, the marble falls through an invisible hole and slips down into another track that goes like this:

People are animals ==> Love is just hormones, just rutting, just chemicals, we fuck whoever is closest to us ==> Reality is thin ==> Fang slipped from the reality of being bonded to you and began to look for a new animal to rub up against, just the same way you got off the plane and saw Johnny Depp and thought: Hello, I'd like a slice of that! ==> It isn't just sex, all of life is this way, we forget everything we know to be true, everything we know to be sacred. Only one rabbi is brave enough to try to stop the destruction of the Great Synagogue. Only one rabbi is willing to have the hose shoved down his throat. The rest of us just shuffle around, hoping it won't be us, hoping to avoid the merciless sword of blind, haggard Justice ==> When death comes for us, it too will be only chemical. Our organism will die and then all light, all narrative, will be extinguished ==> In which case, why not just rut with the animal closest to you? Why not let the Great Synagogue be destroyed? Why not look the other way while your neighbors are exterminated? Why not?

And so I let Daniel kiss me tonight. I didn't just let him kiss me, I courted him into kissing me, I arranged it, I hypercharged the atmosphere until he had no choice but to kiss me. After a deeply bizarre and uncomfortable dinner with that anti-Semitic hick who got so drunk I don't think he could see out of his eye-balls, we all decided to go to a jazz club that Susan knew about.

I had never been to a jazz club, but it was pretty high up there on my list of romantic to-dos for adulthood, so I agreed immediately. Even Judith decided to go. We were all jolly to have gotten rid of Kenneth. And it didn't seem that late because the sun had only just gone down, but of course that meant it was already really, really late.

As for the jazz club itself, I guess I had been picturing a dark bar with little tables and maybe people smoking and everybody crowded together, quietly watching jazz being played by old guys up front, but that was not what it was at all.

It was a straight-up club. Or, like, a clubby bar. There were bright white-and-orange hypermodern chandeliers that looked like dangling globules of pure light. The dance floor was packed with people dancing in the most primal manner I have ever seen. Maybe it is just because mostly all the dancing I have been part of has taken place in high-school gymnasiums or people's darkened living rooms, but these people were sweaty and they had glow sticks and wore body paint and they were gyrating and spasming and it looked less like pretend sex, which is what dancing normally looks like in my experience, and more like people trying to convince God to make it rain. What I am saying is that it was seriously cool dancing.

My dad totally could not get the bartender's attention, so I took over and I barked in Russian at the girl and ordered us five mojitos, which, honestly, it was just the most grown-up drink I could think of and I didn't want to get carded, but she actually listened to me and brought the drinks and I learned a new thing which is that I LOVE mojitos.

I was worried that I would wind up babysitting Judith, but right after we got our drinks we ran into the teapot tenor and she was miraculously absorbed into their group. They all like totally loved her, which, you know, I love her too, but I wasn't expecting random Lithuanian strangers to understand her awesomeness right off the bat. I guess since she met them by buying pot maybe they already had a pretty good idea that she was more than a grandma in boss lipstick. But then it was kind of weird because it was my dad and the Susan lady and me and Daniel, awkward foursome! And we all go to the dance floor together with our drinks because honestly, what else is there to do? There is no way to talk to each other over the music.

And so then, on top of the nerve-racking-ness of trying to seduce Daniel, who is totally older, he's like twenty-six, hell, he could be thirty, I have no idea, and he has no idea I'm seventeen, and the queasiness of feeling at every single second that what I am doing is wrong and immoral and picturing Fang's face if he could see me dancing with this guy, and on top of trying to figure out how to dance to this weird music, which is definitely not jazz but like someone took the idea of jazz and then applied it to pop music and threw in some trance and techno, just, like, for flavor, on top of ALL THIS, I have to do it while watching my father dance.

I mean, on the one hand, it was a spectacular display. I wish I had fucking video. His main move was the handclap, and he would do it big up over his head. But then, at the same time, he was so weirdly confident and so clearly hot for that Susan woman that sometimes his dorkiness would loop back around and become cool again in some kind of ironic, really confusing way. Oh, it was bizarre and impressive and very very funny, and it took me two mojitos to be able to calm down enough to ignore it and just focus on Daniel.

It turns out that twenty-six-year-old guys are exactly like seventeen-year-old guys. All they want is to press up against you and kiss you. It's exactly the same. It doesn't matter how educated they are or whether they would think your thoughts are foolish or if they would judge you for keeping the remains of your Pokemon collection in your room, because in that moment they aren't having any thoughts: All they are is wanting you. All they are is having a hard time breathing normally. All they are is chemicals.

It was reassuring, and at the same time crushingly sad. Like the saddest thing I have maybe ever learned in my whole life.

And thus begins Stage 2. The new part of my life. The part where everyone is just an animal, even me.

THE NEXT MORNING WE ACCIDENTALLY slept through a lecture about Czesław Miłosz that I had wanted to attend. I didn't like skipping out on an event we'd already paid for, but it was also about all I could manage just to sit around with Judith and Vera drinking coffee and eating rye toast. We were all mildly hungover. I felt nervous and ultimately uncomfortable with what had happened the night before. I had wound up kissing Susan. I was pretty sure Vera had wound up making out with Daniel. It was not good parenting. I had tried to talk to Vera about it once we got home, and it had become some kind of un-understandable fight.

"I'm your father," I had said in the suddenly too-bright light of our kitchen. "There have to be boundaries, there have to be rules."

"Do you realize you are yelling at me for being drunk while you are drunk right now?" she said, and pulled out a big block of cheese, cut us both slices.

"I am not drunk," I said, although I was.

"You're such a fucking hypocrite," she said.

"What I'm saying, though, Vera, is that this dynamic of me just trying to be your friend so that you'll like me—it has to change. It can't stay this way. I can't bribe you into liking me."

"So what? You're gonna playact patriarch now? You're gonna make a bunch of rules for me to follow and then feel proud of yourself because you made me toe the line?" She said all of this with a mouthful of cheese. Really, it was all comical, but in the moment I was blinded with rage, made almost inarticulate by it.

"I am the patriarch!" I shouted. "I am your actual patriarch!"

She laughed at me then, hard, the cheese in her open mouth showing. She bent over, hawing like a donkey, slapping her knee. I was shaking, I was so angry with her. A different man would have slapped her. I stood there as she just kept laughing, moaning, trying to breathe. "Sorry," she said, "sorry, that's just—oh, it's too rich. It was too good!"

I looked at her for another shaky moment, then went into my room, slammed the door, and fumed for a while in bed, sure that I would never be able to fall asleep, before suddenly and completely losing consciousness.

The next morning I felt angry, ashamed, confused, sheepish, but mostly incredibly anxious. As I had gotten older, the chief physical symptom of drinking too much became a feeling of intense anxiety the next day, and that made my assessment of the night before confused. All of this combined with other feelings of guilt regarding missing the scheduled lecture, my general tendency to drink too much, my lack of exercise, my inability to grow up, yada, yada, yada.

It was also difficult to tell which of us had even been right. There was no longer any worry about drinking interfering with her medication. She wasn't on any medication! And it wasn't like in America, where Vera was still years and years from the legal age to drink. Here she was, if not technically legal, then

practically legal. Certainly it did not seem like a big enough
deal to have warranted screaming about being a patriarch and
slamming a door. In short, there was nothing to do but try to
wade through all of it until my mental state returned to normal and I could gain the proper perspective.

Still, I would have liked to hear what they said about Miłosz.
I had read Miłosz before, but somehow he had failed to make
enough of an impression. I had vaguely associated him with
dreary Eastern Europe, and never really got the memo that he
was practically the official poet laureate of my grandmother's
hometown. I had only ever read a poem or two. But then Darius passed out a handout with one of his poems on it and I got
curious and started doing some googling.

What I had always loved most about literature was the way
it eased my own loneliness. Even as my mother's son, at my
most awkward and chubby and sunburned, sure I would never
have a girlfriend, there was always Shakespeare. There was the
possibility of having one's most opaque yearnings and vague
intimations transformed before one's eyes into the beautiful forms of perfectly expressed thought. It was like visiting
a mind reader. It was better than having a lover or even a best
friend or a mother. And Miłosz read things in my mind I had
given up on ever being able to express.

I felt like an idiot for not reading his poems every day of my
goddamn life.

I wondered if maybe everything would have turned out differently in my career if I had just chanced upon Miłosz earlier.
If I had decided to write about him instead of Virginia Woolf.

I thought often of my failed dissertation. It was like a maze
my mind continually tried to run, though by now most of
the passageways were so clogged with shame and guilt that I

couldn't make it all the way through to the end of my thought, to that reassuring flush of completion that signaled an idea was functional, that it worked, that it was worth finishing. At times I thought my dissertation was probably the most brilliant thing anyone had ever tried to write about Woolf. Other times, it seemed like everything I was saying was so patently obvious that if I published the thing, everyone would laugh at me. I was not able to hold my perception of it steady, and so my dissertation continually morphed and changed under my scrutiny, like Proteus, only it was just a Word document.

Part of the problem was that I had edged myself out into the frontier between psychology and literary criticism. This excited my committee, since they had been brainwashed by one million faculty meetings into a slavish lust for all things interdisciplinary, but the truth was, I wasn't trained in psychology and I had no idea what the fuck I was doing. I was making connections, but I wasn't able to tell whether the connections were valid. I was trying to take the idea of theory of mind, a thesis in psychology that was getting a lot of press in regards to autism, and apply it to Woolf. *Theory of mind* was kind of a misleading term. What these people were talking about was mind reading. Not psychic-in-a-turban mind reading but the ordinary kind we do every day. We see someone make a mad face, and we say, "Ooh, they must be mad!" We see a girl raise her hand in class, and we assume that she is going to ask a question. We infer people's states of mind from their actions and from the context. The argument was that autistic people had trouble making these same inferences. They weren't able to accurately infer what someone else might be thinking from the external indicators. Other people were as unfathomable to them as aliens or robots.

Some literary critics had proposed that reading novels was

a way of exercising our theory of mind, practicing our mind-reading abilities, our empathic connection to others. When we were able to read minds correctly, we got a little thrill of success, the same kind of kudos we got from being able to run or achieve feats of strength, an assurance to ourselves that we would survive, that we would be able to navigate the world and its complex social hierarchies. The only problem was, after all the literary critics got on board and started publishing books, and after I had my dissertation idea approved by my committee, there started to be an awful lot of dissent in the field of psychology over what theory of mind was, if it even existed.

But there I was, about to write a dissertation on it. Literary critics had been making their careers off psychology's castoffs for ages. Freud's understanding of the subconscious and symbolism was used constantly in literature classes as a way of teaching students how to interpret the "dream" of the text. He was always presented as a formative thinker of the twentieth century, but when I met a psychology PhD one night in a bar, he laughed in my face. "Why on earth would they teach you Freud?" he asked. "He was just plain wrong about, well, everything." So in a way, it didn't matter that theory of mind had lost its scientific validity, and yet it did matter, at least to me.

Woolf was an obvious candidate for talking about theory of mind because of her use of narrative embedding—her characters were constantly inferring, guessing, even narrating the thoughts of others. Her point of view was notoriously unstable, blurring between consciousnesses even as she technically focalized on just one character. But mind reading wasn't just a technical aspect of her work, it was one of her most central themes: the simultaneous possibility and impossibility of knowing another person.

All of it made me think of Vera's question to me on the

plane, about the little men inside her, about the possibility of the self as a swarm or a hive instead of an "I." In particular, I was thinking of these lines from *To the Lighthouse,* where Lily Briscoe wonders the exact same thing: "How, then, she had asked herself, did one know one thing or another thing about people, sealed as they were? Only like a bee, drawn by some sweetness or sharpness in the air intangible to touch or taste, one haunted the dome-shaped hive, ranged the wastes of the air over the countries of the world alone, and then haunted the hives with their murmurs and their stirrings; the hives, which were people." It was the quote I had used as the epigraph for my dissertation.

I looked at my daughter that morning, the hive of her, drinking her coffee, tapping away at the keyboard of her laptop. I thought of Woolf and those rocks in her pocket as she waded into the river because she simply couldn't bear going mad again. The general critical agreement now was that she had suffered from bipolar. Maybe it was only now that I knew Vera wasn't actually mentally ill that I was able to think this, but I thought that even if Vera had been mentally ill, even if she was still, her experiences were real to her and therefore knowable by me. She could tell me about them, and I could understand, even if her observations were about the blue light coming off of Fang's skin. She should never, no matter what, be shut away or deemed un-understandable. No one should force her to stay in bed and drink nothing but milk, which was one of the ways they had attempted to treat Woolf's madness.

Judith was also quietly writing at the table in a little black leather journal. Her gray hair stood out in a poof around her head. I thought of Judith's stories about her husband. I had asked her what he was like, and she said, "He was like me. He was a boy version of me," and then she smiled crookedly. She had followed him all over the world as he pursued his studies. They'd had two children together. She and her husband had understood each other perfectly enough that she thought he was part of her, the male version of her own self. And then he had died and left her alone to wander through the world, through Vilnius, getting lost in the winding streets, unsure how to unlock her own door or locate light switches.

Woolf was always so anxious about whether or not people could truly know each other, and I couldn't help but think it was because people had treated her the way we had treated Vera. Judging her thoughts, trying to control her mind, without ever really doing any proper investigation. And ultimately, if Woolf had truly thought people were sealed away, trapped inside themselves, how could she have written at all? Weren't her books and their characters with their dizzying interior lives proof that mind reading was possible? That as anxious as we were, the feat was right there, on the page, the dangerous crossing already accomplished?

The phone rang. At first none of us knew what it was; we had not registered that the apartment had a landline. It became apparent after several rings that there was a tan hotel-style phone sitting on one of the shelves in the kitchen. Buttons on it lit up when it rang.

"Should I answer it?" I asked.

"It could be the program," Vera said, which was exactly what I dreaded. I worried it would be Johnny Depp, yelling at us for not attending the lecture. Who else would even know the number of a telephone we had not known we had? I decided to answer it.

It was a woman's voice. *"Labas,"* she said.

"*Labas,*" I said, which was Lithuanian for hello.

"This is Justine," the voice said, and I had no idea who Justine was.

"I think you have the wrong number."

"The genealogist."

"Oh, right, right."

Vera got up and was hovering right behind me. "Who is it?" she hissed, but I waved her away.

"Something very peculiar has happened," Justine said.

"Excuse me, what?"

"I am telling you that something very bizarre has happened."

"Oh," I said, "I see." I had my back to Judith and Vera and so was facing the shelves, which I had not particularly examined before. There was a small ceramic statue of a toadstool, gleaming red.

"Your grandmother's brother, Henryk, survived the war."

"He did?"

"Yes, and he had a family, two girls and a boy. Here in Vilnius. They would be your aunts and uncles. And they have had families themselves."

"You're kidding," I said, though I did not think she was joking. Justine was an almost severe and forbidding person to talk to.

"But getting back to the bizarre thing that has happened," Justine said, catching me off-guard: I had thought Henryk surviving and remaining in Vilnius was the bizarre thing. "One of your cousins is my fiancé."

"You're kidding," I said again, feeling instantly like an idiot.

Vera was up out of her chair and tugging on my sleeve. "What is going on!" she whisper-screamed. I blindly waggled my hand behind me to force her away, never taking my eyes off the bright red toadstool. Obviously I would tell her everything when I got off the phone, but Justine had a very quiet voice and a slight accent and I had to pay a lot of attention to hear what she was saying.

"His name is Henryk, too, actually, though he goes by Herkus," Justine said. "Anyway, when I discovered this, I hope you do not mind, but I told Herkus. And he would like very much to meet you."

"That's amazing!" I shouted, and I felt a sudden ripple of joy. But why? I had no specific, conscious desire to have cousins, and yet at the idea of cousins I found I was ecstatic.

"Great. We will meet you at the reading tonight. We can all have a drink," she said.

"The reading?"

"Nikolai Azarin reads tonight," Justine said.

"Right, right, great, we'll be there," I said, and hung up the phone.

Vera exploded, "What IS IT?"

I told her the news, doing a quick recap for Judith. I was careful not to mention the rape when I told of Grandma Sylvia's escape, and it occurred to me that I had created a precarious situation by telling Justine about the rape birthday when I had been keeping it a secret from Vera. I doubted it would come up, but it bothered me. A loose end.

"How wonderful for you," Judith said. "This certainly will be interesting."

But Vera seemed slightly disappointed with the news. Or maybe she was still just grouchy from our strange fight the night before.

"You sounded so excited on the phone, I thought it would be something big," she explained.

"It is big," I said.

"I guess," she said, "but what are you even going to say to this guy? I mean, you don't live here. It's not like you'll become friends or something."

"I know," I said. I couldn't explain how excited I was. It made me feel boyish and embarrassed. On some level I had always longed for brothers, for male cousins, for uncles, for a father, though this longing remained inchoate because it seemed a betrayal of my mother. She was always so quick to avow she needed no one but me, that other people were useless to her, aliens. I knew that Justine's Herkus wouldn't suddenly be my buddy, but the fact that we were blood related must mean something.

"Papa," Vera said, "Judith and I don't want to go to the afternoon thing, either."

"What? What's the afternoon thing?"

"The Holocaust Museum," Vera said.

"I am very sorry," Judith said, holding up her tiny pink hands, which reminded me of mouse paws, the fingers splayed as though to hold off my objections, "but I do not think I can handle it. And I have learned at this age to respect my own fragility. I am an old woman. I have lived in Israel. I have been to my share of Holocaust museums, and I do not need to go to this one."

"Of course," I said. Judith's decisions were her own and needed no justifying, let alone to me, and after the way Vera broke down over the Great Synagogue yesterday, I thought it might be a good idea for her to stay away as well. And yet, the idea of going to the Holocaust Museum alone was like volunteering to spend the afternoon being sad. And I didn't want to be sad. I was already feeling anxious from my hangover, overstimulated and disoriented by the night with Susan, the fight with Vera, and now the sudden news of Herkus.

"What are you going to do instead?" I asked, hoping I could tag along.

"Go shopping!" Vera cried, practically yipping with glee.

"I want to get something for my daughter," Judith explained. "Maybe some amber jewelry. Something."

"I'm going to take her to the store that has the nice amber stuff," Vera said.

"Which one?" I asked. I hadn't been aware that Vera had already zeroed in on the best place, but it had been in my mind to sneak off at some point and buy her a piece of amber jewelry. Amber was a big deal here. The Baltic Sea spat up some of the best amber in the world. It would be a memento of the trip, but I also wanted it to be some kind of emotional gesture.

"It's right there on Gedimino prospektas. On the right before the chocolate shop," she said. I could barely bring up the map of the town in my mind and remember where Gedimino prospektas was. I had no idea what chocolate shop she was referring to, but I committed the description to memory, hoping I would be able to find it later.

"Well, have fun, girls," I said. "Shall we meet for dinner, or just meet at the reading?"

"If you're around when we get back, let's have dinner," Vera said, "but if we miss you, then we can always catch up at the reading."

"Deal," I said.

Judith headed downstairs to get ready, and Vera busied herself with her makeup. Even watching her apply mascara made my eyes water. I remembered vividly the fuss and fury regarding the planning out and orchestration of Vera's bat mitzvah, maybe because it had been the year I seriously reentered her life. Most of the fuss had to do with dresses and caterers and decorations. Kat had been so focused on it. She had wanted that bat mitzvah for Vera so badly, though I had never entirely understood why.

My most vivid memory of the day of the bat mitzvah was watching Katya apply Vera's mascara beforehand. I was sure the entire time that Kat was going to blind the girl. What recklessness mascara was! What madness!

"You're making my eyes water," I said to Vera, as she stroked layer after layer of black paint on her eyelashes.

Her mouth was held open with concentration, so her response was weirdly distorted: "You big pussy," she said.

We discussed the Holocaust with Darius almost every single day. Every part of the city told a part of the story. So I already knew the facts.

When the Germans had occupied Vilnius, one of the first things they had done was hire native Lithuanians to act as their police force. These "police" trolled the streets with trucks, picking up Jewish men and telling them they were being taken to a work camp. Then they would take them to Ponary, an area near Vilnius, where there was a large pit from an unfinished construction project. The men were put in a fenced enclosure. Ten at a time, they were taken to the pit, lined up, and shot in the back so that they would fall in. From the group in the fenced enclosure, another ten would be chosen, lined up, shot, and so on. In the beginning, they were shooting only sixty or eighty men a day, but by the end of summer they were lining up women and children, managing to kill sometimes seven or eight hundred in a single day.

Darius never became emotional as he told us these things, though he waited patiently when people in our group, especially the women, would break down crying. But I did not get the feeling that Darius didn't care. Every statistic, every date, every fact he had gathered was his way of caring. He was a man lit with the fire of remembrance. What a relief it must be to be a man like Darius, I thought. He was probably perfectly in control of the ship of himself, steering through choppy waters, his eye trained on a horizon I had never been able to see.

As I set out that afternoon to meet up with Darius and the group, I already knew that I did not want to go to the Holocaust Museum and that, in fact, I was not going to go though I did not yet know how I would achieve this. I wandered the old medieval streets, a maze through mismatched buildings in pastel colors, affording sudden views of church spires and at other times dead-ending in private courtyards. I got lost, and I enjoyed it. I even hoped I would get so lost that I would be too late and miss the group, but I was not.

As I crossed the street to the lecture hall, I saw that Darius and the group were already outside, standing on the sidewalk, dappled in sun and shade. Susan was there. I felt a surge of luck then, as though the universe were abetting all my most secret desires, providing cousins and walks alone through a sunny city and afternoons with beautiful and fascinating women. It was the kind of feeling that would cause a gambler to bet everything on red. There was no reason not to, no Vera watching, no propriety to maintain, and so I walked up to Susan, leaned over, and whispered into her hair, "Escape with me. I don't want to visit the Holocaust."

Chapter 8

———

Date: 7/16/2014 9:12 PM
From: Vera.Abramov@gmail.com
To: FangBoy76@hotmail.com
Subject: The Shoah and your pretty idiot

Dear Fang,

I got into a horrible fight with Judith after we waited around forever at this stupid poetry reading and now I don't know what to do. I am literally so frantic about it and I can't seem to calm down. You should have seen the way she looked at me. Like I was such a disappointment. Like she was disgusted with me. She had thought I was something, a person, maybe silly and young, maybe even annoying, but someone worth spending time with. She was mentoring me! She was letting me ask all sorts of questions and she was patient with me the way a mother cat is patient with kittens and now I have fucked it all up, I have fucked up everything and she sees me for what I am. Which is . . . a ruined thing. A piece of garbage. Something that could have been nice, but has been perverted, distorted, and is beyond saving.

And you know what? She's right.

I was trying to ask her my question, the "why the Jews" question. Maybe I was getting a little bit strident. I was asking her, I was saying, "Why did the Shoah happen?" She always calls it the

Shoah, I grew up calling it the Holocaust, yet another way I feel like not-a-real-Jew, but whatever. I pointed out that the Native American genocide had a very clear motivation—yes, there was a lot of talk about subhuman savages, but in the end it was about greed: We wanted the land. About American slavery, yes there was a lot of talk about subhuman savages, but in the end, again, it was all about greed: White men were making fortunes off the backs of their slaves and they would use anything, even the Bible, to excuse their behavior. I understand the state that Germany was in when Hitler came to power, I understand that all the same subhuman rhetoric was applied to Jews, that they were dirty, that they were "holding back the motherland from her potential" or something, but doesn't the whole thing seem kind of cracked? It all seems so terribly indirect. Like, exactly HOW were the Jews harming Germany? Show me the money trail, was basically what I was asking.

I mean, I think people who complain about welfare moms in America are just tragically uninformed because we spend way more on rockets and bombs than we do on helping out a few single moms, but whatever, at least they are mad because it is their tax dollars being spent on a group they feel isn't "working hard enough." But the Jews were taking care of themselves. They weren't relying on German handouts or anything. The logic of "if we build a huge expensive killing machine, it will make our economy better" is just way, way out there, right? Except, I guess it kind of did, right? It kind of worked. I mean the Reich hired tons of people and they turned even the bodies of the Jews into products that they made money off of, soap and lampshades, etc., and they confiscated so much Jewish wealth, art, jewelry, gold teeth, I mean, they took it all, so that had to be helping. But still, they could have just motivated themselves to do ANYTHING to create an industry, it didn't have to be exterminating Jews. It just doesn't make sense. I literally don't understand the logic and I don't understand how everyone wasn't just confused. Like, they are following along with Hitler's speeches, and then he's like, ERGO, we should kill all the Jews, and wasn't everyone like, *huh?*

Maybe this is naïve and totally uninformed. I haven't read any of Hitler's speeches and I haven't read *Mein Kampf* because Mama said it wasn't a good idea. So I probably came off as totally snotty and sophomoric to Judith, who after all has been thinking deeply about this her whole life, and anyway, I think she thought what I was saying was that the Jews had DONE SOMETHING to get killed. And it's true, I kept saying it that way, I kept saying, "But why the Jews? What was it about us? Would it have been different if Jews had been more blend-y, like more assimilated? Or was it Jewish success that was making Germans jealous, like if the Jews had been even poorer than the poorest Germans, maybe they would have just felt pity and not the need to turn us into soap?"

I can think of, like, a million reasons now why all of this bothered her, but I don't know which are true or if I am just making them up. Maybe she objected to me casually using "us," as though I were part of the Jewish experience, when really I am a spoiled American girl who hasn't been to temple in years. Or maybe it was just so obvious that I didn't know the very basics of the situation and I was asking for, like, a Sesame Street–level history refresher course from her. Maybe she wondered why I had decided she was somehow my teacher and it was her job to explain the fucking SHOAH to me, of all things.

Anyway, what she said was: "You must never entertain this line of reasoning. You must never allow any conversation to begin that predicates German actions on Jewish behavior. There is no reason for what they did. You must never, ever, ever seek to explain the Shoah by exploring Jewish culpability."

"I'm not saying the Jews are ACTUALLY culpable," I said. "I'm saying the Germans must have thought we were culpable of something or else they wouldn't have tried to kill all of us, and I am not exactly sure what we are supposed to be guilty of except not being blond and usually there is just a better reason than that!"

And then she tried to tell me about Heidegger and about how he had this whole argument that Jews were modern and that in embracing modernity they had actually caused their own destruction. He even referred to the Shoah as the Jewish "self-destruction" as though they were the ones doing it to themselves! He said it was the "supreme fulfillment of technology." But the truth is, Fang, I didn't understand all of this and I don't really know who Heidegger is, though she said he was a philosopher, but who cares about philosophy, no one reads it, it doesn't matter, right? I couldn't understand why she was bringing him up, so I just kept saying, "But I don't care about Heidegger and anyway he sounds crazy too!"

Which, I mean, he DOES, right? Was there something in the water? Was there mold in the rye bread? What the fuck was going on? The supreme fulfillment of technology? It's like a weird *2001: A Space Odyssey* fantasy in which the killing machines just decided to start killing Jews on their own.

So she says, "Any argument that hinges on the Jews doing anything at all to cause the Holocaust is that argument. Any argument that even deigns to entertain that as a question, is already insane and should not be pursued."

So basically she was saying that I was being Heidegger, which I thought was really unfair and I told her so, and she said I was just too young to understand any of this, that I didn't have any real experience with anti-Semitism, which is probably true but still rude, and I said so, and she said she didn't want to talk about it anymore and could I please leave her apartment and take the cat with me, she wasn't fond of cats.

But she said it in this way like she really meant that she wasn't fond of teenage girls and she was just being too polite to say so outright and all this time she had only been barely tolerating both the cat and me. Which is probably true. But she is the one who decided to come on a weird history tour for vacation. If she wanted to be alone, she should have stayed at home. Because let's be honest, she wouldn't be functioning on this trip without me, I am the only one who can open her door and she still can't find the supermarket on her own.

I am being uncharitable.

I just hate feeling like I am not even allowed to ask questions. Isn't there something terribly unsatisfying and obviously FALSE about saying that there can be no line of reasoning that explores why the Germans did what they did? That it has to be this sort of spontaneous miracle of cruelty? That it rose up out of pure evil and it isn't part of the world at all? Because it very much is part of the world. And it isn't just the Germans. It isn't just the Shoah. It's all of history, Fang. The other day, we were walking up these stairs to get to a park and Darius said to look down at the stairs and he pointed out that some of them had inscriptions in Hebrew. The Soviet authorities had destroyed the Jewish cemetery and repurposed the headstones as slate for building projects. Every day Lithuanians literally climb up a hill on the headstones of Jews. Where the Great Synagogue used to be, there is a kindergarten now. I bet there are kids who go there who grow up and go their whole lives without ever knowing there was a temple there.

Like, I am scared to even be writing this down, but if we are going to talk about evil on a human level, on like a one-to-one level, it seems like people generally have reasons for murdering each other. They might be WRONG. They might be stupid reasons. But they have them, and so I think the Germans had reasons, but whenever their reasons are explained to me they make no sense and I feel like someone is hiding something from me.

And here is what I think they are hiding: Humans don't need a reason. In other words, even their reasons are never the real reasons. The idea that we are rational and in control of our actions is a recent and temporary delusion. For most of history, we have totally been murdering each other. We are just violent animals. We like to hurt each other. It feeds some part of our nature. And so we will find any excuse to do it. Sometimes it is greed, like with slavery or with the colonization of America. But sometimes we can kill people for hardly any reason at all. My mom was complaining about social media making us crazy and the world being so violent and on Facebook you hear about every single sad story of a dad beating his kid to death, but I was like, Mom, wake up, imagine what it would be like to hear someone live-tweeting the Wild West. It would be terrifying. Shit is way more under control now.

But maybe it isn't. Maybe underneath all that control is something terrifying and liquid and burning, like lava. Maybe sometimes it just bubbles up.

Poor Judith. Why would I make her have to explain such a thing to me? I am ashamed. She is just a widow, wandering alone through this world, and I tried to force her to articulate the most terrifying truth there is.

I am suddenly very tired.

With love,

From Vilnius,

Your sorry,

V

THANK GOD YOU SAID SOMETHING," Susan said, "because I was going to make myself take my medicine and go, but I really think I would have had a mental breakdown." We were in a tiny Moroccan restaurant where we sat on pillows and where the service was very slow and the food entirely mediocre, bowls of lukewarm lentils, stacks of dried-out pita bread. Even though it was early afternoon, we ordered wine, a red that was inexplicably sweet and metallic-tasting.

Susan told me she stayed up all night the previous night reading the diary of Kazimierz Sakowicz, which described in precise detail the murders at the pits in Ponary. His farm was right there on the road, and he began to keep a record of what he was seeing from his house, and then he buried the pages in a lemonade can in his yard where they were later recovered. It was always a detail like that which defeated my attempt to not imagine these horrible things actually happening: a lemonade can. I pictured a Minute Maid can, though of course it couldn't have been.

"No emotional content at all," Susan went on. "It's addictive to read, you kind of can't stop, but at the same time by two in the morning I was so sick I thought I would throw up and then I just couldn't sleep. The Jews in Vilna finally figured out what was going on because some of the children survived in the pit and then climbed out again at night and walked all the way home. Can you imagine?"

Susan's voice had caught in her throat and she fanned herself with a stiff piece of pita bread. "So then, in the middle of that state of mind, and keep in mind I'm in a hotel, not an apartment like you, so I don't even have a kitchen to make tea in! So then, my ex-husband calls me, drunk, he's obviously relapsed, wanting to talk to me about his business, which he is absolutely running into the ground, and he keeps saying the same things over and over again, how he's so stupid and he's a failure and he should just kill himself. And I'm thinking, 'Why do I participate in this? Why is my life such that this man can call me and make me deal with this in the middle of the night?' I'm sorry—this is too much information, I know, but I haven't slept and, you know—don't think I'm some melodramatic person. I could paint this all in a different light and talk about how I have to have Rick in my life because of my son, and how I try to see the best in people, and blah blah blah. I could make it look good. Or if not good, at least presentable."

"No," I said, "I get it. I don't think you're—"

"A crazy codependent who lets her alcoholic ex-husband ruin her life even when she is taking a vacation by herself focusing on the genocide of her own people?"

I laughed. Susan widened her eyes, smiling now too. "Seriously, though, you don't think that, right?"

"Right."

"Thank God for that!" she cried, and pretended to wipe sweat from her brow. I refilled our wineglasses. Now that we had drunk a glass, the horrible flavor of the wine was more palatable.

"So tell me," she said, "how are you fucked up, dear Lucas? What's your drama?"

I disliked the word *drama*. I almost didn't want to answer, but Susan was so frank about herself. I wanted to be like that too. "The whole situation with Kat—that's Vera's mother—it's easy to pretend that we were just kids being stupid and she got pregnant by accident, but it wasn't that. We got pregnant on purpose."

I let out a breath, afraid to continue, but I saw that Susan was listening, really listening, not even chewing her food or playing with her wineglass. She was just sitting there, waiting. So I told her. I told her about the secret bathroom and about Allen Ginsberg and about the maddening way Katya would eat baby food with a little spoon. I tried to explain about that night, Katya whispering in my ear, "Let's make a baby, baby," and about how I had wanted to, how on some deep biological level it had seemed like the right thing to do, the only sane thing to do. I told her about the road trip that summer and about the commune. I didn't tell her about Chloe, though. In the moment, it seemed irrelevant. Like maybe Chloe had just been an excuse all along, that my real failing had been not being bold enough to love Katya, to follow that road wherever it led. I had never presented it to anyone like this before. Most of the time, I didn't even think of it this way myself—because it was too painful to really allow myself to think of: that the thing between Kat and I had been *real*.

"You can imagine Katya hated me after that," I said.

"Gosh, how interesting," Susan said, and it was a relief that she was interested instead of sorry for me or judging me, almost as though it were a movie, something impersonal. "Because there are those layers of reality: the private, kind of on-the-moon reality of two lovers, and then the reality of the world, your parents, making money."

"But after that, I think," I said, "I was very suspicious of the part of myself that had done that. I didn't feel like I could be trusted, and so I tried to date only girls who were very safe and very ordinary and where no one could get hurt." I thought of Amanda. What a crock of shit. What a liar I was. It wasn't that no one could get hurt, I thought; it was that *I* couldn't get hurt.

"Well, you have lots of time. You could still get married," Susan said. "It's different when you're my age. All the available men are fish that have already been thrown back. Everyone has gotten divorced. They have years of bad habits and resentments built up and you have to try to find someone who is fucked up in the exact matching, complementary way to your own fucked-up-ness. It's very tiring. Excruciating, really. And all the men who want to date me are in their sixties, all the guys my own age are dating thirty-year-olds, and it's like dating Mr. Rogers, I swear to God."

"Could I not be a fish?" I asked.

"Excuse me?"

I cleared my throat. "I would like to nominate myself as a fish."

She considered me. "Why haven't you married anyone? Is it that you're still in love with her, with Katya?"

I considered this. "Possibly," I said. "I think maybe there is something wrong with me, but I can't say for sure what it is."

She motioned to the waitress for the check. I didn't know what more to say, if I should try to make a joke or take it back or break the tension. But Susan just went about stacking plates and tidying our table and when the bill came, she reached for it.

"No," I said, "let me."

She shook her head, slid her credit card in the slot. "I'm going to tell you the truth, Lucas. I don't care why you haven't been able to commit or get married or what exactly is wrong with you. I don't care. Right now, I just want an adventure."

I nodded. I wanted an adventure too.

The bar where Nikolai Azarin was going to read was tiny and absolutely jammed with people. It seemed crazy that the event had been planned in such an unsuitable venue. There was no stage, just a microphone in one corner and wall-to-wall people drinking beer and wine. Susan and I waded into the crowd, holding hands. I was amazed I didn't see more people from the program. Almost all the people were impossibly hip young Lithuanians. Why did they know of and seem to care about the poet Nikolai Azarin? Why had they chosen to cram themselves into this sweltering, tiny space?

At the bar, we had to wait for an eternity, and just when I was beginning to panic that we had not yet found Vera and Judith, I saw them through the window out on the street, huddled against the glass. They must have ordered drinks and then gone out there to avoid the crowd. I brought Susan out with me to meet them once we had gotten our own drinks. The relief from the noise and crush was instantaneous.

"This is crazy!" I said. "Are we allowed to have our drinks out here?"

"Who knows," Vera said.

"I don't know if I can stay," Judith said and took a sip of her glass of wine, which she was holding with both hands, as though it were not a wineglass but a tiny glass bowl with an annoying protrusion on the bottom. "It's so crowded and I'm tired, and I am afraid I don't terribly admire Azarin."

"You know Azarin?" I asked.

"Oh, everybody does. He's always at these things," Judith said. "Po-biz! He's one of the ones who is constantly trying to fuck pretty young things, that's his main line of business. He sees me as nothing but an old hag, I'm sure, and when I was introduced to him on this trip he didn't remember me, but I've met him at least a dozen times over the years, and of course I've read his work, and I'm afraid it isn't good enough to cause me to want to stand upright in an enclosed space with a bunch of drunken Lithuanian teenagers. I find their collective blondness overwhelming."

Susan laughed and Judith gave her an appreciative smile.

"So we might go home," Vera said. She was sipping her own glass of wine, which I didn't exactly like, even if she was voluntarily going home early. But that ship had sailed, rather brutally, the night before when she had laughed at me, her mouth filled with cheese.

"Vera convinced me to at least have a drink and see if it becomes more bearable, and the drink is very nice, but it is not causing anything to be more bearable, I'm afraid," Judith explained.

If anything, things continued to get even more unbearable. An hour past when the reading was supposed to have started, there was still no sign of Azarin and there were more people crowded into the bar than ever. I kept scanning the room for Justine and Herkus, but I didn't see them.

"I'm really afraid we have to take our leave," Judith said finally, even though the four of us had been having a nice conversation standing on the sidewalk. All of our glasses were empty, though, and I understood Judith's desire to go. If I were not waiting to meet Herkus, I would certainly have chosen to go elsewhere.

"I'm actually going to head off as well," Susan said.

"No!" I cried. "What? Really? Don't go!" I had imagined us spending all night drinking and talking and maybe stopping by her hotel on the way home that night.

"I'm exhausted," she said, "I didn't sleep at all last night. I'm sorry. Those pits! But tonight I will sleep for sure. I know it!"

I didn't like that she was leaving, but I was glad she would sleep. There had been a steady electric current between us all night, ever more daring forays into holding hands, touching each other's arms, leaning too close when laughing, and it was all delicious. Maybe it was good to let it be slow. Nothing needed to happen tonight. Even if there were only five days left of the trip. I accepted their empty glasses and kissed each of them on the cheek before they waved and walked away from me, a cluster of beautiful women, all roughly the same height, one young, one old, and one in between. They seemed like something from a fairy tale, as though there was symbolism in their triptych that I must decipher. But even as I was thinking this, I felt the itching need to get another beer, and as I headed inside, feeling like a sweaty bear among all these beautiful young people, I already knew that I was going to get very drunk.

When the reading finally started, I was standing in the crowd, bleary, trying to understand whether the poetry was very good or very bad. Azarin seemed at least as drunk as I was, and that made me feel kindly toward him. There was also a vulgar honesty in some of the poems that seemed slightly magical, which made the otherwise self-indulgent imagery light and playful. One poem that had gone on for some stanzas being about

Putin suddenly ended with the lines, "Or perhaps I only feel powerless because so few women are willing to sleep with me. Who would want to sleep with an old goat like me? Flee from me, beautiful girls! Run away before you catch what it is I've got—that is killing me."

It was really very hard to tell whether or not it was good, but I found myself liking it anyway. When the reading was over, there was no sign of Justine or Herkus. I'd been jilted, but the bar also became significantly emptier and I was finally able to get a seat.

"Another beer?" the bartender asked, and I nodded, though I suddenly felt extremely drunk and worried vaguely about whether or not I would be able to find my way home.

"Lucas?" someone asked, and I turned to see that it was Justine and a man who simply had to be Herkus, so eerily did he look like a better, fitter version of myself. I don't know why I had assumed he would be younger than me, perhaps because Justine was so young-looking, but he was easily in his forties, though he crackled with vitality and health. It was like looking in a mirror and seeing a possible future for myself. He even had the same narrow, fluted nose that I and my mother and Grandma Sylvia all shared. It was a very beautiful, Meryl Streep-ish nose, though in her darker moments my mother referred to it as "the teacup handle."

"We could not find you in the crowd," Justine explained, and she and Herkus took the stools next to me. I was terrified at how drunk I was. I would never have gotten this drunk if I had known there was still a possibility of meeting them tonight. I tried to bring on the sensation of sobriety through sheer force of will.

"So nice to finally meet you," I said.

"I know—so weird, right?" Herkus said, in such a sweet and goofy way that I liked him instantly.

"So your mother was Henryk's daughter?" I asked.

"No, no," Herkus said, "my mother was Sylvia's daughter."

I was confused. Sylvia was *my* grandmother. She couldn't also be Herkus's grandmother.

"I didn't get to this part on the phone," Justine put in. "I thought I should let Herkus explain in person."

"During the war, Henryk had escaped," Herkus explained. "When his family was taken, he was sixteen and in love with a farm girl, so when he escaped from the train—his mother and he had been kept in one of the first-class cabins for some reason, they were separated out, he never knew why—she encouraged him to simply get off at one of the stops. And he did. No one noticed. He just walked right off the train. She said, 'Will you go buy me some candies?' And she handed him all the money she had and he went and that was that! But once he was free, where to go? So he went to the farm girl and threw himself on the mercy of her father who was a good man with no sons to work the farm and who let them marry, even though Henryk was a Pole and they were Lithuanian. So he lived out the war working on the farm outside of Vilnius. Do you want another drink?"

"God no," I said, covering my beer with my hands. "I've had too much if you want to know."

"Oh!" Herkus laughed. "That is okay! Everything is okay tonight! We are family tonight." He reached over and hugged me, which made me feel like I might cry.

"Anyway," Justine said, helping Herkus finish the story, "somehow Sylvia in the forests hears that Henryk has survived. Her brother. And one night she arrives at the farm and she brings them a baby. That baby, Sylvia's daughter, was Herkus's mother. Henryk and his wife raised it as their own, as their eldest daughter. After her they had other children, of course."

I was having trouble processing what they were saying. "But whose baby was it?"

"It was *her* baby," Herkus said. "Sylvia's baby that she had in the forest."

"I think," Justine added, "the story you told me, that she killed her baby in the woods? I was wondering if maybe this was something she made up to tell her forest husband when really she took the baby to her brother."

"I think so," Herkus said, nodding in agreement with Justine.

"But why would she do that?" I asked. I couldn't tell if I was failing to understand all of this because I was so drunk or because I was only finding it out now while Herkus and Justine had had hours or even days to process it.

"To keep the baby safe!" Herkus said. "Who wants to raise a baby in the forest?"

"What do you mean?" I asked.

"You ask why Sylvia takes—excuse me—took the baby to her brother, and I say I think it is because baby would be safer with her brother than in forest."

I noticed he had begun dropping his articles, and it made me fond of him, reminded me of Grandma Sylvia, who would do the same whenever she got flustered or passionate. Justine was nodding, sipping some pink drink on ice through a tiny black straw. "But what I don't understand," she said, "is why she didn't stay with Henryk and the family on the farm. Why go back to the forest?"

"Yeah," Herkus said, smiling and still completely light-hearted, so far away was all this tragic mess from us now, from our little grouping at the bar with our cold glasses of alcohol. "This was always the mystery my mother would talk about—because of course it hurt her, for Sylvia to go back to the forest and not stay with beautiful baby girl. Who would do it?"

I felt like I was dreaming and I didn't know how to make it stop. Sometimes in my dreams I would begin floating and not be able to get my feet back on the ground—I would just fall to the side, skidding through the air. But of course I remained perfectly upright at the bar. "Maybe the farmer didn't want to take on another Polish refugee. It would have endangered them, been more conspicuous," I said.

"No," Herkus said, "the farmer wanted her to stay, begged her not to go. No one had milk for the little baby, see, and they thought she would not live because she was so small, but then she did live—off goat milk!"

"I see," I said. I imagined Grandma Sylvia carrying her tiny, undernourished baby through the forest to find her brother. How long would she have had to walk? "Wait," I said, "where was the farm?"

"Outside of Vilnius maybe fifteen kilometers," Herkus said. I was ashamed that I was too drunk and frankly too ignorant to be able to do the metric conversion in my head, but it didn't matter.

"Grandma Sylvia escaped from Stutthof, but she never made it back to Vilnius—she was in the forests outside of Warsaw by the time she was with the Home Army. How could she ever have gotten all the way to Vilnius?"

"She walked," Herkus said.

"No!" I cried.

Justine nodded. "That has always been part of the story."

It was impossible to imagine.

"How many miles?" I asked. "I mean, how many kilometers? Between Warsaw and Vilnius?"

Justine and Herkus argued in Lithuanian for a minute, and then Justine said, "Maybe two hundred and fifty miles she walked."

"But that's impossible!"

Herkus shrugged. "She said it took her three weeks."

"All the more of a puzzle as to why she would not stay," Justine insisted. "Why walk two hundred and fifty miles all the way back?" She used her straw to stab a maraschino cherry that was lost in the bottom of her glass.

I thought for the first time that Grandma Sylvia must have been angry. I had never pictured that part before. The young girl, raped and set free, who would not want to take care of a baby, who would not want to be saved, but who wanted to go back into the forest and kill Nazis. The girl who simply could not bear to just be normal again, who could not fit in on a happy farm with her brother who only knew her as his little sister, not this wild, half-starved, violent thing she had become. Maybe it was a blood vendetta. A chance to avenge her sister. Maybe she just wanted to die.

I had only known Grandma Sylvia when she was an old woman, her past reduced to a series of stories as familiar and safe as episodes from a beloved television show—*I Love Lucy*, or *Gilligan's Island*. I had never understood the rape-birthday cake, but I thought I understood it now. She was not celebrating the rape but the fact that she survived it. To be ninety years old in Southern California, licking the thick lard frosting off a knife as you eat a cake from the supermarket, encrusted with improbable blue roses, talking happily with your daughter about the latest episode of *All My Children*! The extravagance and unpredictability of life was beyond comprehension. The memories burned me, were too hot to touch. I didn't know how to explain all of this to Herkus and Justine in that strange and suddenly very dark bar. When had it gotten so dark?

"Back then," I said, "she must have been so angry. After the rape, I can imagine that she may not have wanted to survive. Perhaps she was hoping to die in the forests, fighting. She was young, sixteen or seventeen when they were taken. So by this point she must have been—what? Eighteen?"

"She was fourteen when they were taken. Wait, what rape?" Herkus asked.

"Oh," I said. I explained about the guard at Stutthof, surprised Justine hadn't already done so. She kept giving me warning glances as I told the story of the SS officer raping her and setting her free, but I wasn't sure why. I was still reeling from the idea that Grandma Sylvia was only fourteen. I had never pictured her as being fourteen at Stutthof. The way my mother told the story, she had seemed older, in control, the protagonist of the story. It had been because of her great beauty that the guard was overcome. Now it seemed that she was just a child having horrible things done to her. I thought of Chloe, then pushed the memory out of my mind. I thought of Justine's objection: That Grandma Sylvia could not have been beautiful. That it was something stranger or more sinister than desire that had moved the guard.

"So probably timing-wise," Herkus said, "the baby was from the forest husband, not the officer." I understood now what Herkus was trying to piece together, why Justine had been shooting me warning glances. Herkus's mother could have been the child of that SS officer. Which would mean that sweet, goofy, beautiful Herkus had a Nazi for a grandfather. A rapist Nazi even.

"I am sure," Justine said, "that your mother was the daughter of the forest husband."

"Yes," I agreed, because it was the thing to do, the thing to reassure Herkus. But I imagined that if the baby were the Nazi officer's child, Grandma Sylvia would have had even more reason to leave the baby with her brother and not stay, even more reason to turn her back and return to the darkness of the forest. There was a compelling psychology to this explanation that I couldn't entirely let go. And maybe it was just because I was so woozily drunk, but when I looked into Herkus's face, his eyes seemed uncannily blue, merciless. It seemed like a foregone conclusion, almost, that he was the progeny of that SS officer. It was, I felt, a terrible tragedy, but also an unavoidable one, like the ending of *Romeo and Juliet*.

It was closing time at the bar and suddenly we were on our feet and being herded to the door. I realized as we were almost outside that I hadn't paid for any of my drinks.

"Don't worry about it," Herkus said, patting me on the back. "They are my friends here. On the house."

"No," I said, "but I didn't just have this one beer—I had— I need to pay."

"Next time you treat me!" Herkus said. Herkus had put on a brown leather jacket that was cool and buttery soft when I hugged him. It was raining very lightly outside, but it was still warm.

"Will I see you again?" I asked, confused, misty-eyed, as though Herkus and Justine were angels who had visited me and might not come again.

"Of course! Of course!" they said.

"I will call you," Justine said.

And then I was walking down a street by myself. The rain was pleasant. I wandered for what seemed like a long time.

When I came to the River Vilnia, I realized I was lost and I should not cross it. I knew for certain that I didn't live on the other side of the river, so I doubled back the way I had come. I thought of Grandma Sylvia in the forest, killing Nazis. She killed four Nazis. That had always been the story I was told. One of them she stabbed in the neck with a knife while he was taking a shit in the forest.

At one point, I realized I was outside of Susan's hotel. I stood in the gutter, swaying, looking up at the darkened windows. I didn't even know which room was hers. I wished desperately that I could go to her, that I could tell her everything I had learned from Herkus and Justine, that I could put my head on her lap and she would stroke my hair and possibly give me a glass of water and some Advil.

"Inadvisable," I said to myself, still swaying, looking up at the dark windows.

But I realized I now knew where I was and I could find our apartment.

Once my key was in the lock of our front door, I understood that I had been terrified for hours, unsure if I would ever be able to find my way home. My mind had not registered the fear, but my body was full of it, and I was shaking and unable to breathe normally.

Inside, I sat on my bed in the dark and looked out at the moon as I listened to my heart pounding like a lonely drum in my ears.

Chapter 9

—

"Off the Record"

Word doc
Created by User on 7/17

I have been thinking more about the possibility of there being no self at all. My mind goes in two directions. One is that if my perception of my self is determined by my brain chemistry, which seems like a duh since the invention of SSRIs and anti-depressants, then I am really just a pot of bubbling chemical soup and my consciousness is just a by-product of my being. Which means that consciousness isn't some magic pebble that only human beings, made in God's image, possess. Probably all biological beings have varying levels of consciousness and self-consciousness: there is something it is like to be a dolphin or a pig or a dog or even a clam or a bug. The complexity of the self-perceived self is probably just a reflection of the overall complexity of the organism. In other words, maybe even rocks have really simple primitive rock-consciousnesses.

It is five in the morning. I have not slept and I don't think I am going to. It is bright as day outside. My father is snoring in the next room and it is so loud it is impossible to believe he is actually making that sound with his body.

The other direction I head in, is what if we are not single people but, like, genetic collages, so that part of my grandmother goes on in me, or part of my great-great-great-uncle. I mean, genetically that is EXACTLY what happens, but I am just saying: We have this illusion that we are somehow separate from our ancestors as though our stories have nothing to do with their stories and maybe that is an incredibly stupid thing to think. Maybe people who remember "past lives" are actually remembering their ancestors. What is ancestor worship all about? I know it is a thing, but I don't know much about it.

After my fight with Judith, I couldn't sleep and my dad was still out, so I decided to maybe go find him, only I ran into Daniel at a café, so I sat down with him. He had been out running, I guess, because he was wearing a T-shirt and running shorts instead of his usual pirate outfit. He was drinking a vanilla milk shake. I knew as soon as I laid eyes on him, "Oh, this is the night I have sex with you. I was wondering how this all was going to happen, but this is the way it transpires." Sometimes I know things like that, and everything feels gentle and predestined, and all I have to do is let it happen.

A lot about Daniel is confusing. For instance, going on a run and then stopping for a vanilla milk shake on your way home. That's a weird thing to do at ten at night. Also, he is incredibly physically attractive: tan skin, dark hair, a robust, almost phallic-looking nose, and a really wonderful body. And yet he wears the pirate shirts and those khaki Dockers that come all the way up to your belly button. I think the shirts are cut the way they are because currently he is living in Saudi Arabia, or at least that's what he told me the night we went to the jazz club. So I guess it isn't his fault, but still. It is even weird that he is living in Saudi Arabia.

"What do you think about what's going on in Ukraine?" Daniel asked me. The lights of the café where we sat were bright-hot neon and it reminded me of a carnival against the swimming darkness outside. I sighed. So he was going to make me work for it. I would have to be intelligent in order for him to have sex with me. He knew about my Russianness and now I would have to perform for him. I resented it, even as I knew I would oblige.

"I think Putin is winging it," I said, quoting almost exactly from a *Times* article I had read and just praying like hell he hadn't read the same one. "Everyone keeps analyzing what he's doing, but I don't think analysis will help. There has to be an underlying pattern in order for you to analyze something. But Putin is just winging it and when he gets scared he tends to double down."

"The CIA released something where they had some analysis of him done in secret and they think he has autism," Daniel said.

I shrugged. I didn't care if Putin had autism. The man was cracked. Maybe autism was part of it, but it barely seemed like useful information to me.

"Maybe the CIA leaked that because they knew it would irritate Putin to hear they thought he was autistic."

Daniel took a sip of his milk shake, raised his eyebrows, nodding, but then when he swallowed, he didn't say anything. We sat there for a while. It seemed like maybe I was wrong. Maybe he wasn't even interested in me and he was thinking about how he wanted to get home and go to bed and digest his vanilla milk shake in private. But then he said, "Would you like to come to my place and get a massage? I studied Zhi Ya massage when I lived in China and I haven't gotten to practice in a little while."

Granted, it was an incredibly weird come-on line, combining the oldest and most blatant sexual overture with a weird professional explanation, but at least I felt like I knew what was going on. Sure, I said. Let's go to your place and you can practice your acupressure thing on me. All the way there he kept chattering on and on about the principles of Zhi Ya and his time spent in China. He had made a vow, a personal commitment, he explained, to live in seven countries and learn seven languages before he turned forty. He had already lived in Chile, China, and now Saudi Arabia, and he claimed he was fluent in Spanish, Mandarin, and Arabic as well as English.

Like my dad and me, he was living in a little rented apartment instead of a regular hotel room, though his was just a studio with a tiny kitchenette in Užupis. He didn't have a washing machine, he explained, and he was going to have to figure out where a Laundromat was soon. It was clean enough in there, though it smelled like boy. I wondered how old he was. I was thinking that since he had already lived in three countries and learned three languages, he was probably close to thirty, but he didn't have any wrinkles. He had me lay down on the bed, and I went to take off my shirt, but he said no, he could do it through my clothes. I was almost offended. Who stops a girl from taking her top off? But this was his weird-ass rodeo and I figured he was in charge of making up the rules.

I was wearing a white T-shirt and jean shorts and flip-flops. I kicked off my shoes and lay facedown on his bed, which smelled even more like boy. He climbed on top of me and straddled my hips. "You have really nice calves," he said. "You can tell a lot about how a woman is going to look naked from her calves."

I just made a noise into the covers in order not to have to answer. He was rubbing me now, and it was clear he wasn't lying about having been professionally trained. He definitely had a system and within ten minutes I was no longer having conscious thoughts and he was making things hurt and things feel good I didn't even know were there. He spent a long time pinching around in my armpits and then he made a noise like he was really satisfied with himself. "That was a good release," he told me, as though I had done something.

When and in what way this was going to turn sexual was entirely a mystery. I could feel he had a hard-on through the thin, almost crunchy fabric of his running shorts. It was rubbing all over my back when he moved to work on my shoulders. "Maybe I should take my top off," I suggested again.

There was a silence. He was breathing kind of heavily. "If you want to," he said. So I reached down and tugged my T-shirt up and over my head, still lying on my tummy, but I left my bra on. "Do you have any lotion?" I asked.

He scrambled off me and went to scope out the bathroom. I could hear him opening cabinets and then opening his mini-fridge. "I have butter," he said.

"Like cocoa butter?"

"No, like dairy butter."

Whatever, it didn't matter. I didn't say anything, just shrugged, and he clambered back on top of me and began to rub the cold stick of butter into my skin. It felt good actually. I was sure that now that I was half naked and covered in butter, things would begin to speed up, but they didn't. He just kept rubbing me for maybe an hour, and then he announced he was done.

"How do you feel?" he asked.

"You're really strange," I said, directly into his mattress.

"What?" he said. My voice had been muffled by the covers.

"I said you are really very strange."

He laughed and climbed off me. "How so?"

"You live in all these countries. You speak all these languages. You are clearly ambitious, but not about anything normal like money or a career. For fun, you go on history tours with a lot of old people by yourself. You give out massages that should turn into sex, but they never do, and then you climb off and you say, 'How do you feel?' I'm just saying, you're strange." I had rolled onto my side, and he could see my breasts spilling a bit out of the cups of my bra. It was a good bra.

He laughed again, sitting on the bed beside me, his massive hard-on clearly visible in his running shorts. I felt almost resentful of the size of the hard-on since it seemed increasingly that I wasn't going to have the chance to actually see it. I had only ever seen three penises before, and none of them had been as big as his looked to be. I was just curious. He rubbed his forehead with his hand for a minute, and then looked up at me, his face suddenly candid. "I guess," he said, "I'm just a little worried about how old you are. I've been avoiding asking."

"That's a good instinct," I said. "You should keep doing that."

He let out a sigh, shaking his head like he'd lost a big bet. "So does that mean you aren't twenty-one?"

"I am not twenty-one," I agreed.

"But you are eighteen?" he said.

"Like I said, you are better off not asking," I said.

"Oh fucking crap."

I nodded in what I hoped was a knowing way. I had gotten the impression that most men wanted to have sex with "barely legal" girls, so I was really hoping this wasn't a deal breaker. I had never read *Lolita,* I had never even seen the movie, but I did have a vintage movie poster of it in my room and I got the gist. Lollipops and everything. "I'll be eighteen in a few months," I said, in as husky and sexy a voice as I could manage.

He hid his face in his hands for a minute and I knew he was deciding, and I was positive, absolutely positive he was going to decide in my favor, but when he looked up, I knew. There was pity on his face. And I hated him.

"I'm sorry," he said. "You're beautiful, but you're just a baby. You're a baby!" He held out his hands, gesturing at my body like it was beautiful but also like it made him sad. I was like cake he couldn't eat. That was what his look said.

I was so angry it made me start trembling. I grabbed my T-shirt from the floor by his bed and whipped it on.

"Don't be mad," he said.

"I'm not mad," I said. "Thank you very much for the massage. You're talented." I wanted desperately to get the power back, but I wasn't sure how. What was just revealed was that I was willing to have sex with him but he wasn't willing to have sex with me, and it was humiliating. I hadn't really wanted to have sex with him in the first place! I just wanted to get back at Fang and forget about Judith and have an adventure and see a new penis. But he was weird. What a baby, to order a vanilla milk shake.

"I'm sorry, Vera," he said.

I didn't want him apologizing to me. "For what?" I asked.

"For leading you on, I guess." He shrugged. He no longer had an erection, I noted. I was standing now, in the middle of his room, and he hadn't stood up with me. Evidently I was supposed to find the door on my own, which was fine, it was just right there, but it was still awful, like I was a servant being dismissed.

"You didn't lead me on," I said. In order to keep my voice level and unemotional, I pictured a steaming pile of dog shit. It was a trick I had learned in therapy. I could talk about anything in a level voice by now. Really, I wanted to punch him in the face. It suddenly seemed stupid to me that he had such a cartoonishly huge dick. It was probably what made him feel so entitled.

"All right," he said, shrugging. "I'm sorry all the same. Can we be friends?"

"Of course," I said, because there was no other option. If I told him no, he would have the impression this had been upsetting for me, and I would lose even more power.

"Good," he said. "Are you safe getting home?"

He wasn't even going to walk me home, I realized. I mean, I hadn't expected him to, it actually hadn't occurred to me that he would. But now he wanted verbal acknowledgment that he didn't need to, when he knew perfectly well that I was seventeen and wandering around in a foreign city at what was now midnight. "Of course," I said. "I'm perfectly safe."

I didn't even know how to get home because his apartment was in Užupis and I got totally confused. I wandered around for fucking forever. At one point I saw a bar and there were lots of young Russian guys in it and I thought about going in there and fucking one of them, but I was feeling too scared and upset about how lost I was. Finally, I found myself on Žydų gatvė, but I only knew it because I saw the kindergarten where the Great Synagogue used to be.

I sat down in the grass in the middle of the playground. It was a little muddy from the rain earlier, and I knew my shorts were getting wet, but I didn't care. I just sat there and let my mind unclench, and it felt like knowledge was being poured into me. It was just this feeling of transmission, of images or facts, flickering by so fast I didn't know what they were. I felt that God was there with me on that playground. The universe was being explained. I plucked at a lock of my hair that had gotten stuck in my mouth as I was walking. The moon was small and high above me. I wish I could describe it without using language. If anything, what I was receiving were images, thousands upon thousands of images, flickering through me, and each one was a code for some tremendous truth.

Daniel didn't matter. Judith didn't matter. My father didn't matter. Fang didn't matter.

Your mother birthed you through her hips, a voice said in my mind. I pictured myself sliding out of Mama, and her sliding out of her mama, and her sliding out of her mama, all the way back. We were like *matryoshka* nesting dolls. We were thousands of years old.

It was funny, I thought, the way women let men think they ruled the world. That was the bargain they made: You take the world, and we'll take life and death. Sure, fight wars. Make up countries. Call them whatever you want. Make up laws. It all sounds good.

But that was only to distract them so that they wouldn't try to participate in the women's work, which was the pulling of souls out from the darkness and the projection of light into the future. Women were making time, they were weaving it in their wombs by building consciousnesses to experience it. Let the men have their tanks. Let them have their statues. Let Putin ride his horse shirtless.

We would be here all along, quietly guiding the light out of the dark.

I T TOOK SEVERAL CUPS OF COFFEE and four Tylenol before I could even be convinced to shower and get ready for our trip to the castle at Trakai. It was a long bus ride out to the castle and Judith was there, but both Susan and Daniel were conspicuously absent. Vera was humming with energy. She was chattering about the forest and what a magical place it seemed like. *Primordial* was the word she used. It was true; the country cottages, dachas, were like something from a fairy tale, and as we passed open meadows there would often be a fat old woman wearing a head scarf stooping to pick mushrooms or flowers. I was close enough to Vera that I noticed her teeth were yellow and visibly coated in plaque.

"Jesus, Vera! When was the last time you brushed your teeth?" I said. The rest of her was perfectly coiffed, her makeup precision perfect. It was unsettling.

"God," she said, elbowing me. "Nosy!"

"Seriously," I said. "Buy some gum or something just to get the top layer off."

The castle was not nearly as impressive as a castle ought to be. The grounds were beautiful, though, a large lake with swans. An inordinate number of weddings seemed to be taking place. Brides were posing for photos everywhere you looked.

Darius took us around the castle, pointing out what was of interest, explaining that this was wedding season and that many couples had been waiting for summer so that they could get married at Trakai. The castle itself was stone to about the first story and then brick going all the way up after that. It made the building look like one of those flip-books where you can put the legs of an elephant on the body of a deer.

"The castle needed renovations," Darius explained, "and of course the Soviets would never have allowed us to build a fortress, a castle, thinking it would be part of a rebellion. Well! So the Lithuanian officials came up with a scheme to rebuild the castle anyway, and they told the Soviets they needed building materials to build new schools and then they used the bricks that were sent to rebuild the castle. Too bad for the schoolchildren, but oh well!"

Vera was in such high spirits that she kept turning cartwheels as we wandered along the green lawn. I noticed that Kenneth was watching her, sneering, as though her cartwheels were a direct rebuke or rejection of him. After Darius released us to explore, I just wanted to get away from the group. I wasn't interested in the castle. I was getting bored of history, to be honest. "Let's go get some coffee or something," I said, and steered us to a small café on the lake.

We ordered coffee and fried dough. Dragonflies buzzed along the edge of the water and something about the expansiveness of the space or the properties of the lake muted all sound. Even though there were many other people around, we could only hear their conversations or laughter as a hush. I thought about Herkus. I was going to have to tell Vera about what had really happened to Grandma Sylvia. I had decided that much already.

"Vera," I asked, "did you write a paper about rape for English class?"

She closed her eyes for a long slow blink, then opened them, said, "I had forgotten I did. It feels like that was so long ago. It was in another life."

"Well. At the time, you were upset about it. And your mother told me about it."

"God, Mama, way to be a busybody," she said.

"And she asked me not to tell you something, a thing that I think is important, and that I feel like you have a right to know because it's part of your lineage." I was the only one eating the fried dough, and I tried to lick the powdered sugar off my fingers before telling her the story, the real story, of how Grandma Sylvia escaped.

Vera listened with a stagy but quiet stoicism. Her manner was affected in a way that reminded me of my mother, as though she were playacting hearing the story.

"This doesn't surprise me," she said, when I was done. "How else is a woman supposed to escape with her life?"

I thought this was an odd reaction.

"I mean, really," Vera said. "The story before didn't make any sense. He just set her free because she was pretty? Like freeing a butterfly out of doors that has accidentally gotten in your house? It didn't add up."

I nodded. It was true that the edited story I had told her was psychologically problematic, presenting the SS officer as some motive-less do-gooder, but I thought the issue of combining rape and freedom was just as hard to fathom.

"Oh, I don't think so at all!" Vera said. "Rape is really like the perfect act to encapsulate what he wanted to say to her: Fuck you for being so beautiful and forcing me to want you.

Fuck you for not being something I can just kill. Fuck you for making me look, for making me *see*."

It was an interesting point. I didn't want to bring up the other hypothesis, the one that Justine had introduced into my mind, that the guard had been moved not by Grandma Sylvia's beauty but by pity. There was something terrible about pity, something dirty and terrifying about it, that I did not want to discuss or bring to Vera's attention. Instead, I asked a question.

"Why did you write that term paper, Vera?" I asked her. "Why were you even thinking about rape? I mean, what was the assignment?"

"Oh, rape wasn't the assignment," Vera said. "That was part of why she failed me. I have no idea what the assignment was supposed to be, but I figured, like, ugh, it's just a hoop to jump through, you know? They want you to do a certain amount of work and show you know how to format a bibliography, but then she got almost like *personally* offended that I hadn't done the assignment."

I nodded. Sometimes when I tried to picture Vera interacting with the world, the real, official, boring world, I got a nervous, almost giggly feeling and it made me want to cover my eyes with my hands. God only knew what that teacher made of her.

"But I guess it was just a way for me to think through what happened to me at the mental hospital."

I reached across the table for her hand. "What happened at the mental hospital?"

"Oh, chill—no!" she said. "I wasn't raped. I mean, like, sexually. But there are things you can do in this world that make other people decide you don't have a right to your will anymore. I didn't have a right to choose when I wanted to eat, when I wanted to sleep. I didn't have a right to think my thoughts. I didn't have a right to feel my emotions. It was the most complete form of rape imaginable. I didn't want to take that medication, but they would make me. If I tried to resist, they would hold me down and inject it into me with needles."

"So talking about rape was your way of talking about all that?"

Vera nodded. "But I mean, I don't really believe that—that there is no such thing as consent. Obviously there is. It's just in a different class of being, than, like, trees and rocks and stuff. I mean, consent is, like, fairly imaginary."

"What?"

"Consent is just a nice idea. Like freedom or liberty. Or justice. It has reality and importance as an idea. And we should strive to make our real lives mirror those invisible ideals. But at the same time, you know, it's not real like gravity. If consent were real the same way gravity is real, it wouldn't be possible to rape anybody. Or maybe you could, but it would be much harder, I think."

While what she was saying was uncomfortable, and could possibly be construed as wildly offensive, it was still intriguing. That was the thing about Vera. She was always coming at things from an unexpected angle. "Listen," I said, "I just can't shake this feeling that Herkus's mother was the product of that rape. With the SS officer." I told Vera what I had pieced together with Herkus and Justine the night before.

"But you don't know for sure," she pointed out. "And what does it matter anyway? Might as well let him believe his mother was the child of the forest husband."

"But it just makes too much psychological sense of why she

would leave the baby, why she wouldn't want to raise it herself."
I was also aware that I was upset about something I would
never have said to Vera, which was that I was upset that the
Nazi had been evolutionarily rewarded for raping Grandma
Sylvia. He had snuck his way into our chain of being. His
genes were threatening sweet Herkus from the inside. It was
an insane idea, I knew this.

"Maybe, and maybe that's why she left the baby," Vera said,
"but there's no way of knowing for sure."

Still, it occurred to me that there was a way of knowing for
sure. I knew the date of Grandma Sylvia's rape birthday, had
known it my whole life, had eaten cake with her on that day
when I was a child. All I would need to piece it together was
some idea of when Herkus's mother had been taken to the
farm, what her birth date might be. If they were nine months
apart, then I would know.

"Yeah," I said, "but doesn't that just seem like too much of
a coincidence? She gets raped, has a baby, but the rapist isn't
the father?"

Vera shrugged. "It's not as easy to get pregnant as all that.
You're only fertile, like, three days a month."

But it *was* as easy as all that. I thought of my own mother
and father, who'd had sex only the one time. I thought of myself
and Katya. Sometimes it was incredibly easy to get pregnant.
Sometimes the stars aligned just so. Still, statistically speaking, Vera had a point.

"Did you know that chimpanzee males rape females all the
time?" she said.

"No, I didn't know that."

"Fang and I watched a documentary. I put it in my English
paper. And the male chimps kill the babies of their rivals so

that the females will be fertile again quicker. So to deal with that, the female chimps mate with as many males as they can so that there will be confusion over who the father is."

"That's terrible," I said.

She shrugged. "They commit genocide, too. Just like us."

She looked so grown up these days, with her clear skin and new clothes. But I was worried about her. I was worried about what being in the mental hospital had done to her. What it had cost her when none of us believed her.

"You know, Vera," I said, "all your, you know, 'delusions' were really just metaphors taken a little too far, but they were *good* metaphors. The blue light on Fang, the rotting cheerleaders—all of that was insightful. There *is* way more to life than being cool in Rancho Cucamonga. And we really are all going to die someday. But if you focus on that, it will make you go crazy."

"So you're saying don't think about it?" Her disdain was quick and cutting.

"No," I said, "I'm saying—I don't know what I'm saying. Just: It's part of our obligation to go on living and wanting and becoming. I used to not understand this—how could Grandma Sylvia, after all that, how could she move to god-damn California and become a housewife, of all things! How could she possibly do it? But that's what you do. That's the heroic thing to do: To choose to be happy. To take your kids to Disneyland. To drive your station wagon through the orange groves and let the past *go*."

"I'm sorry, Papa," Vera said, "but I just think that is really very stupid."

I thought maybe she was right. Maybe it was stupid. But possibly because I had eaten so much fried dough or else because there was a sleepy magic to Trakai, I didn't worry too much about whether I was right or wrong. There was no way, sitting there at that lake, looking at my daughter, to second-guess myself. I could only think the things I thought, just as the dragonflies could only be dragonflies buzzing. I shrugged. "I'm just saying, Vera, now that you're not insane, what are you gonna do with your life? Are you gonna go to college?"

"Don't even talk to me about college," she said, her voice bitter like the words tasted of pennies. "Nowhere good will take me now."

It was true that the public universities of California had become almost impossible to get into in the last decade. In order to be accepted as a freshman you had to have perfect grades, extracurriculars, the whole nine yards. Even B students had to spend a few years at a junior college before transferring in. And her grades this past year—they would be a lot to explain. "You could look at private schools," I said. "Or go out of state."

"With what money?"

"I could help with money. I'm sure my mother would help. We could take out loans. We'd patch it together."

Vera just stared at me. I stared back at her.

"You would do that?" she asked.

"Of course," I said, amazed she didn't already know.

I snuck out that afternoon to buy Vera an amber necklace. I wanted nothing more than to take a nap, but we only had four days of the trip left, and I was worried I wouldn't have another chance. I told Vera and Judith I was picking up some groceries, and I went out to find the jewelry store Vera had described on

Gedimino prospektas, a long, broad street where vendors laid out wares on tables or on blankets on the ground: a multitude of amber baubles, tiny lacquered wooden boxes, hand-carved wooden kitchen implements, fur hats, Soviet trinkets, old war medals, painted canvases hawked by middle-aged artists absolutely reeking of alcohol and cigarettes. Not the fresh smell of alcohol spilled but the citrusy, rotting smell of alcohol that cannot be processed by the liver, now seeping out of the pores as some new poison. Ink, I thought, and wondered if I smelled like that too. I needed to get the drinking under control. I was always intending to get the drinking under control, but I never actually did. It was another thing that made me feel helpless, the lack of progress I made on my various schemes to better myself. My body was just one more dissertation I wasn't going to finish.

I couldn't find the shop Vera mentioned, but I found *a* shop, and I was assured by the high prices that the amber was real. I was not normally very good at picking out jewelry. It wasn't that I didn't like jewelry or couldn't tell when it was pretty, but I knew there was a whole other fashion part of it that I didn't have a handle on. But with the amber, I was less nervous. It was just like trying to pick a pretty shell at the seashore or a pretty rock at the lake.

I didn't like the pendants, just one big gob of amber on a chain, and I finally settled on what I thought was the prettiest thing in the store: a necklace of perfectly polished, large, round amber beads that ranged from the lightest, palest honey all the way to the darkest, pitchy red-black, perfectly arranged like a rainbow. I could picture it on Vera's neck. I knew it was the right one, and I bought it, practically in a haze of exhaustion. I am sure the woman who ran the shop thought I was completely insane; I was barely able to count my money to pay for the thing. Sadly, I needed a beer. I knew having a beer would cure me, but I was unwilling to have one and admit what was wrong with me.

When I got back to the apartment, having bought a useless hodgepodge of groceries as cover, there was a note on the table in Judith's spidery hand:

Your daughter is acting as my chaperone on a night out. I am unable to work the locking mechanism on my door and so I need her in order to enter and exit my apartment. She has an excellent sense of direction! Don't wait up.

XOXO, Judith

PS: I am kidding, we will be home early. I am an old woman.

I didn't even need to think about it. I opened the freezer, poured a shot of vodka, chased it with a pickle, brushed my teeth, put on fresh clothes, and set out for Susan's hotel.

It was luck that she was there. I brought her a bag of little black plums I had bought as part of my cover-story groceries. My mother had always said never to show up to a woman's house without bringing a gift. I held out the plums, not knowing what to say, just standing there at her door. I wanted her so badly I didn't even know how to flirt or coerce or beg. I could only hold out the plums and hope she knew what I meant, why I was there, what I needed. It wasn't just sex I needed, either. It was something I didn't have a name for.

She was wearing an oversize man's shirt and pajama pants. "I was writing," she said. "Sorry I skipped out on Trakai without telling you." Her hair was wet from the shower. I wanted to lick her ears. I wanted to bite her hair. She took the plums and motioned me inside. "Sit," she said, and gestured at the bed.

I sat. It was late afternoon, almost evening, but the sun was still bright outside and her curtains were pulled against it so that her room was dim in that very particular way that a sickroom is dim. She sat beside me and reached into the bag of plums, plucked one for herself, then offered the bag to me. I reached inside, my hand awkward and trembly in the plastic, and took one of the little fruits. When I bit into it, juice ran down my chin. The skin was puckeringly sour and the flesh disgustingly sweet. I almost choked on my own saliva. Susan made no game of eating her plum suggestively, but she didn't have to. It was a frankly, undeniably erotic activity, eating those plums on her bed.

"Are you ever going to kiss me?" she asked.

My mouth was full of plum. I had failed again. I had waited too long. She laughed and reached over and kissed me.

My usual pedestrian concerns during sex—wondering if she was liking what I was doing, wondering if I would make her come, trying to keep from coming myself—were absent. Susan didn't try to say dirty things to me, and I didn't try to say dirty things to her. Kat and I had had sex something like this, wordless, animal sex, but there was none of that teenage fumbling or frantic lunging between me and Susan. Our sex was slow, almost decorous, and yet verging on delirious. I felt like I had a fever. Naked, her body was small and firm, but she was not skinny. She reminded me of a cat, that kind of contained, graceful plumpness. After she got me undressed, she wanted to look at me for a long time and I felt silly. "Golden fur everywhere," she said and touched my chest hair.

"Sorry," I said.

"No, I like it."

When we were done, I pulled the amber necklace out of the canvas grocery bag and gave it to her. I'd brought it with me only because I didn't want to leave it in the apartment, afraid Vera would find it.

"Are you serious?" she said, holding the beads which almost seemed to glow in the low light.

"Yeah," I said. I thought that I could always go back to that store and buy something else for Vera. In that moment, I just wanted to give Susan something and the necklace was what I had.

"But this is so beautiful," she said.

I helped her put it on. She sat on the bed, naked except for the amber at her throat, and ate another plum. I thought that I would remember how she looked for the rest of my life. Her hair was the same brassy red-gold as the middle beads of the amber necklace. Her skin was dewy with sweat. Her room had no air-conditioning and there was sweat at her temples too, making her hair curl. It was clear from the easy way she sat cross-legged that she was comfortable being naked. She was not nude, not like some European painting of coy, pale butt cheeks. She was graphically, powerfully naked, like a fertility idol.

"What are you doing?" she said, and snatched away the bed pillow I had used to cover my crotch.

I laughed. "It's just a reflex. When it's erect, it seems obvious to be naked, but when I'm soft I feel like I should cover up."

"I think he's very handsome, sleeping like that," she said,

gesturing to the way my penis slumped over my thigh. I had never had a lover refer to my penis as "he," like it was a separate person. I thought it was cute of her.

"I like you so much," I said.

"Oh, don't start with that," she said. "You'll get me all confused."

"But I really do like you," I said.

"I know. I like you too." She fished another plum out of the bag and threw it to me, then got one for herself. "These little plums are amazing. I could eat all of them. They're so sweet, they're like candy."

I ate the plum. We were going to talk only about the plums. Normally I was all for avoiding such conversations because women were so often hurt by whatever I was really thinking or feeling, and so talking after sex involved a lot of white lies. But to not talk about it with Susan now seemed perfectly absurd, like we were both ignoring bombs going off just outside our window.

"I'm not going to get you confused," I finally decided to say. "This isn't just a lark for me. I haven't felt like this about someone in a long time."

"Oh, just shut up!" she cried. "You'll ruin it!" She threw her plum pit at me and burst out laughing.

"No, I won't," I said, brushing the wet plum pit off my chest and onto the floor and then lunging for her, tackling her on the bed. "It can't be ruined! That's what I want to show you. That's why I'm talking about it."

"You're young," she said, but she was smiling, a little out of breath, her eyes darting back and forth like she was trying to look in both of my eyes at once.

"I'm young," I agreed, and I kissed her.

Chapter 10

Date: 7/17/2014 4:30 PM
From: Vera.Abramov@gmail.com
To: FangBoy76@hotmail.com
Subject: Another sunset

Dear Fang,

    I was very interested in your letter about Virginia Woolf, and I assume it is an olive branch. You always know best how to please me. I accept your gesture of intellectual rapprochement. I think it is very civilized of you. I also know you prefer brevity in writing and so for you to write me pages and pages like that was really impressive. It meant a lot to me. Even though I suspect you just got weed from your cousins and were stoned with no one to talk to. Still, you could have done anything with that time. You could have jerked off to porn of dragons fucking cars, for instance. The Internet makes anything possible.

    But for now, lay your suspicions to rest: I am fine. I give you my solemn word.

    There have been a few interesting developments here, however.

    For one thing, my father says that he might be able to help me pay for college. And I got the sense, Fang, that he wasn't saying it to get me to like him. It wasn't a bribe. He was saying it because he genuinely wanted me to be able to go to college.

It just brings up all these possibilities that I had assumed were off the table, and it makes me feel very differently about starting school because if I could get good grades in the fall, then maybe colleges would see that last year was just a blip. I know you probably don't like the idea of me going out of state. But you could too! I mean, couldn't you? Why not? Why does everything have to be California California California?

I get so torn, Fang. About humans. About what we are. About whether God exists. Sometimes I am so hopeless about it, and then other times I feel blinded by this realization of exactly what we are. The truth of what we are. The beauty of it.

One part of me thinks I am just a collection of cells and hormones and hair. The idea that I am entirely a Jew because it was my mother and not my father who was Jewish—as though there is a metaphysical baton that she has passed me—well, isn't it insane? I am equally my father's daughter, and so half Lithuanian. Or Polish. It is always unclear to me whether we are Lithuanian or Polish. But isn't Grandma Sylvia's blood in my veins, too? It seems so obvious now that I am here, my connection to her. I was not aware of it, but I think my whole life I have been pretending he is not my father on some level. I have been pretending that he has nothing to do with me. But he does.

It turns out that Grandma Sylvia was raped by an SS officer and that is how she really escaped from Stutthof. This guy saw her naked when she was in line for the gas chamber, decided he wanted some of that, yanked her out, fucked her, then sent her off into the woods with his coat and some money. Which just goes to show you: Human beings, in the end, are nothing but a bunch of chimps.

And yet. Sometimes something will happen, like my father will offer to pay for college and I'll think: But what beautiful, noble chimps we are. And it seems like we are more than animals, after all. I still don't understand what beauty is. What it indicates, exactly. But it must mean something.

Do you think that we are made in God's image, Fang? What does that idea even mean?

When I was eight, I told my mother I was an atheist. It was ridiculous, really. We were having a fight about the sunset. She said, "Just look at that. So beautiful. It looks enchanted, don't you think?"

And I said, "It's just what happens when the sun hits the atmosphere at that angle. There's nothing magic about it. I read about it in science at school."

"I'm just saying, there doesn't have to be beauty," Mama said.

"Are you saying beauty means something?" I asked. Because I didn't know what a pretty sunset could possibly mean, but I did recognize that it was an appealing idea. Actually, I was very into the idea of EVERYTHING meaning something. Like, I would look at three candles burning, and I would think: Those three candles represent Dedushka Pavel and Babushka Inna and Mama, and that is why two of them are very short and one of them is long, because Mama still has many years to live and Dedushka and Babushka will die soon.

"I suppose that beautiful things always make me think of the divine," she said. She was driving me home from piano.

"I don't believe in God," I told her. Which, I had never actually thought that before, but it seemed like such a daring and interesting thing to say, I just couldn't resist.

"You don't?" she asked.

"No."

And she asked me why not, and I think I said something lame about how there was so much suffering in the world, how could there be a God who would allow it, if there was a God he was a sadist, basically. I don't think I used the word sadist. I think what I actually said was that if there was a God, he was the kind of boy who liked to pull wings off flies. Anyway, she said that God gave us minds to question with and that she was proud of me, but that she took my atheism as yet another sign of the existence of God. Which, maybe she just said that to irritate me. That would be very like her. Or maybe she really did see it as a sign of God's existence. Maybe it was this whole stupid conversation that made her want to send me to Hebrew school in the first place.

My dad wants to believe that Grandma Sylvia being raped is some big meaningful event, some kind of mystery that sums up all of human existence, but I am very afraid that it is just another sunset. It seemed like what you were proposing in your letter is that God is a kind of larger collective mind that is using our individual minds as neurons. And that strikes me as the most exciting and beautiful idea of all. I will try my hardest to believe in it.

I'm going to try to go to sleep.

With love,

From Vilnius,

Your fellow neuron in the mind of God,

V

I WANDERED HOME after dark had fallen, worried. I had used Judith's note as an excuse to shirk my fatherly duties, though on the other hand, Vera was nearly an adult and all she was doing was hanging out with Judith. I guess it made me anxious not being able to use my cell phone. What if she had needed me while I was at Susan's? What if something had happened? When I got to the apartment, I was relieved to see that Vera was already back and painting her toenails at the kitchen table. Judith had not been lying about coming home early.

"How was your night?" I asked.

"Where should I start if I wanted to read some Virginia Woolf?" she asked, not looking up from her toes. She was painting them black, or some version of brown-red that was nearly black.

"*Mrs. Dalloway* or *To the Lighthouse*," I said. "Why?" I assumed she and Judith had been talking about Woolf for whatever reason.

"Fang said I should read *The Waves*," she said, looking up finally, and screwing the little cap on the nail polish.

"Why on earth would Fang tell you to read *The Waves*?" I said. I had always staunchly defended *The Waves* in graduate school, but it was a weird book, and I did not particularly enjoy reading it, if I was being honest. It wasn't even really a novel. Woolf had called it a "play poem" and it was a series of soliloquies from six different narrators who were not, Woolf maintained, separate characters per se but merely six facets of consciousness that were really continuous. It was slow and very poetic and opaque. The fact that Fang was recommending it was bizarre.

"He said it's the best thing he's ever read," she said. "He said Virginia Woolf was the first European he had ever read who had spit out the lie of, you know, thinking we are all separate people."

I hesitated. "But we are all separate people."

"Well, but that could be an illusion," she said. "Ants might think they are separate people, unaware that they act as a colony. Maybe humans only think they are separate, but really we might be like cells or bacteria, and collectively there might be a thing that is thinking, using us as, like, neurons."

I sat down at the table. I wanted to get out the vodka, but I did not. The drinking had to stop, it just had to. I wanted my body back. Something in the sex with Susan had made me want that, to be a physical specimen again. To be frank and naked and unashamed of myself. Or maybe it had been meeting Herkus and seeing in him such an uncanny facsimile of a self I had already given up for lost. "Does Fang think there is no such thing as separate people?" I asked.

Vera squinted, looking up at the light, thinking. "Maybe not 'no such thing'—like, that makes it sound like there are no individual ants, and of course there are—just more that what is actually interesting might be something we are unaware of about the way we are all connected. And he thinks that the idea of individuality is like a disease that has infected our culture. Basically."

"Is this a Tongan thing?" I asked. "Or a Mormon thing?"

"I don't think so," she said. "I think it's a Fang thing."

"Why is Fang named Fang?" I asked suddenly. "I mean, is that his real name?"

"No. It's because he can open a beer can with his teeth."

I considered this for a moment. "Well, then, you should read *The Waves*." I held up my hands, shrugged. "It's kinda boring, though. And she talks about the connectedness of people's minds in the other books too. That's what I was writing my dissertation on."

"No shit? So you don't think Fang is insane?" she asked, narrowing her eyes at me in a dramatic way that made it hard to take her seriously.

"No, why would I think that?"

"I just thought maybe you might," she said.

"No," I said.

"But you still think *I'm* insane," she said.

"No," I said, shaking my head. It was almost as though the past few days hadn't happened for her. I was confused. She looked at me, searching for something. "I really don't," I said.

"All right," she said, but I didn't get the feeling it was settled in her mind.

"You told me you were on acid," I said, trying to give her a replay of my understanding of our mutual reality. "And I believed you."

"Oh, how great of you to 'believe' me," she sneered.

"Well, Vera, what else am I supposed to do but believe you?"

That seemed to stop her. She shook her head. "I don't know," she said. A glass that had been on the counter suddenly fell to the floor and shattered. We both jumped as though someone had fired a gun.

"What the fuck!" she cried.

"I don't know," I said, "it must have been on the edge and then fallen."

"Or there's a ghost," she said. I stood to sweep up the glass, telling her to stay sitting since her feet were bare. She propped them up on the table, her newly painted toes splayed, as I swept under her chair.

"There's no ghost," I said.

"Maybe it was Grandma Sylvia," she said.

"Why would Grandma Sylvia be here? Wouldn't her ghost be in California?"

"I don't know," she said. "I have no idea how ghosts work."

"Well, I don't believe in ghosts," I said. But I had no explanation for why the glass might have fallen.

"I'm sorry I was so weird," Vera said. "About believing me. That wasn't fair of me."

"That's okay," I said, down on my hands and knees with wet paper towels, trying to get the smaller shards.

"So you think I should read *Mrs. Dalloway* first?" Vera said, and it took me a minute to remember we had been talking about Woolf in the first place.

"Sure," I said, crouched at her feet, holding the dirty wad of paper towels, still scanning the linoleum for shards. I had lost the thread. Nothing was making sense. Other people's moods were changing too quickly for me to track. It was late and I needed to go to sleep.

"Justine called," she said. "I told her we would skip out on our afternoon event tomorrow to go meet your family."

"My family?"

"Yeah, I guess it's Herkus's cousin's birthday or something. And everyone will be there, his mom, his aunt and uncle, like everybody. Big family gathering in the country."

"And you didn't lead with this news?" I said, as I struggled to stand and throw away the wad of paper towels. My body was stiff. I felt old. "This wasn't the first thing you thought to say when I entered the room?"

"Ugh, Papa, not everything is about you," she said. "The address is by the phone. I figure we can take a taxi."

I nodded, feeling overwhelmed. I didn't have a number for a taxi service. We would figure it out. Tomorrow was still an entire day away.

A bit later, she went to bed and I retreated to my room. I could hear her playing music in there on the tinny speakers of her laptop. Lady Gaga, it sounded like. *I wanna take a ride on your disco stick.* I thought about writing my mother, but didn't. I should tell her about Herkus, but it felt like too much to explain, and I was exhausted even thinking about getting out my computer and typing it all.

I wondered about my mother. I wondered what it had been like to grow up as Grandma Sylvia's daughter, what glasses might have shattered on that floor. The transition from forest fighter to housewife was perhaps only a smooth one in retrospect. I wondered what my mother hadn't told me about growing up in that house, what things she had left out of her stories.

One of the things I had never told my mother was that I decided to find my father when I was living in New York. I had never told anyone, except Katya in one desperate letter sent after the fact. But since then, I had tried to contain it and keep it from spreading by not even thinking about it myself, as though it were a disease under quarantine. All these years, I had just sort of grown around it, the way skin will swallow up a splinter of glass.

It was the second winter I was in New York alone, and graduate school was already beginning to seem like a pointless exercise in pretension and one-upmanship. The loss of Vera seemed very final. My life was deeply hollow. I had been dating a girl named Crystal, but we had broken up and I was on a crash diet. Wrestling had done that to me, given me the bug of bulking up then starving myself to my lowest weight. That winter I survived on a diet of frozen chicken tenders, bowls of broth and hot sauce, and extra-large Diet Cokes. I knew my father was an actor. I thought maybe there was a chance he lived in New York. Most actors did, either there or LA. It was only because I was alone in the apartment too much that I even started thinking about it, decided to look him up. He had a pretty unusual last name, and when I looked in the white pages online, there were only five listings, and one of them was for an R.

Robert. That was my father's name. Robert Cogle. I called and left a message on his machine, amazed by how cool and collected I sounded, how casually I mentioned that I might be his son and that if he ever wanted to have coffee or something I now lived in the city.

He called me back the next day. He invited me to his apartment, which was downtown. He had two bedrooms, and his rent must have cost a fortune. I wondered if my mother had been accurate in saying his career hadn't been successful. The furniture was a hodgepodge of hypermodern and antique pieces he had saved and restored himself. He liked to find things on the street. He explained that the paintings on the walls were his own. He was just a dabbler, though, he said. The paintings were not realistic renderings or anything like that, but bright whimsical things, a red and green watercolor of a rabbit that looked about to melt and dissolve into thin air, a still life of a candelabra and some fruit done in different shades of gray. What struck me most, when he ushered me in, was that I looked nothing like him.

He was tall and narrow and dark-haired with a big booming voice. His eyebrows grew into fiendish, pointed tufts. I was very aware of the physicality of him, aware of our differences, but also eager to see any way in which we might be the same. We kept crossing our legs at the same angle, laughing at the same moment, in a way that was intriguing. Being raised by a single mother had made me a fervent believer in nurture over nature. I had wanted to believe that my father had absolutely no influence over my life, over who I was. But now that I was in the same room with him, I could feel a biological relatedness, a kind of hum of sympathy between our beings that was uncanny.

We made small talk, and I told him about my PhD program, hoping he would be impressed, though he didn't seem particularly interested. "That's good, that's good," he'd said. It did not seem the time to belabor the point that it was such an exclusive program, that I was excellent at what I did. I also did not tell him about Katya or about Vera. I presented myself as a successful scholar, an ordinary sort of guy, worried he would find me questionable or neurotic if I revealed more.

When the subject of why he had never been in my life was inevitably broached, he began to embark on a project of persuading me, trying to paint the picture from his point of view. I was more than willing to hear him out. I wanted to know, to know what reason he could have had. I had wondered all my life, after all. I had always imagined his decision not to be in my life as happening on a darkened stage, just him and me in a spotlight, a man incomprehensibly walking away from a baby who could not have yet committed any sin to make him go.

For one thing, it turned out that my mother had told other people before she told him, and so he heard about her pregnancy secondhand instead of from her. I could see that this would be off-putting. He went on, explaining that they had gone out to dinner to try to talk things through, and she had seemed to think they were on a date, and at one point told him she might be in love with him, which was absurd, he pointed out, because they had only slept together the one time and hadn't even been dating. "She was obsessed with me, I'm afraid," he said. His fingers were long and elegant and I was distracted looking at them as he gestured. He had always suspected she had gotten pregnant on purpose, to trap him. "Do you know what it's like to be with someone who is just—Christ, it was like she was in a romantic comedy and she kept expecting me to kiss her! We couldn't have a real conversation about any of it. She'd devolved into being a teenage girl." He said the word *devolved* as though it disgusted him, as though it denoted a gross metamorphosis like something from Kafka.

I could see that all of this was entirely possible. I could see his point of view, even. He didn't know this woman, and here she was, seemingly overly attached to him. His instinct had been to free himself. He claimed my mother began showing up at his apartment, loitering at the theater near his dressing room. They were members of the same company back then. "I couldn't work with her anymore, and I told the artistic director that, and of course it made her think it was my fault she wasn't getting any roles, and she turned quite spiteful after that. Honestly, she haunted me for years. I would be up for a big audition, and she would call ahead of time and spread nasty rumors about me."

I had a hard time imagining my mother doing this, but I nodded and sipped the coffee he'd given me. He asked if I minded if he smoked. He smoked Nat Shermans. Even now that oxblood-colored box is burned into my memory, as were all the details of his apartment: the dark blue mid-century sofa, the glass kidney-bean-shaped coffee table, the peculiar odor of lacquer or paint drying, a resiny smell overlaid with brewing coffee. It surprised me that he smoked. So few real adults did by then. I lit up with him. "It wasn't about you," he said, "you see? But how could I try to raise a child with some-one like that? We couldn't see eye to eye on anything, and any inch I gave, she took a mile. I couldn't trust her."

There were many things I wanted to say. I wanted to say, "If you couldn't trust her, why would you let her raise your child?" I wanted to say, "But my mother isn't insane. She just factually isn't. So maybe she was hurt because she had a crush on you, and she was scared and pregnant." But I felt intuitively that if we were going to have a relationship, my allegiance to my mother would have to be covert. I was not going to try to argue him into understanding that he had been wrong. And I could also see that my mother's flair for drama, her ten-dency to overplay the intimate moment, could strike a man as strange, could keep him from understanding that underneath she was really very practical, almost brutally so, and also, of course, very tender. Very easy to hurt.

I left that day feeling on edge from all the coffee and ciga-rettes. I remember I wasn't paying attention as I crossed the street from his apartment, and I almost got hit by an ambu-lance. I thought that was remarkable at the time, that I hadn't heard it coming, that I was so inside my head I had been deaf to the sound of sirens. Probably very few people had been run over by ambulances, and I had almost been among them. He lived near the Hudson River, just a few blocks in, and I could hear the seagulls screaming after the ambulance passed. I didn't feel like my father had really seen anything of me. That first day had all been about him, about presenting himself to me. But I thought that would change as we got to know each other. The important thing was that I had met my father. And he painted pictures of bunny rabbits turning into air. And he liked to restore old furniture. Everything about him was just painfully cool. And he was my father.

We spent the next three or four months meeting for coffee or lunch every two weeks or so. He was very charming. A good storyteller. Nice to me. We both loved Shakespeare. "What's your favorite play?" he'd asked.

"*The Tempest*," I said, without hesitation, and he had crowed: "Mine too!"

And I felt so proud, proud that we had the same favorite play by Shakespeare. He showed me a novel he was writing and I was dismayed to discover that it was excellent. By that point, I had given up on ever publishing my writing, but I still did write and I could see immediately that my stories, foolish, awkward things about dating girls and not feeling enough for them, were nothing compared to his half-finished novel, which was set in Shakespeare's time and had a decidedly fabulist bent, told from the point of view of a child who could remember things from the moment he was born. "I don't know if I'll finish it," he'd said, waving my compliments away. His excellent novel was just a lark, a side project.

"No," I said, trying to get him to understand. "But this is brilliant. You *must* keep working on this."

I never knew if he did or didn't. Whether he was pretending not to care to draw compliments out of me, to underplay his achievement the way kids in high school will pretend not to have studied when they ace a test, or whether he really could just toss off such brilliance as if it didn't matter.

Gradually, though, I began to feel as if I were behind a partition of glass and Robert could not hear anything I was saying. He never took an interest in *me*. He rarely asked questions about my life except in the most cursory way. He was always polite about it, but it was clear that I wasn't very interesting to him. He was the interesting one. That was where he was most comfortable: being the raconteur, being the genius, being the star. For Christmas, he gave me a taped recording of himself playing Iago in *Othello*.

He also began to be more and more careless about saying nasty things about my mother. He assumed, because I did not say otherwise, that I was his confidant, that we were bonded together against her. "And I think we both know Rose is a little cuckoo," he would say. Or, "And my hat is off to you for turning out so well, being able to handle her." Most of the time it didn't bother me. I thought of the woman he had known as being entirely separate from my actual mother. He simply didn't know what he was talking about. But I found it annoying, presumptuous. I was beginning to see that he was arrogant. A bit of an ass. Quick to assume the worst in other people.

Once, I accidentally slipped and called him Dad. I was just a young guy, twenty-five, wanting to connect with my father, yet I can still feel ashamed when I think of it, that burning, searing shame associated with early childhood. I remember once playing dogs when I was four and licking the leg of a babysitter, the way she turned on me, suddenly serious, and told me no. There had been a warning in her voice that scared me: I had crossed a line I hadn't even known existed. I felt that way when I accidentally called Robert Dad, that confusion over what I had done that was wrong, that hot fumbling flush, but there I was, a grown man. "Hey now," he had said. "We don't know that for sure. We ought to have a DNA test done."

"Why?" I asked.

"I've never been entirely sure I was the father," he said. I noticed he said "the father" and not "your father."

"But who else would be my father?" I asked.

"Who knows?" he said. I realized he was implying my mother had been sleeping around. Given the fact that I had been conceived during a one-night stand at a party, I could see that it was a reasonable inference that my mother might be sleeping with other men. In fact, she had never told me she wasn't. But I was incensed anyway. Didn't he see himself in me? Wasn't it obvious in the way we crossed our legs, the way we laughed at the same time, the way we both loved *The Tempest*? And if he truly thought that I wasn't his son, then why on earth was he having coffee with me all the time?

"So you really don't think I'm your son," I pressed.

"I have no way of knowing," he said. And then, as though to make sure I understood he was being perfectly reasonable: "I'm not ruling it out by any means. I'm not saying you *aren't* my son."

I just stared at him. I was like Schrödinger's cat then, half alive and half dead. I was nothing but a thought experiment, someone who might be but was also possibly not his son. I wasn't real to him at all.

I didn't exactly cut off our friendship, but things became awkward after that. I felt hurt when he forgot my birthday, but then I realized he might not even know when it was. He stopped calling, I stopped calling. By the time my mother came back the next summer, the whole thing was over. I never told her. I didn't want her to know. The nasty things he'd said about her and the way I had listened, not objecting. The way he had failed to notice me or see me or claim me. The way I had been so bitterly disappointed. I felt foolish and exposed.

After that, I scoured myself for any possible influence from him. In part because I looked so much like my mother on the outside, I suspected myself of being more like my father on the inside, and I was absolutely sure that I was genetically destined to become a blind, arrogant, hurtful asshole. It was part of why I second-guessed everything I did, everything I wanted. The part of me that burned, that thought of Grandma Sylvia in the gas chamber, that quivered when I read Virginia Woolf was the same as the part of him that painted pictures of rabbits dissolving into air, wrote novels about boys who could remember being born, played Iago so cunningly I had become nauseated watching him and had to stop the tape halfway. What a shitty Christmas present.

What an embarrassment, to be that man's son.

Chapter 11

—

Date: 7/17/2014 11:34 PM
From: Vera.Abramov@gmail.com
To: FangBoy76@hotmail.com
Subject: Marginalia

Dear Fang,

I have been contacted by Great-grandmother Sylvia's ghost. At first, I didn't know that's what was happening, but now I feel almost certain. There have been thoughts, insights really, that I know are beyond my own capability, and I think they are her consciousness working through mine, just as we have been discussing.

Tonight she made a glass fall right off the counter in our apartment.

Maybe it is a coincidence, or maybe not. I have no explanation for how mental energy could affect physical matter, and at the same time, I have clear evidence that it does: How is it different for me to think of raising my arm and then do it? Aren't I using my mental energy to create a chemical cascade that results in the movement of physical matter? I have no idea if there are other methods of doing this besides brains and bodies, but I don't think the idea is totally whackadoodle.

Also, almost every single culture has a mythology about ghosts. Where there is smoke, there is fire, no?

Anyway, I have a lot of reading to do to try to make sense of things. Darius loaned me a book of poetry and some guy named Daniel gave me a book about Tesla and also told me the very interesting and very tragic life story of Alan Turing. It's all connected. Especially to what you were discussing regarding the Woolf. I will try to write it out cohesively and then send to you, but in the meantime just do some Wikipediaing of those names: Nikola Tesla, Alan Turing, and oh, Hedy Lamarr. I think she is also connected, and of course Woolf, too. Each of their lives contains an echo of a single truth.

I got an interesting image the other day. I pictured a giant ice wall with people's heads frozen in it. I walked up to it and it was frosty, and I wiped away the frost, and I could see all these heads just frozen in it, their faces contorted, and I kept wondering what it was. Some kind of astral object? A metaphor? What is an ice wall full of heads?

Also, I've been thinking of starting a Tumblr that is just pictures of whales photoshopped to be wearing sunglasses. I was even thinking there could be music videos to go with it. Wouldn't that be funny? If I do go to college, what do you think I should major in? I've been thinking maybe biology!

With love,

From Vilnius,

Your ghostbuster,

V

THE MOMENT I LAID EYES on Herkus's mother, Grandma Sylvia's other daughter, I was sure the SS officer was staring right out at me. She had wide, Teutonic, milky-blue eyes, white hair as thin as floss that she wore with bangs in front, the rest pulled into a bun. Her name was Agata. "Yes," Herkus said, when he was introducing her. "Sylvia named her after her sister, the one who died in Stutthof." I took Agata's soft, pale hand. So now I knew the name, the name of the girl who had not been beautiful enough to live.

Agata was much older than I had thought she would be. I'd been thinking of her as my mother's age, but of course my mother had been born in the 1950s and Agata must have been born in 1943 or '44, which explained why Herkus was older than me. She accepted my handshake, but then held her arms open and kissed me twice on the cheeks. She said something in Polish and Herkus translated, "She says she would give anything to meet your mother."

"She would love to meet you, too," I said, though I wasn't sure if this was true. My mother's sense of her history was like a beloved stage prop, a fan she used to hide coquettishly behind or a shawl that she posed with in lavish repose. I wasn't sure how she would handle having it changed, suddenly having to contend with a sister, which is perhaps why I had avoided telling her about meeting Herkus in the first place. We were standing in the kitchen, which was just one corner of a large room decorated like a lodge with leather couches and wood paneling. The house was made of red-stained wood, a long simple rectangle with a pitched roof that had been done over in some ecological way so that grass was growing on it. I did not know if this was an old tradition or something very modern.

"She says," Herkus translated again, "that she wants to call you son because you are her sister's child. She says she loves you very much."

Agata reached again for my face and kissed me full on the lips, then let her hands rest on my cheeks, just staring at me. She smoothed my eyebrows with her thumbs. She said something again in Polish, and her face was pink, her eyes misty.

"She says you and I are like twins," Herkus said.

"I'm the big twin," I said, and patted my belly.

"Hey, no," Herkus said, "I am older than you. I would have been the big one. It would have been me dunking your head under water and pushing you off couches so you broke your arm."

I laughed, imagining a childhood spent being beaten up by Herkus, here in the Lithuanian forest. Everywhere I looked, there were little blond children running around. A toddler was naked, his penis bobbing as he ran, and there was a girl who must have been about four in a fairy costume, sparkling wire-and-mesh wings strapped to her back. The party was huge, maybe thirty or forty adults and then an infinity of children.

Vera and I were introduced around and given kisses and emotional embraces by everyone, though I was uneasy because

I could not keep track of their names and most of them began speaking to us in Polish or Lithuanian, not knowing or caring that we couldn't understand. Sometimes Herkus translated, sometimes he just smiled and nodded, perhaps forgetting that we didn't know what was being said. The party spilled out of the house and onto the deck and then all over the lawn. Beyond that were pine trees. Pop music was playing out of a gray boom box with hot pink trim that must have been from the '80s, sitting on the railing of the deck. Justine was there, wearing a denim dress that made her seem like a different person entirely. No longer severe, no longer a scholar, she sat in the grass, legs splayed, and let a little boy sprinkle grass on her head.

Vera was having an easier time making conversation than I was because of her Russian, and so I found myself drifting toward the picnic table that was laid out with dish after dish of food. There was dark rye bread, little latkes and blini, a dish of orange caviar, a dish of sour cream, cabbage rolls, strawberries and blueberries and some other berry I couldn't identify. Big platters of sliced tomatoes and onions and some kind of salami. It reminded me of parties I had been to at Katya's parents' house. I had been tentatively invited to these after reentering Vera's life. Vera's sixteenth birthday had been hosted at Inna and Pavel's house, a smorgasbord of food and toasts. Russians loved toasts and even the men would go on, openly crying, making long speeches in Russian that I had to sit through comprehending only the simple verbs: "go," "do," "make." That was all that was left of my high-school Russian: a vague sense of motion in a chaos of unknown nouns. The only thing I could still say in Russian was "I love you." The only thing I knew how to say in Lithuanian was "hello." And in Polish, I could say absolutely nothing. I loaded a plate and went back to wandering, smiling at whoever smiled at me.

Who were these people? My family? This was the kind of family and belonging I had always wanted. What my father had been so arch about, so unwilling to give, these people extended in a heartbeat, without thinking, as though it were all for free. "I call you son," Agata had said. "We are family," Herkus had said. But I still couldn't carry on the simplest conversation with any of them. I was an alien, floating alone in my pod through their happiness.

I had never identified as either Polish or Lithuanian in the same way that Kat had identified as Russian. Even Vera felt herself to be more distinctly un-American than I ever had. If anything, I had felt disappointed at how easy assimilation had turned out to be, how quickly whatever strings of blood or fate connected me and Grandma Sylvia had been cut. Why was I then so bothered by the idea that Herkus might be the grandson of a Nazi, that Agata was staring out at me through loving, murderous eyes? Maybe it didn't matter who our fathers were.

I didn't figure out until it was time for the birthday cake that Vera had gotten it wrong: We weren't celebrating some cousin's birthday. It was Agata's seventieth birthday and everyone had gathered to celebrate her. Suddenly the huge party, the endless children, made sense. This was their matriarch. This was their Grandma Sylvia. Her birthday marked the passage of time in their world.

I did the math rapidly in my head. Grandma Sylvia's rape birthday had been January 18, 1943. If she had gotten pregnant on that day, she should have had the baby sometime in October. I did the math several more times to make sure. There was no way that Agata was the daughter of the SS officer, not if we were celebrating her birthday in July 2014, and not if she was turning seventy years old. Herkus's grandfather had been the forest husband after all.

It had been a ridiculous thing to focus on, this idea of Herkus being the progeny of a Nazi rapist. And if I had been truly anxious about the possibility that Agata was a Nazi's daughter, then finding out the truth should have brought me relief. But it didn't. In fact, I felt more anxious than ever. I stood holding my paper plate in the bright sunshine, smiling vacantly.

Agata sat in a special chair garlanded with ribbons and flowers, and a girl, maybe a grandchild or niece, brought her a special pink sash to wear. Everyone sang a song that bore no relationship to "Happy Birthday" but was clearly the same thing, and I was happy to clap. For my mother's birthdays, I just took her out to brunch. Our family consisted of only us two. Christmases were so lonely, we didn't even bother anymore. Katya did not like Vera celebrating Christian holidays, so even when I reentered Vera's life, our gatherings hadn't really gotten any fuller. I wished my mother could be put on a garlanded chair and sung to by a bunch of happy, drunk people. I wished there were children running around for her to laugh at.

As the afternoon wore on, there was dancing and a lot of drinking and Vera danced with many boys. They were probably technically her second cousins, but no one seemed concerned about it. All in all, it was a success, and I did not even get drunk. Herkus, on the other hand, was a sloshy mess by the time he was loading Vera and me into our cab.

"I love you," he said, and moaned. "Oh, it is terrible that you are leaving so soon. You must come back to Vilnius!" Indeed, the tour was almost over and our flight home was on Monday.

"I'm sure we will come back," I said.

"Are we brothers?" he asked. "You and me are brothers."

"Of course," I said, laughing at his jokey grief.

"Until we die, you big, fat bastard," he said, slapping the hood of the taxi, and giving a final wave. Vera and I were silent in the back of the cab for a time, lost in our separate worlds, jouncing along the forest road. It was late afternoon and the sun was streaming through the trees, filtered by the pine needles. The skin on my face was tight and itchy, and I was pretty sure I had a sunburn.

"Did you have fun?" I asked.

"Yeah, sure," Vera said. "That Herkus guy is a big jerk though."

I looked at her harshly. "Why on earth would you say that?"

"It's just shitty to be married for that long and then to cheat on your wife with a girl half your age and then leave her and start all over like you don't have three kids. I don't know. I know divorce isn't a crime or anything, he just seems kind of immature."

"He had a wife?" I asked.

"Yeah. You didn't see those kids hanging all over him?"

I had seen Herkus giving piggyback rides and faux-wrestling with some kids, but I hadn't known that they were his. Vera's Russian had evidently given her a lot of information and context that I had missed.

"Was the wife there?" I asked, wondering if I had met her without knowing.

"No. And everyone was really sad she wasn't there, but she didn't feel comfortable."

"That *is* shitty," I said. The splitting up of families had become normal, the word *divorce* acceptable and clean, but each time it happened it was like a tiny world exploding. Obviously, I didn't know the half of it. I didn't know Herkus's circumstances, and I had never even been married myself, but three kids seemed like an awful lot to leave. He and I were brothers after all, it seemed. More deeply than I cared for.

"Agata isn't the product of the rape, by the way," I said. "I did the math."

"See," Vera said, smiling. "You don't have to be the grandson of a Nazi to be a total asshole."

When we got home, I didn't want to go to dinner, I didn't want to take a nap, I didn't want to write my mother or Kat or do any of the things I was supposed to do.

I wanted to go see Susan. She had sent me an e-mail that she would be in her room writing all night if I wanted to stop by.

"Listen," I said to Vera, "Susan invited me to go hang out with her."

"That's fine," Vera said.

"Are you sure? I'll give you some money. You can go out to dinner with Judith or something."

"Sure," Vera said. She was writing something on her laptop and she had the book on Tesla that Daniel had given her out on the table. She had become very studious lately. It made me proud of her. Darius had even loaned her a collection of Miłosz poems.

I sat down. "Are you positive?" I asked. "Because I really don't have to go. If you'd rather I stayed."

"You don't have to babysit me, Papa. I'm almost eighteen."

"Right," I said. In my mind I was already out the door.

———

When I got to Susan's, I was disappointed to find that she was sad.

She didn't say she was sad. It was just apparent. She sat on her bed in a green silk bathrobe. Her laptop was glowing, open on her desk, the amber necklace lying in a sine curve beside it. There was a half-eaten box of sugar cookies open, and she gestured toward it in case I wanted any.

"Why are you sad?" I asked.

"I'm not sad," she said. There were little pillows of skin under her eyes. She wasn't wearing any makeup. She hadn't showered. She wasn't smiling. All of these were signs that she was sad. She hadn't hugged me or kissed me when she opened the door.

"You certainly seem sad," I said.

She laughed a little. "I'm just disappointed," she said. "But no big deal. I don't know what I expected even."

My first thought was that she was disappointed in me.

"What did I do?" I asked. "Because you have to tell me these things. I don't always pick up on signals, and I might do something without even knowing."

"Oh, God, Lucas, no!" she said. "It's not you. It's this trip. The genealogist couldn't find anything about my father's brother. That was why I came here. And it just feels—oh, God, so much is lost. It seems impossible, like one of those nightmares where you are searching for something and you don't know what it is, but you feel like you'll die if you don't find it, or the world will end."

I had just come from spending the whole day with my family, my new extended family, and Susan had spent the day in this room, having to give up on finding hers. She had not been kissed and had her eyebrows smoothed. She had not stuffed herself with blini and watched her child dance among cousins. She had been alone with the blinking eye of her computer.

"They couldn't find anything?" I asked. I don't know why I said "they" like it was some impersonal board of distinguished men in robes or suits, when we both knew perfectly well it was Justine we were talking about, Justine with whom I had just spent the afternoon, watching a little boy, who may or may not have been one of Herkus's children, sprinkle grass in her hair.

"No. There's record of my grandfather because he was a pharmacist, but there isn't even any record of my father or his brother. Nothing. The Germans were fairly big into record keeping, but a lot of it was burned or destroyed by the USSR later. I could check the Bad Arolsen archives in Germany, but I'd have to change my flight and spend a few hundred dollars I don't have, and . . ." She trailed off. "I mean, what's the point? We advertised in every city in Europe, we put ads in every major Jewish newspaper and magazine, we've even done the online stuff. If he was alive, we would have found him."

So many people must have been searching after the war. Trying to find the children they'd sent into hiding. Trying to find brothers, mothers, sisters, lovers. So many worlds torn apart. But not Grandma Sylvia. She had known exactly where her brother was. And she had not wanted to return, had never wanted to even send a letter. For all I knew, Agata had been posting such ads for years, and Grandma Sylvia had been stubbornly not scanning the papers in search of them, refusing to even wonder what had become of her other daughter.

I asked Susan how her father had escaped, and she told me. It was her own Grandma Sylvia story, I could tell, a story that had shaped her family, become mythology, changing the way they saw the world.

Her father's name was Josef, and he had been ten years old when the Germans occupied Lithuania. No one had been expecting how rapidly the USSR would cede, and a struggle everyone expected would take weeks or months was over in a matter of days. For a time the Germans were too occupied with fighting the Russians and setting up bases to bother with the Jews. Josef and his brother, Saul, and his mother and father hid out on a farm owned by their aunt in the country, afraid to return to their apartment in the city. The farm was far from Vilnius, nearer to a town called Kaunas, but the techniques employed there were similar to the ones used at Ponary. There was a call for all Jewish men over age fourteen to assemble in the town square of Kaunas. Saul was fourteen, but their father insisted he stay and made him hide under the bed in case any of the Lithuanian police came to check the house. Their father knew he was going to be slaughtered and he told the children so. He left his wallet and wedding ring and papers at home. They never saw him again.

The next week, there was a call for all of the women and children to assemble in the square. Both boys went with their mother and aunt, her children, and their grandmother. They didn't know if they would be killed or imprisoned or just made to register or wear a patch. "My father was still too young to understand how bad it was. Even though their father had told them he was going to die, he didn't quite believe it. But Saul knew and he kept saying he should have gone with his father that day, so they could have died together," Susan said. She reached for one of the sugar cookies in the box.

The boys and their mother and aunt were sent to a work camp in Batakiai where they stayed for two months. There were rumors that the camp would be liquidated, and Josef's mother and aunt and grandmother sat the boys down and told them that they must escape. They were young and strong and had the best chance of surviving if they were unhampered by women and children. Their aunt had her three-year-old and a six-year-old with her in the camp. "Be like rabbits," their mother told them. "Hide in the woods. Get word to the rest of our family and they will take care of you." They had family in Australia, and their mother wrote down the address for them on little pieces of paper that she sewed into their underwear. Josef begged their mother to come with them, but she would not.

The two boys set off at midnight. They zigzagged through the camp, and managed to climb the fence and get safely into the woods. From there they did not know where to go. They spent a crucial three days undecided, starving in the woods. Luckily it was summer, so they were not cold. Eventually, forced by hunger and thirst to explore deeper into the woods, they found a road. They argued over which direction to go, but finally decided to head south. They were picked up almost immediately by the police. Saul, for reasons unfathomable to Josef, refused to talk. "My brother can't talk," Josef told the police officers, the lies simply sprouting from his lips. "He is simpleminded. We were sent out to the market by our father to fetch medicine for my grandmother who is gravely ill."

Josef swore up and down that they were Catholic and was smart enough to give them the Lithuanian versions of their names: Salius and Juozas. But the Lithuanian police pulled down their pants and saw at once that they were circumcised. The boys were arrested and placed in holding cells until they could be transported back to the camp. The police station was a commandeered farmhouse and the "cells" they were placed in were closets, a linen closet for Saul and what must have once been a pantry for little Josef.

That was what it would all hinge on: the lack of windows in a linen closet. In Josef's pantry there was one tiny window up high. It did not open, but he discovered he could climb up to it by bracing himself against the walls, and the casement, when he knocked on it with his knuckles, was loose. Late at night, he took some dusty old cans of fish and carefully tap-tapped the casement of the window entirely loose. He climbed down with it, but fell the last few feet. He waited, unable to breathe to see if anyone had heard. He had fallen on his ankle in a bad way, but it was only sprained, not broken. "He always said if he had been just one day older, he would not have been able to fit through that window," Susan said.

Hungry and scared and crying because he was leaving his brother and he suspected the rest of his family was already dead, Josef headed into the forest to try to be a rabbit as his mother told him. He almost starved to death there, and he once got very sick from eating the wrong kind of berries. He found a farm and he observed the woman working in her garden every day. He stayed in the woods, afraid, watching the family for more than a week. There was one man and one woman. They were both in their fifties. At night, he would sneak to get water from their well and steal carrots and fruit from their garden. They went to church on Sunday, and over the period of about eight days, he convinced himself they were good people. One morning he approached the woman in her garden. He must have looked like a ghost, appearing among her black currant bushes, half starved and dirty-faced. "Please," was the first word he said to her. Then, "My family is dead."

She took him in. It turned out that her husband was a member of the Lithuanian police force working for the Germans, but he too agreed to hide the boy. They hid him in the attic whenever anyone came over and the woman taught him how to knit. That was how he spent the war, knitting in the attic. He became an excellent knitter and could make even complicated cable-knits and fine sweaters, impossibly tiny socks, anything. "I still have sweaters my father knitted me," Susan said.

"So you've been looking for Saul," I said.

She nodded. She brushed powdered sugar from the cookie off her chin. "My father spent the rest of his life feeling so terrible about not saving Saul. He would tell me how wonderful Saul was. How smart. How brave. I thought if I could find him, or even just find out what happened to him . . . I don't know what."

"Is your father still alive?" I asked.

She shook her head. "Stroke," she said. "Last January." So she had come here to mourn her father as well as to search for Saul. I reached out and grasped her calf. The skin was cool and smooth under my hand. I squeezed the muscle.

"This searching, this constant searching, it's like a disease of the mind," she said. "Trying to piece things together, but none of it can be put back together. But you can't stop searching. It's a compulsion."

I kissed her foot. She looked at me. I kissed her toes, one by one, light little kisses. She smiled. She arched her foot, and I kissed her heel. I kissed her ankle and then her shin bone. She laid back on the bed and spread her legs, and I kept on kissing upward.

She was the descendant of a sly rabbit of a boy, and I was the descendant of a wild, murdering girl. What did it mean about

Iphone

us, on this rented mattress, in this rented room, in this world that would be ours for such a short time?

"Please," she said, "just keep me from being me for a little while. Just make me stop thinking. Just make me—" She broke off.

I didn't want to be me, either. I didn't want to think about Agata or Grandma Sylvia or Katya or Vera. I didn't want to think about my father, his arched eyebrows, his Iago, his rabbits dissolving into air. I didn't want to think about Chloe, who still burned in my memory, crying on the bed, saying, "I just miss my mom. That's all. I just miss my mom."

I wanted only Susan's thighs, Susan's globed breasts like dangling fruit, Susan's amber hair in wet curls, Susan's salt, Susan's cries, Susan's lip pulled back over her teeth. I wanted sour-plum skin and ripped fruit. I wanted to be nothing but a body moving over Susan's body, nothing but our cells, dying and dividing, the chemicals of pleasure rolling loose into our bloodstreams.

Chapter 12

———

Date: 7/18/2014 5:34 PM
From: Vera.Abramov@gmail.com
To: FangBoy76@hotmail.com
Subject: Re: re: Are you ignoring me?

Dear Fang,
    Please do not give up on me. Please. I'm sorry. I take back everything. I am the same as I always was. I am yours. Please. I need you so badly.
    With love,
    From Vilnius,
    Eternally,
    V

WHEN I GOT BACK to the apartment it was dark, and the waitresses in the restaurant downstairs had turned off the light in the stairwell and I couldn't find the switch, so I ascended in such pitchy black that I couldn't even tell if my eyes were open and kept blinking to make sure. I pushed open our door, which was unlocked, and bumped into a wire drying rack covered in wet men's clothes. I recognized the drying rack, but not the clothes. Why were another man's clothes drying in our apartment?

"Vera?" I called. There was a light on in the kitchen.

"Papa, go away and come back later," Vera yelled.

"Please come in here, sir," said a male voice.

I tried for a second to just edge the rack by pushing with the door, hoping it wouldn't tip, but then I heard the man's voice again, "Please, Lucas!," and realized it was Daniel. I opened the door hard, knocked over the rack of wet clothes, and tripped over it on my way to the kitchen.

I saw Daniel sitting in a pair of running shorts, shirtless at the kitchen table. I saw Vera in a nightgown holding a large butcher knife. She pointed it at me as I entered the room, the tip following me like the barrel of a gun.

"What's going on?" I asked.

"You, sit," she said, gesturing with the knife at the other chair at the table. I hesitated.

"Sit!" Vera screamed, and slashed at the air with her knife.

I sat. "What's going on?" I asked Daniel. He didn't say anything, just gave me a long look that I couldn't entirely interpret. It was a look of pleading, but not entirely a look of panic.

"I know about the conspiracy," Vera said. "I know about the Great Synagogue and I know what's underneath. I know you want to help me, Daniel. Or why would you have given me that book?"

Daniel sighed. "I gave you that book because I thought you would think Tesla was interesting."

Vera laughed, a big, rich stage laugh. "Oh, get real," she said. It was becoming clear that I was walking in on an interrogation. "You don't want to fuck me, you don't want to date me, you just thought I would think Tesla was interesting?"

Daniel nodded. "That's why I gave you the book."

"Vera, can you back up and tell me what's going on?" I said.

"Be quiet," she told me, flicking the knife in my direction. "The thing about you, Daniel," she went on, "is that you have no idea how obvious you are about what you are hiding. You think you are wearing normal clothes, but you are not. You think you are behaving as all people behave, but you are not. You do not belong to any system of power that I am aware of. You are operating mysteriously outside of the regime. It is obvious just looking at you."

Daniel sighed. "Yeah, you keep saying that."

I had never before been so aware of how physically small Vera was. She was tiny, but she was practically vibrating with energy, and being in the room with her felt more like witnessing a horrible storm or a flood than talking to a person.

"We are alike in that way. Cut loose of our places in the social hierarchy. I was deemed medically unfit. They were going to chemically alter me. But I think you already knew that."

The words were pouring out of her now, not in response to either Daniel or me but almost as though she couldn't control the ideas that were multiplying in her brain, forcing their way out of her mouth as sentence after sentence. "Darius was lying when he said that the Soviets used the lot of the Great Synagogue to build a kindergarten. Think about it. Why would the Soviets take a place of such immense spiritual power and just destroy it? Think about how much rock or gravel or earth it would take to fill in that hole. The Great Synagogue was five stories tall, but dug into the ground. They would have had to haul in truck after truck after truck of soil just to fill it in. There's something underneath, there's a secret building underneath that kindergarten, and Daniel knows what it is."

I looked at Daniel. He shook his head at me. He had no idea what she was talking about. "I don't think Daniel knows anything about it, Vera," I said. "And can you put the knife down? It's really freaking me out."

"Papa, don't make me slit your throat." She walked toward me with the knife. I don't think I had understood she was insane until that moment. In a way, I knew the second I walked in on her holding the knife that she was having an episode, but I hadn't known until she walked toward me with the knife that she was unreachable. As unreachable as a bird or a fish, her pupils so dilated that her eyes were all dark mirror, her hands not so much shaking as vibrating.

"I don't want to kill you, Papa," she said. "I was just starting to actually like you."

"Put down the knife, Vera," I said. "You're not going to kill anybody."

She sighed, whirled away from me and back to the counter,

her arm extended so that the knife cut through the air. There was something childlike about the gesture. "Death isn't permanent," she said. "There is no self, Papa. I don't know how many times I have to try to explain that to you. You are so dense, you know that? I try to feed you just tiny morsels of new ideas and you spit them out like a toddler. It's exhausting. But I won't give up on you, I promise."

"I'm so sorry," I said to Daniel. "She's been through a lot and—"

Vera turned on me. "Don't talk about me like I'm not here! God! What disrespect! Am I not a person? Have I not ears?"

"I'm sorry," I said. I could hear the washing machine chugging in the bathroom with another load of clothes. It clicked over into the spin cycle and the kitchen was filled with the high-pitched whine.

"What I'm trying to explain, Papa, what I've been trying to tell you ever since we got here, is that there is no such thing as reality. Everything is a metaphor. All of this is just shadows on the cave wall. What is real is something else, something that we can't see. Don't you get that? If I kill Daniel, or look, even if I were to cut my arm—" She gestured with the knife and I winced, but the knife didn't cut. The blade just rested there, kissing her skin. I could see the bulge of flesh above where it pressed, and I thanked God the knife was dull. All of the knives in this stupid apartment were dull. "It's just like a line in a poem: It reflects something real, but the words are not the same as the actual objects. I am part of God and you are part of God, and even Daniel is a part of God. That is what is real. These are just bodies, like puppets. Even the dragon is a part of God!"

"The dragon?" I asked.

"She keeps talking about a dragon," Daniel said softly. "I haven't been able to figure out what she means."

"Dragon is the name of the project," Vera said. "The Great Synagogue project. But Daniel already knows that."

"That's the problem," Daniel said, clearly exasperated. "I *don't* know that."

"So what are you doing here?" Vera asked, gesturing around us at the kitchen with the knife. "Why did you come over here?"

"You said I could use your washing machine," Daniel said.

"No, I mean in Vilnius."

"I don't know!" Daniel yelled, clearly on the verge of losing it. "What do you want to hear? We've been over this a dozen times already. I came here because I think Vilnius is interesting! I like history! I came here because my girlfriend just broke up with me because I'm a loser. I don't know, Vera! What do you want to hear?"

Vera growled with exasperation. The black eyes were unnerving. It seemed impossible that she could see out of them. "You are making me do this by lying to me! Don't you get that? Please stop, please stop lying to me!"

The spin cycle paused, then started again. No one spoke. She had said it herself: We were making her do this. It occurred to me that she didn't want to be holding that knife. That she was scared and out of control, and if I could simply take the knife out of her hand, she would let me. She was just a girl and we were two grown men, pretending to be hostages. I could walk up to her and take the knife out of her hand. I outweighed her by a hundred pounds or more. The worst that would happen is I might get cut badly enough to need stitches. I stood up.

"What are you doing?" Vera asked.

I didn't want to telegraph what I was doing in case she decided to fight me. "You're tired," I said.

"I am," she said, nodding.

I walked over to her, and I wrapped my hand around hers, the one that was holding the knife. "You don't need this," I said. She relaxed her hold. With my other hand, I removed the knife and dropped it in the sink. It made a loud clatter as it fell, but she didn't react, almost as though she hadn't heard it.

"You're right," she said. "The knife was silly. Daniel will either tell me the truth or he won't." She was about to continue her interrogation, unaware that the spell had been broken, that the knife had been her only power.

"I'm calling the cops," Daniel said. He was already over by the phone on the shelves.

"Please don't," I said. I had no idea what the ramifications would be, what they would do to Vera. Obviously I had made a grave error about her medication, but I could fix it. We just needed to get her home to her doctors. "She needs her meds—they're in the bathroom. Just get them," I said.

"You have her meds and you didn't give them to her?" he asked, stunned, his hand still on the phone. "You knew she was sick?"

I didn't know what to say. I just looked at him.

"You're as fucking crazy as she is," Daniel said, and he picked up the phone and dialed.

Vera had turned in toward my body and stayed huddled against the front of me. I wrapped my arms around her. She was jittery like she had drunk too much coffee or done too much coke.

"I'm sorry," I whispered to her.

"I'm so tired," she said. "I'm so tired and I can't sleep. I haven't been able to sleep for days."

On the phone, Daniel spoke in an orderly way. He had to wait until they found an operator with fluent English. I would not have been so coherent if I had been the one making the call. Now that I was holding Vera in my arms, all my muscles were shaking, exhausted, as though I had been lifting weights for hours. "Not sure if we need police or an ambulance. There is a girl here suffering from a psychotic break. She's been threatening people with a knife." He paused. He looked up at me. "No, she is currently unarmed. No, no, I don't think anyone wants to press charges, we just need to transport her to a mental hospital or a psych ward or something. She's sick. She needs to be seen by a doctor."

"Papa," Vera whispered into my neck, "don't let them take me away. Don't let them."

"I'm going to stay with you the whole time," I said. "I won't let them do anything bad to you."

"Do you believe me? About the dragon? I know you do—I've known this whole time that you knew. That's why you brought me here. That's what this whole thing has been about."

I didn't know what to say. I just held her. I couldn't look at Daniel. He could have easily pressed charges. He could have made things a living hell for us. What he had done was the right thing, no more and no less. And I had told him not to call. I stared at the little red ceramic statue of a toadstool on the shelf beside his head. I was burning with shame.

He hung up the phone. "Someone will be here in ten or fifteen minutes."

I nodded. "Vera," I said, "do you want to put on different clothes?"

She looked up at me. "Yeah, I don't want to go in a nightgown. I'll put on jeans or something." She slowly untangled herself from my arms and floated off toward her room. "I think this is actually a good thing," she said.

"You do?" I asked.

"I'm excited to talk to them. I think they will understand what I'm saying. There is just too much I have to catch you guys up on and as hard as I try to explain, you don't get it! It's so exhausting!"

Daniel and I stared at her. She smiled as though she were filled with great peace and took a deep breath. "I'm going to get changed," she said, and went into her room.

For a moment, we just stood in the silence.

"Thank you," I said to Daniel. He shook his head, shrugged.

"I want you to know," he said, "I never thought she was actually going to stab me. I didn't really think that."

I nodded, sucked my lower lip into my mouth and ground it with my teeth. "Let's get your clothes packed up," I said. Together we picked up his wet clothes from the knocked-over drying rack in the hall and stuffed them into his laundry bag. We went to see if the washing machine was done with the second load. There were a few minutes left in the cycle, it seemed. "I'll wait," he said. "I might have to give a statement or something anyway."

I nodded. We were both standing in the tiny, brightly lit bathroom, staring at the washing machine.

"Do you want to check on her or something?" he asked. It was like being startled awake. I rushed to her door, already panicked.

She wasn't in her room. Her window was gaping open, letting in the velvet night sky. I stuck my head outside, screamed her name. I looked down into the courtyard, but I couldn't see anything, any sign of her. Then I heard whimpering, and I turned my head to find she was right there next to me, hugging the sloped roof on her belly, terrified.

"I don't know how to get down," she whispered. "I'm really scared."

Her feet were braced on the roof gutters. She was barefoot and still in her nightgown. The way our rooms were deformed by the gables of the building was extreme, and the window I was standing in was at a steep angle and was almost like a skylight. With my hips pressed against the window frame, I was already halfway out on the roof. I turned in the opening of the window, tried to keep my legs and hips facing forward as I arced my torso over toward her. I knew that if I sat on the window frame, even though it would get me closer to her, it would also make it possible for me to fall backward out of the window. There was a little radiator under the window and I stuck my feet under it, flexing them to try to create some kind of lock, as I reached my arm out toward her beside me on the roof.

I could just barely wrap an arm around the back of her waist. "You've got to edge back this way," I said.

I heard Daniel behind me, saying "Holy fuck" over and over in a harsh whisper.

"I feel like I'm gonna break the gutter if I move," she said. "I can't move. I can't move."

"I've got you," I said. I had my right arm around her waist, but if she fell there was no way I could hold her weight. The angle was too extreme. She edged toward me with baby steps. The gutter made a loud sound and she screamed, stopped moving.

I heard pounding at the door of our apartment. "For God's sake," I shouted at Daniel, "let them in!" But he was already doing it. The apartment filled with low voices asking questions in Lithuanian.

"Just a couple more steps, baby," I said. She was looking only into my eyes. I tried to smile. "You can do this," I said. "I've got you. I've got you."

She was close enough now that I had my hand linked all the way under her other arm, tight around her back, and I pulled her to me, trying to get her to budge a little bit, come a little bit closer. Instead, she gave a hiccuping little leap sideways, and I got my arms around her, but there was a teetering moment where I thought she might pull us both out of the window. My feet were still wedged under the radiator, flexed, but my legs were shaking from trying to keep us both from falling. She was entirely in my arms now, and I could feel the weight of her, the pull of gravity, the light breeze outside ruffling her nightgown. For a moment, we both remained perfectly still, just breathing, and then I was able to shift one of my legs, and I found my balance again, knew I could hold her. Slowly I pulled her inside, hugging the top of her body as the window ledge scraped the front of her thighs, then her knees and shins, until she was inside.

A circle of paramedics and two police watched us. *"Labas,"* I said, which was the only word in Lithuanian that I knew. I imagined this was some kind of weird Greek tragedy and these men were the chorus. I was embarrassed for us. Embarrassed of Vera's nightgown and madness and my own awkward delivery of her into the room. No one should see such things. It was like they had caught us shitting together.

I held up one finger in what I hoped was a universal gesture that meant "wait." I grabbed a pair of her jeans from the floor and held them open for her. She stepped into them, one leg at a time, as though she were a child. I had never dressed her before. I had missed all of that stuff. The diaper changes, the putting on of pajamas, the bath times, the cuddling. I had never been a father to her in that way, and it struck me now, as I pulled the jeans up over her legs, which were goosefleshed and shaking, that I had missed everything. I had missed the whole thing and never known it. I handed her a sweatshirt even though it was hot.

"Can you help me?" she asked, her voice barely above a whisper. I knew the police and paramedics in their professionalism, their sudden official-ness, scared her. They were just watching me dress her. She was too flustered to be able to figure out how the sweatshirt worked. I held it open and pulled it over her head, holding open the neck hole so she could find it, pulling it down when it got stuck on her ears. She was able to find the armholes herself, but I fussed with the cuffs anyway, making sure her hands got free. There she stood, in jeans and a nightgown and a giant sweatshirt surrounded by police and paramedics in that dark, slant-roofed room, her eyes black, black as the eyes of a deer.

I didn't know what would be next. We would go with these men to where they took us. Eventually we would find someone who spoke English. There was nothing to do but what they told us to do. I took her hand and nodded at them that we were ready to go.

The emergency room they took us to was adjoined to a mental hospital, a combo I had never heard of before, and as emergency rooms go it was pretty tiny, more like a triage unit. There was no hustle and bustle, no other patients, just a waiting nurse, who looked as plump and peaceful as a chicken sitting at her desk when we came in. She wrote out the forms with a pen that had a big orange plastic flower on the end, as the paramedics filled her in on the situation in a stream of Lithuanian that flowed over both Vera and me. I signed everything she gave to me, even though I couldn't read any of the forms.

Then she led Vera and me into a little cubicle behind a curtain with a hospital bed where Vera perched. She had to get one of her arms free of the sweatshirt so they could take her blood pressure, but she didn't want to take the sweatshirt off, so she just snaked her arm up through the neck hole. Everything was absurd. I noticed Vera had mascara under her eyes, and I wondered when she had been crying. Had she been crying when she held Daniel at knife point? Had I failed to register that? Or had she been crying before that? Or only later in the ambulance? I couldn't remember her crying in the ambulance. The nurse told us something in Lithuanian, and we just stared at her. She tried Russian, and Vera nodded, sniffling like her nose was getting clogged up, snaking her arm back in her sweatshirt. The nurse left.

"The doctor will be in here in a minute," Vera said, sniffling again and sighing. I noticed that she wasn't trying to explain her vision to the nurse. That plan seemed to have faded or receded in her mind.

I nodded.

"I hope they give me a lot of drugs," Vera whispered.

"Why?" I asked.

"Because I'm scared."

A lot of things were only now occurring to me. That at some point, I would be asked to leave and she would be alone here. That she would be with other mental patients who didn't speak English. That I would be essentially abandoning her in this strange place. The building was large and clearly very old. I wondered who had built it. If only Darius were here to explain things to us. It felt like the kind of building that would have ghosts, if there were such things as ghosts. I had been more in the mind-set of a trip to a hospital where, since she was a minor, and I was her father, I would be allowed to follow her, to spend the night at her bedside. But mental illness wasn't treated like physical illness for reasons that seemed newly unfathomable to me. I squeezed her knee because her hands were unreachable, tucked up inside the sleeves of her sweatshirt. I had lost Vera so many times. I had lost her when she was a baby, I had lost her when she was four, I had said goodbye to her at the end of every weekend we spent together, sending her back to her real life, to her mother and school and friends, and none of it had felt like this. I was panicked to let go of her.

"Don't cry," she said. "Seriously, don't."

"I can't leave you here," I said.

"Well, you're going to have to."

The doctor, when he came a few minutes later, spoke English and so I was able to relieve Vera of the burden of talking, and I explained her past mental history, the current episode, at least what I had seen of it. Luckily, the police had suggested I bring Vera's medication with us when we were still at the apartment, so I was able to give the ER doctor the prescription bottles that included Vera's doctor's name and phone number. Vera sat through all this patiently, her eyes far away. The questions were unending, and then suddenly they weren't.

"Probably because of the use of the knife," the doctor said, "she will be asked to stay for at least forty-eight hours, but this will be decided by the administrators tomorrow. Because she is a danger to herself and others, it is a policy. But they will decide tomorrow."

Vera and I both nodded. I looked at her to see if this was okay, and she shrugged. It was what I had been expecting, since pretty much the exact same thing had happened when she was hospitalized in the States, and I guess she had been expecting it, too.

"We don't have insurance here," I said, "so how will we pay?"

"I don't know the exact details of that," the doctor said, "but some of the nurses can help you when you come and visit her tomorrow and the administrators have had a chance to review her file."

It all seemed very humane. In America, the first thing you did at an emergency room was figure out how you would pay or give them an insurance card. The idea that such matters could be left until tomorrow was an unexpected, almost lavish kindness.

"Visiting hours are ten to noon," the doctor said. "You can wear your clothes in the ward, but if you want we have some pajamas you can wear for tonight. If you don't wish to sleep in your clothes."

Vera nodded. She was still wearing her nightgown over her jeans and under her sweatshirt, but it was thin and had lace in the front. I could understand why she wouldn't want to wear it.

"I will have the nurse bring you some," the doctor said.

"Can I go and see her room?" I asked. "Can I at least see where she'll be?"

"I'm afraid no one is allowed in the ward except during visiting hours," he said, and gave me a polite smile. He was tall and balding. "Because it is the junior ward, the adolescents— the rules are more strict. But a clean transition is better. We will take very good care of her." He stood there, nodding and smiling.

"Fine," Vera whispered.

But I didn't feel like it was fine. I felt like I was abandoning her here.

"The nurse will be right in with some pajamas and can show Vera to her room, but I'll give you two a chance to say goodbye."

Once he was gone, I hugged Vera where she sat. She didn't wrap her arms around me back, just let herself be hugged, her arms at her sides. They had given her a strong sedative and I could tell it was kicking in. Her face looked thick and frozen. "I'm so sorry," I said.

"It's okay," she said. "I'm pretending it isn't happening."

We swayed back and forth, me standing, her sitting on the creaking hospital bed, not talking.

"I love you," I said. I had said that to her before. I had said it a million times. I said it as she was getting out of my car at her mother's, as we said goodbye on the phone. I had said it a million times, but this time it seemed to be shredding my vocal cords.

She didn't say anything back. When the nurse came, she was holding a pair of gray pajamas that had been washed so many times they were almost white. Vera climbed off the bed and accepted the small bundle, and together the three of us left the little curtained room. The nurse said something in Russian and gestured me back the way I had come, as she steered Vera down the hall in the opposite direction. I just stood there, watching as the woman guided Vera by the shoulder. Before they rounded the corner, Vera turned back to me and mouthed, "Dragon. Go find the dragon."

Chapter 13

———

"Revelations"

Word doc
Created by User on 7/18

It is unclear to me yet whether Dragon is merely the name of the project, or if it is a metaphor (for that which is on fire, that which is molten and chaotic, yet housed within a scaly exterior, just as murder/genocide/etc. is, i.e., an irrational principle cloaked in the disguise of reasonable behavior), or if there is an actual literal dragon. Not sure about the line between literal and metaphorical in general. Could be a trick, way the government is duping us, possibly convincing all populace that reality has only one layer, whereas clearly it is multilayered as evidenced by metaphysical activities like falling in love, etc. And about dragons, I am unclear what kind of creature is indicated. The Hebrew word for dragon is *tannin,* which is also the word for serpent, but I need to look up which word is used in Genesis, because if Eve was tempted by the dragon, then that would be a very interesting thing to know.

Pits are another interesting feature. The huge, unfillable pit left by the Great Synagogue. The pit full of bodies in Ponary. If there is a hole, something will rush in to take its place. A vacuum. This is how Tesla comes into things, maybe. But curious as to the relationship between pit in the ground and pit in a fruit. Connection? Coincidence? Even if they are not etymologically related, aren't they still phonically linked? Possibly there is no such thing as coincidence?

And I saw a beast rising out of the sea, with ten horns and seven heads, with ten diadems on its horns and blasphemous names on its heads. And the beast that I saw was like a leopard; its feet were like a bear's, and its mouth was like a lion's mouth. And to it the dragon gave his power and his throne and great authority. One of its heads seemed to have a mortal wound, but its mortal wound was healed, and the whole earth marveled as they followed the beast. And they worshipped the dragon, for he had given his authority to the beast, and they worshipped the beast, saying, "Who is like the beast and who can fight against it?" And the beast was given a mouth uttering haughty and blasphemous words and it was allowed to exercise authority for forty-two months.—Revelation 18:1–18

Hitler ==> Modern Germany ==> European Union ==> Internet ==> Tesla ==> Daniel

"Ways to Keep Papa from Noticing"

Word doc
Created by User on 7/15

1. Remain calm and collected at all times
2. Do not let him notice the way strangers have begun to respond to you

3. Feed his ego by letting him feel close to you
4.
5.
6.
7.

I READ THROUGH these documents and more on Vera's laptop as I sat on her bed, in her little slant-roofed room that was so similar to my own but which felt entirely different. It had taken me only three tries to guess the password to her computer log-in, and then her laptop was completely open to me. The password was "FangBoy76," which was easy to guess because it was also her Pandora password that she had given me so she could play music on my stereo at home.

Her room had a little chair by the door and her dresser was wider and lower than mine was. These two tiny differences seemed enormous, maybe because I kept assuming I was in my own room as I read and then getting startled that I was not. I read her e-mail first, skipping around in time, then finally deciding to go all the way back to the beginning of our trip and read linearly forward. Then, once I had a better idea of the narrative, I started to go through her Word documents, of which there were literally hundreds. Some of them went on for pages, some were only a few lines. Lots were from before our trip, but a shocking number of them were from just the last few days. Yesterday she had created twenty-three new Word documents.

It was like watching an instant replay of a bad fall. There

was an almost physical revulsion to reading bad logic, like looking at pictures of people badly wounded or deformed, and I realized, reading, that I had always been afraid my own thinking was like this. Writing anything was to stare this kind of madness in the face. All you could do was move through the links between one idea and the next, testing each one out, hoping they held. You were all alone with the words and the page, going further and further away from anything social, civil, conventional, or agreed-upon. At times, I came away from reading my thesis thinking it was like this. I would close the document, horrified, revolted. And that had been a well-formatted academic paper.

Her ideas were something like this:

The persecution of the Jews was not a historical accident. (How could it be? How weird was it to hate Jews? Why hate, they were like everyone else?) Instead, the Jews, in their worship of God, had created a positive polarity, which, by virtue of some physical law (enter Tesla), had engendered the dragon as a corresponding negative polarity. There were incomprehensible math equations trying to explain all this. Nazi Germany had harnessed the power of the dragon, but after Hitler's fall, those dark powers had only been shattered, not slain. The ghosts of those slain in Ponary had tried to bind the dragon to their bodies and sink him in the pits, but had failed precisely because the Soviets had destroyed the Great Synagogue. Again there were references to Tesla, trying to argue that spiritual energy operated by similar principles to electric energy and that Tesla's work had been repressed because it was too dangerous. She suggested that the Soviets had found a baby dragon somewhere in the region (there was some supposition in the text that the dragon had actually been Grandma Sylvia's lost child, and that Agata was a fake planted later by the EU) and had built a secret laboratory in the ruins of the Great Synagogue where they could keep the dragon and study it. For some reason I could not understand, she had decided that in the global power vacuum created by the crumbling of the USSR, the EU had become a kind of dream team of power-hungry scientists and Freemasons, who were also secretly trying to suppress Tesla. They had taken over the care of the dragon, but eventually the dragon would grow too powerful for them to contain.

The poor girl didn't know a thing about alternating or direct currents and she kept trying to guess what the "War of the Currents" was about. Clearly she had been reading the book Daniel had given her, but her brain had been too exhausted from the mania to take much in. In the end, she decided that Daniel was acting as some kind of agent for the EU (because of the pirate shirts, or at least the pirate shirts figured prominently on a list of reasons Daniel might not be a "real" person) and that he had been planted in the history tour to discover how much she, Vera, "knew" so that the government could decide whether or not to kill her.

"I wouldn't mind if they killed me," she wrote, "but it would make Fang so sad. For his sake, I must somehow untangle all of this." It was a herculean task she had set for herself, impossible if it were real, but even sadder and more impossible because it was not. In addition to this, there was a lot of speculation about whether or not human beings were animals or if there was such a thing as a higher self, a soul. The more manic she got, the more able she was to believe in the soul, in God, in beauty. This struck me as profoundly tragic. I did not want madness to be her only way in to believing in those things. I did not want her choices to be between No Meaning, a desert landscape presided over by bland Dr. Carmichael and his vials of pills, and Too Much Meaning, a lightning storm of connections that amplified and built upon one another until everything was connected to everything else and the government was hiding a dragon in a kindergarten.

I had been so busy. I had been so busy with Susan and with history and even with Judith and the stupid cat, with blini and beers and glasses of wine and shots of vodka, with thinking I was such a great father and I was going to vanquish the absurd foe Dr. Carmichael, that I had failed to notice any of this.

Then again, what kind of father snoops in his daughter's laptop? What kind of asshole would I have been if that was how I treated our new intimacy? Hacking her password that was her boyfriend's name and jersey number?

I had let her drink. I had let her go off her medication. I had let her go out unsupervised with Judith. She and Judith had smoked pot! I had almost forgotten about that. Why hadn't I asked her how she was doing? But maybe I had. We had been spending every day together. We had been talking. She had seemed fine. Maybe it was because she had always been so insightful that it had been possible to overlook her madness. Vera had always been able to see through people. Like at that birthday party when she was just a child: "If you wanted a birthday party so badly, maybe you should have thrown one for yourself." I was so confident in her assessments of reality, in her ability to penetrate and see the truth, that it took a delusion as ridiculous as a conspiracy involving a dragon to make me actually believe, really and truly believe, that she was sick.

It was a bitter, burned-tasting irony that clear-sightedness and insight, her greatest gifts, were the very things that had been taken from her.

I set down the laptop next to me on her bed and rubbed my eyes. I had not slept at all. I had come straight from the mental hospital and begun reading at around one in the morning. Go find the dragon, she had said. And I had.

Now it was bright out and about 4 a.m. So it would be 6 p.m. in California. Dinnertime.

I turned on my cell phone and dialed Katya.

She was less interested in recriminations than I expected. I choked out my story, and mainly she wanted to go over the details again and again, what had happened, what had Vera said, what had Daniel said, what had I said, what had the police said, what had the doctor said. It was hard to keep it all straight, I was so hollow-hearted and dizzy by that point, and she grew frustrated with me.

"I'm so sorry, Katya," I said. "I'm so sorry I let all of this happen. You have no idea how guilty I feel."

Katya tsked, loud, annoyed. "I don't care about you, Lucas. I don't care right now what you should have done, what you could have seen or noticed or done different. None of it matters. What I care about is Vera. The fact that I'm not there is—" She broke off. "I need you as absolutely together as you can be. I need you to sleep. I need you to be her father. I need you to have lists of questions for her doctors. I need you to write down what they say so that you can tell me exactly. I need you to make it so that it is like I am there, as much as possible. At least until I can fly out."

"Oh, don't fly out," I said. "They're only holding her for forty-eight hours. By the time you even got here, she'd be released and we'd be heading home."

Katya was silent. "I just want to get on a plane," she said. "That feels like the only thing to do."

"I know," I said, "I know. But it doesn't make sense. Just wait and we will come to you. I will get her home. I can promise you that much." I was sitting on the foot of Vera's bed with my eyes closed. It would still be hours and hours before I could visit Vera in the mental hospital.

Katya was silent, then sighed. "This dragon business is, well, it's baffling, don't you think?"

"It is the hardest part," I said.

"So Christian," she said, though that wasn't what had occurred to me as difficult about it. I hadn't noticed that dragons were a particularly Christian element, though once Katya pointed it out, I could see it.

"You would be happier if she were having a more Jewish delusion?"

"No," she said, "I would just be able to understand it better."

"Well," I said, "*Puff the Magic Dragon,* Dungeons and Dragons, fuck, *Game of Thrones,* dragons are just part of the larger cultural collective at this point, I think."

Katya groaned as though this bothered her. She did not want to share a cultural imagination with anyone else. She did not want her daughter to be sharing a mind with unrefined American cinema, with TV shows and comic books, a soup of high and low, holy and unholy. But that was how it was. That was the world now.

"Is she scared?" Kat asked. I wondered if she had her eyes closed too. Her voice seemed so near, it was almost like it was inside my own head.

"I think she's terrified, but she was handling it really well. At least last night. Maybe it was the sedative, but she was incredibly brave."

"I know it doesn't make sense for me to come," she said. "But it's so hard to accept that. It's so hard to stay here."

"You must hate me," I said.

"I never hate you," she said. She must have her eyes closed, I thought. I pictured her in her house, in her kitchen with garlic hung above the sink, the dishrag printed with little pigs. I pictured her dark hair, now cut short. Her face that had grown pointier and more feral and even more beautiful as she had gotten older. I closed my own eyes tighter.

"You hated me when we left the farm," I said.

"No, not hate." She sighed. "I was disappointed. But you did what you were going to do, you know? You were a Lucas being a Lucas. You didn't like that place. I was foolish to think you would, but I was a young girl and I didn't understand people then. I didn't understand things seemed so different to different people. I thought you and I were the same person. But it turned out better, don't you think, Lucas? You were right. We couldn't have stayed there."

"Do you ever think about Chloe?" I asked.

"Chloe? Who is Chloe?"

"The girl on the farm."

"Oh," Katya said, "I had forgotten her. You still think about that girl?"

"All the time," I said. A breeze was drifting into Vera's room through the open window that I had failed to close after pulling her back into the room. I had not told Kat that Vera had tried to escape by climbing out onto the roof. I had not told Kat about the moment I had Vera in my arms, but knew I wouldn't be able to keep her from falling if she slipped. "I wonder how she is. If she stayed there, or where she wound up. If she ever got to go home. She kept saying she missed her mom, and I've always wondered about her mom, and about what made her run away from home in the first place."

"You worry too much about such things," Kat said.

"Probably."

"I never hated you. Who could hate you, Lucas? You are too full of light."

"I always felt guilty. I left you stuck with all the responsibility. The guy always gets away scot-free, the girl has to raise a baby. It's not fair. I got to go to college, I got to—"

Katya laughed. "No, Lucas. You got nothing. I never thought that, that I was stuck with her. You would send me these desperate letters, and it was so clear you had nothing. I had everything. I had her."

I opened my eyes. I was looking at a jumbled pile of Vera's clothes. I saw the pretty purple sundress I had bought her.

"But you are a very good person, Lucas," she went on. "You don't have even an ounce of meanness in you. Your whole life, I am willing to bet there is not one single person who hated you. Sure, I was mad at you because you didn't do what I wanted you to do. But you are really a very good person. The joke is on you if you don't already know that."

The joke was on me. That phrase kept coming back to me as I walked to the hospital, as I climbed the steps past a melty bronze statue, as I waited in the waiting room to be taken to Vera. I was impatient to see her. I had brought a notebook in which I had written down all of Katya's questions and where I could take down everything the doctors said. I also brought a slice of chocolate cake and a plate of cabbage rolls from a bakery/cafeteria thing I found on the way, as well as some clothes for her to wear, casual things, jeans, T-shirts, some frighteningly skimpy underwear that appeared to be the only kind of underwear she owned. I didn't bring her any books or her laptop. The hospital, when I called to check that I had the visiting hours right, had said that I could bring books, just not the laptop, but I didn't think it was a good idea.

But when I got to the ward, they wouldn't let me see her. At first I couldn't get anyone who spoke English, but after a while they found someone for me.

"She is too agitated for visitors right now," the nurse said.

"But I'm her father," I said.

"She can't have any visitors," the nurse said again. She was a blonde in her forties with a wide, practical mouth. She'd had to deal with family members like me a thousand times, her look said. "Right now she is very agitated and she is in the quiet room."

"She's in isolation?" I asked. I imagined the quiet room as the padded cell so often depicted in movies, Vera straitjacketed and flailing. Last night she had been so calm, it was hard for me to understand why she needed to be locked up by herself. What had they done to her?

"Someone checks on her every fifteen minutes or so," the nurse said.

"But you're saying I can't even see her. I can't even visually ascertain that she is actually here?" I had made a horrible mistake. I should never have left her here. These people were not to be trusted. They were holding her hostage, practically. "Can I at least look at her? Can I just watch her through a window or something?"

"As I said, she is too agitated." The nurse was clearly getting irritated with me. Her English was really very good. It was weird that my brain could register being impressed by her at the same time as I was starting to get really and truly frantic.

"Can I speak with a doctor?" I asked. "I need to speak to a doctor."

"It's the weekend," the nurse said, "so we don't have much staff on, but I will see what I can do. Maybe I can find a doctor to talk to you."

"Maybe you better," I said, in a tone that was so childish and impotent that I was immediately embarrassed for myself. The nurse just stared at me for a beat and then sighed.

She left me in the waiting room for a long time, and I sat, awkwardly cradling my sweaty paper bag of cabbage rolls and chocolate cake, the duffel of Vera's clothes at my feet. There were surprisingly good oil paintings on the walls. But then, it seemed painters were abundant in Vilnius. You could buy an oil painting for thirty bucks off a blanket on Gedimino prospektas. Art was easy here. Alcohol was ink.

It was a different doctor than last night, not the tall, bald man with the shiny pate, but a woman in her early fifties with dark hair in a braid. She was short and trim, almost girlish, and she bounced on little leather loafers as she led me to her office. In American hospitals, mental or otherwise, my consults with doctors had usually taken place in hallways, waiting rooms, or at the foot of the patient's bed. Grandma Sylvia's death, a protracted process, had been full of such conversations, my mother and some doctor in a hallway, as I sat on the floor, leaning against a wall, reading a sci-fi novel.

But here I was led to an actual office, filled with books and simple furniture, an academic's office. It reminded me of my own office at Orange Coast College. But the doctor had very little information. She had diagnosed Vera as bipolar I. They had not yet contacted her doctor in the States because such contact had to be made through written official correspondence. She listed Vera's medications and their dosages, and I wrote them down studiously in my notebook, as well as the doctor's name, which I had her spell for me twice but which I was still pretty sure I had gotten wrong. All of this was attended by a peculiar physical sensation that my chair was slowly sinking into the floor as though into sand.

"Why is she in solitary?" I asked.

"Sometimes when a patient is first admitted with acute mania, the drugs that block the production of dopamine initially cause the brain to go into overdrive producing more and more dopamine to try to fix the blockade. This can result in an intensification of the existing mania, and in your daughter's case, very acute psychosis."

I stared at the doctor. It appeared that what she was saying was that the drugs they had given Vera had actually made her worse. I almost wanted to laugh, it was so awful. "What did she do, though? Surely she must have done something?"

"I wasn't on duty at the time, I only got here in the morning, but my understanding is that she removed her pajamas and she entered the rooms of other patients naked and was trying to wake them up and assemble them so she could ... give a kind of sermon, or a speech."

I nodded. I thought of the video Fang had shown me of Vera naked, claiming to be God's daughter. I thought of the way she had talked to me and Daniel, oratorical, unstoppable, her knife almost an afterthought, a kind of shiny, dangerous conductor's baton. I understood suddenly that even if this place was stupid, even if their medication didn't work, even if they kept Vera in padded cells and refused to let me see her, I still had no choice but to put her here. Because I didn't know how to take care of her on my own. My mouth was incredibly dry.

"When will I be able to see her?" I asked.

"It could be hours, it could be days."

———

I left the duffel of Vera's clothes with an orderly and threw away the chocolate cake and cabbage rolls in a trash can on the street. I had nowhere to go, but I found the idea of returning to the apartment repugnant. I began walking, and walking felt like the answer, felt like the only thing that could help me, and so I just kept doing it.

It turned out that you could traverse pretty much the entire old town of Vilnius in a big triangle, simply by making lefts on the three main drags, so I did this for maybe three hours. At times I stopped and bought coffee. Once I bought a cinnamon bun that I immediately threw away. I bummed a cigarette from an old man. That seemed to help. I walked until the balls of my feet were on fire and I had blisters on my heels.

On Gedimino prospektas there was a small museum, a portrait gallery, and I paid thirty litas to go inside. I wandered through the paintings. Most of them were of men, historically or locally significant men. They were fat and red-nosed and jowly, or else thin-necked and hollow-eyed, like mean turkeys. They all looked like alcoholics. They all looked incredibly sad. I kept picturing them as babies for some reason. They looked like babies holding broken toys, trying not to cry. One of the uncanny things about the actual experience of walking around Vilnius was that everyone looked the same. City of diversity though it was, Poles and Lithuanians and Russians and Belorussians looked remarkably alike. In the States, there were so many kinds of faces. In California, there were people from all over Asia, people from Mexico, people from Polynesia. Black people, white people, all colors and shades of brown people. But here, all of the people looked related, like one huge extended family. The men in these portraits could have been brothers or cousins. And they all looked like me.

Katya had called to accuse me of having the genes for mental illness on my side of the family because she knew about my father. She was the only one I had told. I had written her a letter, pouring out the whole truth at the end of that summer, and it was the only one she had responded to. "He sounds like a nut job," she wrote. "Try to forget him." At the time, I thought it was hilarious that Katya of all people would impugn someone else's mental stability. She was herself such a nut. But the idea stuck with me. There was no proof that my father was actually mentally ill, but there were details that suggested it. When he had shown up to that "date" with my mother, he had been wearing a trench coat, and he kept asking her questions then scribbling her answers in a small notebook. She found out later he was also tape-recording all their conversations. Was he really mentally ill? I didn't know. But I worried about it enough. Enough so that when Vera was first diagnosed, I felt guilty.

It was my greatest fear—that I was carrying his genes like undetonated grenades, and I had given them to Vera by mistake. Maybe that was why I had wanted to believe Herkus was the grandson of a Nazi. I wanted to believe there was someone who was more genetically tainted than myself. Or I wanted to believe that genetics didn't matter, that even though my father was inside me, in every single cell of my body, he couldn't touch me. He didn't know me. He had nothing to do with my fate, with my life, with my choices. I had to believe that or else the quarantine that I had spent my life building against him would be for nothing.

I left the portrait gallery when I started to feel like I couldn't breathe. Outside, it was bright and sunny. I realized I was in front of the jewelry shop where I had bought the amber necklace that I had given to Susan, and the guilt was immediate and lacerating. I had given Vera's necklace to someone else. I had taken something special, and I had given it away like it didn't matter. Obviously it was absurd to think Vera wouldn't have had the episode if I had just given her the necklace, but I couldn't shake the feeling. I went inside, determined to buy Vera something. It was the same woman who had helped me before. She had long curly hair and she wore glasses on a chain around her neck.

"Back again," she observed, and I only murmured, not wanting to talk. I was scanning the cases and cases of jewelry, looking. I ran my fingers through some necklaces hanging on a stand on the countertop and they seemed too light, made of plastic. Was any of this amber even real? It all looked so cheap.

I left without buying anything. A blister had burst on my heel. The blood and fluid had stuck my sock to it. I walked quickly, finally understanding where I was going, where I had been trying to walk all along.

I banged on the door to Susan's hotel room with my fist like I was in a rainstorm, waiting to be let in, but there was no answer. I don't know why I had been so sure she would be in. Perhaps because I needed her to be. Feeling weirdly off script, I wandered back downstairs and was just about to leave when I saw her eating lunch in the hotel restaurant. When she saw me, she waved, delighted.

I sat down at her table. I felt like I was intruding into another world. She was wearing a white button-down shirt that seemed too white, impossibly white, and she was eating salmon carpaccio and drinking mineral water. Her skin was visibly moist and soft-looking, as though she had just applied lotion. The sun shone in her hair. I felt like a crusty monster and I had an instinct to hide my hands under the table even though they were perfectly clean.

"I'm so glad to see you," she said. "I've been having the most gorgeous lunch and then what could be more perfect but that you show up! Order something. I'll get you a menu."

"I'm not really hungry," I said. I would have preferred to have this conversation in her room. I felt exposed in the bright and airy restaurant.

"Is everything all right?" she asked, and I was grateful to be given such a clear cue to begin my narrative. I told her as best I could about the night before, about the situation with Vera, her episode earlier in the fall, all of the complicated reasons we had taken this trip together. She listened sympathetically, nodding, her brow knit. And the more she listened, the more I let the story pour out of me. The sense that there was something tainted in our very bloodline. My growing unease with Grandma Sylvia and who she may have been. What did it mean to escape with your life? What did it mean to live through all of that? Was it possible ever to heal?

"I just feel like an utter failure as a father," I said, "and an utter failure as a human being." My eyes were hot and stinging and I worried that soon I would begin openly weeping at her table.

She nodded, pressed her lips together. I waited, but she didn't say anything. "I'm sorry," I said, suddenly aware that something was wrong. "Should I not have told you that?"

"No," Susan said. "No, I think it's very natural that you would need to talk about all this. And it seems like you've had a very traumatic experience with your daughter. And I'm very sympathetic. I am."

"I knew you would be," I said. "I was just feeling so completely lost and adrift in this city. You know, when you're in a strange place you don't have any cues as to who you are, and I thought: Susan is the only person I really know here."

She grimaced, then smiled, a confusing combination. "See, that's where I feel like we aren't quite understanding each other."

I stared, stupidly, my ears already burning hot. I had a hard time listening as she spoke. "See," she said, "as you were talking, I realized, you know, I've done this a hundred times before. Not with you, I'm not saying you've done this to me a hundred times. But in my life, I've listened to a man cry and sob and bemoan what a failure he is or what a bad person or tell me how tragic his life is. And I have always let my heart go out to them, and I have always tried to mother and to fix and to help, but you know what? It never actually works. I'm just getting too old to keep doing it, Lucas. You can't imagine how surreal it was, as you kept going on and on, it was like I was trapped in a scene I had played a thousand times. And the truth is, we don't really know each other, do we? It's not my job to leap in and help you get your life sorted. You need to grow up and do that on your own. We're just strangers, really. We're both only here on vacation."

I nodded. "Right," I said, my mouth dry, my voice cracking. "You're right."

"You're going to be okay," she said, and she reached out and squeezed my hand. "I'm going to go pay my bill and go to the afternoon tour. It's the last one, and then there is the goodbye dinner after. Are you going?"

"No," I said.

"I know I'm being harsh," Susan said, withdrawing her hand.

"Yes," I said, "you are being harsh. But I understand."

"I'm very sorry about your daughter," she said.

But I couldn't make my throat work to answer her, so I just nodded again and stared at her plate of half-finished carpaccio, the beautiful streaks of olive oil, yellow green against the white of the plate and the pink of the fish, gleaming in the sun.

It was only when I got back to my apartment and I felt the familiar buzz of my phone notifying me of an e-mail or some kind of status update that I realized I hadn't ever turned it off after calling Katya that morning. The roaming charges would be insane. I was about to shut it off when I saw that I had four new voice mails, one of which was from Fang and was dated day before yesterday. I listened.

"Hey there, Mr. Lucas," Fang said, and then continued so solemnly and carefully that I wondered if he had written out what he wanted to say ahead of time. "I hope I am not out of line in calling you, but Vera has told me that you know about weaning down from her medication, and so it is my belief that there are no secrets between us anymore. I'm worried about her. She has been sending me long, occasionally incoherent e-mails. I worry that she is manic again and that it is my fault. At the same time, there is little that I can do from this distance. I hope that you will attend to this matter. Hopefully, I am wrong, but I do not think so. Thank you for allowing me to call you."

And then he hung up.

What a simple and straightforward warning. One day too late.

I sat with the phone in my hand for a moment, dazed. Then I called Katya.

"Just get on a plane and come here."

Chapter 14

———

Date: 7/14/2014 11:16 PM
From: FangBoy76@hotmail.com
To: Vera.Abramov@gmail.com
Subject: Re: What's done is done

My Lovely V,

As you can imagine, defending myself against your recriminations is wearying and agonizing and weirdly boring, all at the same time. It is not that I hold them against you. I understand that we are far away and you are insecure. But let me be clear: I do not care if you do not forgive me because there is nothing I need to be forgiven for. NOTHING HAPPENED.

I am profoundly relieved that you have confessed all to your father. It is a weight off my shoulders, perhaps more than you imagine. I was also quite taken with your description of him as simple. I like your image of him as perfectly transparent, like some kind of crystal or very clean water. It is summer in California as you well know, and when you go off on such tangents it causes small cascades of thought, flights of fancy in my mind that keep me from sleeping and give me that sense of late-summer magic. Indeed, you above all other people convince me that magic is real. Not the cheap transubstantiation of handkerchiefs into doves but the abiding ontic mystery of june bugs dancing under yellow streetlights.

Vera, we are lucky that we found each other. Before the spectacle of you, I become a toothless baby clapping in delight. Or maybe it is that you animate me, so that I become a friendly snowman instead of a pile of lumpy snow. Whatever it is, doll: You are my magic hat.

Still, I am unhappy, lover. Your obsession with the photograph of me and Stephanie Garrison appears to be ongoing, and I do not know what to do or say to break you of the habit of that train of thought.

Think instead of this: That we are all as simple as your father. That we are all, at heart, so breathlessly childishly clear. That is our true nature, Vera. Everything else is a mask.

Yours truly,

Fang

Date: 7/17/2014 1:30 AM
From: FangBoy76@hotmail.com
To: Vera.Abramov@gmail.com
Subject: Re: The Shoah and your pretty idiot

My Lovely V,

I wish you could know how helpless I feel when you present me with your wild emotions and I am able only to read them on this blinking blue eye of technology as all around me the household sleeps, except for the occasional somnambulistic pilgrimage to the kitchen by my mother. She keeps a key lime pie in the freezer and feeds off of it in the night, like a pie vampire. She prefers it frozen. She does not want it thawed. She passes by me here at the computer without saying a word. I believe she knows that I am writing to you and that I am like a love-sick puppy.

It is time for me to confess what I have been withholding. If only it were as simple as having kissed Stephanie Garrison! You can't know how badly I wish I had done something so straightforward. But we are not straightforward, you and I.

I have been harboring in my heart, Vera, the secret and treasonous suspicion that all is not well with you. I try valiantly to keep from viewing you with a distance. I do not wish to become your doctor or your keeper. I dislike the idea of evaluating you, as though everything you utter to me, every idea, must be judged fit by me. I am not your judge, nor do I wish to be your jailor. And yet I am filled with the icky certainty that something is going wrong with your brain chemistry.

Please reassure me and tell me that I am wrong.

In either case, I am very sorry that you fought with Judith. But I would also remind you that she is your elder and that listening to her wisdom will serve you more deeply than getting to practice running your mouth. You can practice running your mouth on me.

Yours truly,

Fang

Date: 7/17/2014 11:15 PM
From: FangBoy76@hotmail.com
To: Vera.Abramov@gmail.com
Subject: Are you ignoring me?

My Lovely V,

There has begun to be a disconnect in our letters. I write to you with my concerns. I cite passages in your letters, explaining why I am worried, and you ignore these and persist in writing me as before. Now you say the ghost of your grandmother is contacting you.

I am concerned.

I am afraid for your safety.

But I am also increasingly angry. We have always said that we were a team. We were a team before your episode, we were a team afterward. Together we waded through it all, the drugs, the disbelief of your parents, the unfortunate situation at school. Even at your most lost, I felt I could count on you to be honest with me. We were in this together.

But I no longer feel that this is the case. Worse, I feel you have cast me in some villainous role that I cannot escape from. I cannot spend all day worrying about you. By the way, I was recently fired from Fat Burger. This does not seem like the proper venue for the story, but I assure you it was both humiliating and rather humorous. Suffice it to say, I am not a good multitasker. I was supposed to be working the grill station, most abhorrent and hellish of tasks. I do not understand how other people, people far more stupid than I am, are so good at these menial jobs. Truly, I am baffled by it. I am like a tortoise among them, trying to manipulate burger tongs with my digit-less hands.

I am not having a good summer. Sometimes I feel the strain of trying to be myself in my current maladapted life, along with worrying about you, feeling somehow responsible for you, and yet helpless to actually do anything to assure myself of your well-being. Sometimes the strain of all this makes me feel I will snap.

Did you know I considered lying and telling you I did kiss Stephanie Garrison, just to make it stop? Just so I could be cut free and no longer tied to the heavy anchor of my love for you?

Are you really determined to tug me to the bottom of the sea after you?

Wearily, I will follow, for I do not know how to stop.

Yours truly,

Fang

PS: I am sorry I refused to ever acknowledge the note you left in my underwear drawer. I did receive it, but the effect was perhaps more claustrophobic than you intended. I have no desire to "turn into you" or to be your mental twin. That was never the plan. I wanted to love you, but as myself, and for you as yourself. Do you understand the difference?

Date: 7/18/2014 5:21 PM
From: FangBoy76@hotmail.com
To: Vera.Abramov@gmail.com
Subject: Re: re: Are you ignoring me?

V,

I no longer believe there is anything I can do for you through e-mail. I have left a voice mail for your father, explaining my concerns. I cannot do this anymore.

Please stop writing me. It is torturous for me. I cannot take any more of it.

I hope some day you forgive me.

As ever, just more distantly,

Fang

AFTER I GOT THE VOICE MAIL from Fang, it occurred to me that I had not really read his half of the e-mail exchange with Vera. Feeling much more like a snoop than I had the first time, I logged on to her computer and started to go through her mail folder. As I tried to piece together their whole correspondence, what she wrote to him, what he replied next, what she had said to that, I found that I couldn't, and that was when I realized that a lot of his letters to her and her letters to him had been deleted. But they were right there in the trash folder of her mail program. So I read those too, and gradually a fuller picture began to emerge.

In a way, I think Fang would have figured out what was going on even earlier if he hadn't been so thrown off-balance by Vera's jealousy over the Stephanie Garrison debacle. I hadn't gone on Facebook to actually check, but it seemed that the picture in question was totally harmless: Fang smiling for a picture in a group, his arm thrown casually around the girl who happened to be standing next to him. But for Vera to be irrationally jealous was not something Fang would immediately connect to her bipolar, especially since he himself was convinced she had been misdiagnosed. Vera was quite capable of being volatile and irrational all on her own, and jealousy can cause anyone to seem insane.

But the letters she sent to him during their fight were vile. And there were even more of them in her trash file, as though she had been aware that she should not have sent them and wished they could be stricken from the record. Fang must have been enraged by these letters, even as he sought to comfort and console her.

Ultimately, Fang was an even stranger and more interesting person than I had guessed. It was easy to see why he and Vera had fallen for each other. I in no way blamed him for wanting to try to disentangle himself from what seemed to him the crushing moral weight of being Vera's sole guardian, but at the same time, the idea of the two of them truly severing ties made me sad. And the timing of it. She must have gotten his last e-mail right before Daniel came over.

I shut the laptop and rubbed my eyes. The cat jumped down through the window and came to lay beside me on Vera's bed. The afternoon was wearing interminably on. Katya was coming, but she wouldn't be here for almost two days. I thought of Vera in the quiet room, her padded cell, and suddenly hoped Fang stuck by his resolution to be done with loving her, to let go the heavy anchor. No matter how weirdly right they were for each other, I wouldn't wish *Romeo and Juliet* on her and Fang. I wouldn't wish for him to be the one waiting to see her at the mental hospital, or the one who has to realize she doesn't actually want to be holding the knife, the one who has to find a way to take it from her hands. No matter how smart he was, he was still just a seventeen-year-old kid.

I was also experiencing an almost physical sense of revulsion caused by some complicated aggregate of spiritual wrongs I had recently committed. I felt like a spy for reading such intimate exchanges between two people who would never have wanted me to read their correspondence. I felt embarrassed by Vera's psychosis, and so added to my unease while snooping was the embarrassment of being let in on someone else's shame.

I remember my mother had a lover once, not Jerry, but someone just after him, who would let his house get horribly, disgracefully messy. He would keep buying new clothes so that he didn't have to do laundry, so the dirty clothes in his back bedroom got to be waist high almost. The kitchen was unusable and putrid. My mother recruited me once to help her clean his apartment and it took us three days. I remember finding an open can of cat food among the clothes, a bag of gummy worms that had mysteriously begun to liquefy. It was appalling that a human being could live like this, and both my mother and I had an instinct to never voice to each other, nor to her boyfriend, how upsetting his house was. It was like that reading Vera's trashed e-mails. I wanted to delete them even more permanently, to keep anyone else from ever reading these things and knowing how unreasonable she was capable of being.

It was a horrible, queasy feeling. And dancing over this feeling were images of Susan, retinal burns almost. I could still see her plate of carpaccio in my mind, her knife fallen across the little rectangles of raw fish. She had told me she only wanted an adventure. She had told me I would ruin it with feelings. "You're young," she had said. And I had thought it was a compliment. I had misread her completely. Just as I had misread Vera.

Had I misread Katya all those years ago? Was I really so bad at knowing what was real, at discerning what was true?

I napped, disconcerted, the rest of the afternoon, the ownerless cat curled up beside me.

———

By evening, I did not know what to do but return to the mental hospital. Visiting hours were long over, but I went to the desk and asked if Vera was still in isolation and if she was not, could I please be allowed to see her. The nurse could not understand a word I said. I wrote my request on a piece of scrap paper, handed it to her to do with what she would, and then sat down in the waiting room and waited. I waited for three hours. Finally, at about nine o'clock, someone must have taken mercy on me or finally deciphered my note, because the nurse called me over and an orderly took me to Vera's floor and let me see her in her room.

She was lying on her bed, not like a sick person tucked under covers and propped up neatly, but like a mannequin that has simply been set down. She was fully dressed in some of the fresh clothes I had left for her, and her eyes were open. She gazed steadily at the ceiling. When I approached her bed and whispered her name, she did not sit up or turn to me, just lifted her eyebrows and said, "You decided to come after all."

"I've been trying to see you all day," I said. "How are you?"

She ignored this question, but continued to stare at the ceiling.

"They told me they put you in solitary," I said. I wanted her to tell me about it. To tell me it had been awful, or to tell me it was not so bad, or to tell me what color the padded walls were. I pictured them blue. Were they blue? Probably they were tan.

"You are afraid of me," she said finally, with a queer little smile that made me shudder. Her body was nearly comatose, but her mind was still spitting up oracular little psychotic particles.

"No," I said, "I wanted to see you so badly. I was furious when they wouldn't let me see you earlier."

"Do you know the book *Hop on Pop*?" she asked. "The children's book?"

I didn't. Possibly I had read it when I was a child, but I had missed those years with Vera and so my memories of children's books were dim and murky.

"Two little bears jump on their father's tummy. They hop on Pop. That was always how I thought of you. That was what I thought I was missing: having someone who would be magically immune to the pain I would cause them so that everything would just be hilarious all the time."

"That's funny," I said. "I never thought about not having a father that way."

"I always forget that," she said, closing her eyes. "That you didn't have a father, either."

"Yeah," I said. And we remained there like that, Vera lying with her eyes closed on the bed, myself sitting hunched over in a chair at her side, until the orderly came to get me and tell me I had to leave.

"Your mother is coming," I told her, right as I was leaving. But she didn't say anything, only shrugged, as though it didn't matter to her at all.

The next morning was Monday, and Judith came to say goodbye before she left for the airport. I had seen her in the hallway the day before and awkwardly explained about Vera, and she hadn't insisted on knowing more or talking. But an hour before she was supposed to leave, she showed up at my door offering me the rest of her coffee and tea. "Since you're staying," she said, "I thought you might need these." I had, of course, canceled Vera's and my flight and our future was so uncertain that I had yet to book a new one. An ongoing supply of coffee and tea was a blessing.

Judith had on her red lipstick and her red beret. She was, as my mother would say, "ready to be seen." She had survived this trip, this foray out into the world as a widow, and she looked happy. I was genuinely glad for her. I invited her in. "You don't still have any of that cheese?" she asked.

"Indeed, I do!" I said. Vera had made fun of me for buying it at the store. "It looks like someone tried to make soap out of cottage cheese," she'd said. But Judith and I had both become swiftly addicted to the farmer's cheese. I sliced some for us now, along with a huge red tomato, and we ate from a large platter with our fingers.

"I feel very badly," Judith said finally, "about the way things ended between Vera and myself."

I nodded. I didn't know how much to say. I knew about their fight only because I had read Vera's e-mails, and I didn't really want to get into that right now. All I wanted was to absolve Judith as quickly and resoundingly as possible.

"Don't spend even a second feeling bad," I told her. But she went on speaking as though I hadn't.

"I, of course, did not know she suffered from mental illness and that what I was seeing was part of a manic episode, but in retrospect it seems very clear. She kept asking me about being a Jew. She kept asking me if it was really important to be born a Jew, and I didn't get it because her mother is a Jew so even by Orthodox standards, she's a Jew."

I nodded, listening. This seemed like a very different conversation than the one Vera had reported in her letter to Fang. But perhaps it was foolish to try to piece together reality from letters. Maybe Vera had been censoring herself, not wanting to seem so manic in her summary to Fang. Or maybe there had been two distinct fights, and it was I who was trying to force them into congruity.

"Anyway, this did not comfort her for whatever reason, and she had some idea that she was a new kind of identity, a thing she kept calling a post-Jew. Which, if I am being totally honest, I found both appalling and amusing because how could she not know that I myself am a post-Jew? I mean, she was coming to me as though I were some bastion of traditional wisdom, when the truth is that I am just a hippie who has patched together her own sense of Jewishness, mixing it with Buddhism and modern poetry and all sorts of things as I saw fit."

"Listen, Judith," I said, "none of this is something you should feel bad about. There wouldn't have been any right answer you could have given. She has delusions of grandeur and—"

"Well, I know," Judith said. "That's what I'm trying to apologize for!"

I was starting to feel really anxious and sick, but I wasn't sure why. I ate another piece of farmer's cheese.

"She was getting agitated and she was talking about Jews being the chosen people. She was really hung up on that word: *chosen.* I said what I usually say, which is, Yes, but did God choose the Israelites or did the Israelites choose God? But she wasn't interested in that question. It seems so painfully obvious now that I could just kick myself, but at the time I was irritated and overtired, and I felt like she was being a melodramatic teenager. Unsatisfied with my un-flashy old woman's truths. She'd asked me the secret to true love and she hadn't liked that answer either!"

"What is the secret to true love?" I asked.

"Oh. To be nice to each other."

We sat in silence for a minute. To be nice to each other.

"That's actually the secret to raising children, too," she said. "You just try to be nice to them. Not to coddle them or spoil them, not to be afraid of their anger or disappointment, but to be *just* to them, to be *kind*. Or at least, that's what I think."

It occurred to me that I ought to go out and buy one of Judith's books and read it.

"I have no idea what I could ever do that could be of help to you, but please know that you can always call on me," she said. "I will do anything I can for her. And for you."

I didn't know what Judith could do to help us, either, but I was deeply touched that she had offered. "Thank you," I said.

"I should go downstairs. Adam called me a taxi, that sweet boy, so I wouldn't have to try to find one myself. It's supposed to be here at ten." It took me a moment to realize she was talking about Johnny Depp. I had forgotten entirely that his real name was Adam.

I offered to walk her out and help her with her suitcase since I was on my way to the hospital anyway, and thank God I did because I have no idea how she would have gotten that enormous suitcase down the three flights of stairs by herself. Judith seemed to exist in some kind of special space where the things she needed just appeared: someone to carry her bags, someone to find the light switches, someone to sell her pot. It was tempting to believe the world was like that. All you had to do was need something, and it would appear, like the SS officer flinging open the door and saving you from death, or like your soul mate suddenly walking up and shaking your hand.

"Wish me safe flight!" Judith chirped. I wished her a safe flight, kissed her on the cheek, and left her at the curb to wait

247